Simple Gifts

Also by Janie Franz

The Bowdancer Saga

The Bowdancer

The Wayfarer's Road

Warrior Women

The Lost Song Trilogy

Verses

Refrain

Coda

The Premier

Sugar Magnolia

Ruins Discovery

Ruins Artifacts

Ruins Legacy

Handful of Dirt

Simple Gifts

Janie Franz

Simple Gifts
Book 1 of the Granny Woman Tales

Published by Per Bastet Publications LLC, P.O. Box 3023
Corydon, IN 47112

Cover art by T. Lee Harris
ISBN 978-1-942166-82-5

Available in trade paperback and DRM-free ebook formats

Simple Gifts

Dedication

This book is dedicated to the late Bob Seidel and his lovely wife Dixie Evans for their welcoming presence in this book.

And to my ancestors on both sides of my genealogy for leaving an indelible imprint on my life.

Acknowledgements

No book would be possible without research and the input of sources with insightful knowledge.

First, I want to thank Kari Taurig, a Norwegian folklorist, singer, educator, and researcher. Her insights and knowledge helped me keep track of many of the creatures in this book. With kindness, I borrowed a few of her stories to share in this book and the shaping of Bella Anderson.

I want to thank the Firehall Theater in Grand Forks ND, the Hatton Community Theater, Frost Fire Summer Theater, and the former Federated Church for exposing me to a variety of plays and musicals and the opportunity to participate in them, especially the late Linda Christianson and her husband Duane Christianson. Those experiences added color to this tale.

I also want to thank Miss Bella Giganta, formerly of Santa Fe, an extraordinary drag queen who has the most exquisite voice. Her charm was the inspiration for Charleen in this book.

In addition, I want to thank a variety of musicians and singers who informed this work and shaped my understanding of Spirit and the place of song within its expression. I have comprised a playlist of the songs referenced in this book so that readers can add flavor to their reading. That will be available on my website: janiefranzauthor.com

And finally, I want to thank my wider family in Tennessee and Kentucky for the stories I grew up hearing that have influenced other tales within this larger telling and those that will come.

Thank you all. Without your help, this book would not be so rich in lore.

Chapter 1

Day 1: Dark Hollow, TN

Sephronia Hill rocked to and fro on the porch of her cabin in Dark Hollow where an ancient river had cut a gorge long ago into the cliffs. All that remained of that river today was a creek, meandering through the woods that had grown in the patches where the sun crept between the rocky bluffs around her. The woman's face, full of freckles and liver spots, crinkled with happiness as she watched the yellow and black swallowtails flit among the dappled branches, dancing in counterpoint to the music of the water trickling over the rocks and submerged branches of old storm fall. The peacefulness here allowed her to think without her sister Agnesia's constant preaching about how she was going to Hell.

Sephie, as she was called by her friends and some family members, had built the cabin five years ago in response to Agnesia's constant presence. Sephie's husband had gone to Glory a decade ago from a sudden heart attack when he was 75. At her daughter's urging, Sephie had agreed to open her home to her sister, who was also a widow. Agnesia had never seemed to benefit from her childless marriage, turning into a wizened old prune with a heart as shrunken as she was. The only thing that drove her to put her feet on the floor every morning was her mission to bring her sister to the throne of Grace before the Rapture came.

To avoid spending her sunset years arguing with the old biddy or truly endangering her immortal soul by putting Agnesia out of her misery with a feather pillow, Sephie had enlisted the help of some local college boys to help her build the cabin she'd ordered as a kit from a building supply store. It took those boys most of the summer to figure the plans out, making Sephie snort over college educations one moment and hide her tears in another. It was what her husband with his German ancestry would have done — read everything thoroughly and then watched a video on the things he didn't know how to do. They'd remodeled their home with those building supply videos, even plumbing in a new bathroom. Sephie herself preferred to MacGyver something with duct tape and chewing gum.

The cabin became her retreat. Though it had no modern conveniences, Sephie used technology and old knowledge to make her stays there safe and comfortable. She put in a wood burning stove, a composting toilet, and a heavy-duty water purification system that trapped rainwater and made it potable. She even had a small propane fridge installed so she could sip iced lemonade, laced with a little gin that she'd had to hide down in the cabin from her sister's teetotaler eyes.

Sephie could have stayed there overnight if she wished, but she usually didn't. Every evening, she made her way up the steep path to see if she needed to call the doctor or the undertaker for Agnesia. Mostly, she just called the preacher so he could help Agnesia pray for her sister's wayward soul. Sephie thought the old woman planned her "spells" for when Sephie came home just so she'd have to call the preacher.

This particular evening, Sephie tasted her lemonade, finding it had a little more kick than usual. She'd added two fingers of gin instead of one because her hip osteoarthritis had flared up again. The old woman had spent far too much time that day traipsing through the woods hunting for goldenseal and chamomile. She hadn't been as successful as she'd have liked because there just weren't as many plants in their usual places. Sephie had been careful to harvest only a few at a time and at several different sites. She didn't want to over-glean them and have nothing for the next year. The old woman knew how delicate the balance of nature was, even here in this protected gorge. She'd seen too much clear cutting of the forests in these Appalachian foothills and far too much strip mining that leveled some of the beloved mountains she'd grown up around. Sometimes, Sephie would find herself disoriented when she'd follow a trail up to a ridge and look out and not know where she was. It was like waking up one morning and not recognizing herself in the mirror.

Sephie had washed her herb finds for the day, and they lay spread on newspapers on the kitchen table, letting the Scott County News soak up the excess water before she hung them up to dry. She'd do that first thing tomorrow. Sephie smiled. She'd have a few good teas from her gleanings that day.

Finishing up her lemonade, she heaved her plump body out of the rocker and into the kitchen to wash her glass and tidy up before making her way up the path. Inside, she ambled past strings of other herbs hung on twine across the low rafters, drying in the summer air. Some of them emitted pungent scents as she passed. They reminded her of the basil from the garden plot next to her house that smelled green and spicy when she'd cut it, only to protest bitterly as it gave up its moisture, scenting the air with an acrid aroma.

Sephie wondered if Agnesia had ever had a spicy thought in her youth. She smiled, thinking that perhaps she herself had. As the years passed and the dew of youth left her, Sephie saw herself now as an old woman whose body creaked and complained, unable to do what it once had, producing pain out of contrariness. But she had certainly not dried into a bitter old shell like her sister.

Sephie closed the windows of the cabin and shut her cabinet full of jars of herb salves, teas, and the special tinctures she preserved with moonshine. It didn't take her long to set things right for the night and lock up her cabin. Grasping her polished cedar walking stick leaning against the door, she trudged up the path, making her way around boulders and over the fallen tree trunk that intruded on her path.

A half hour later, she rested at the top of the cliff, looking across the meadow at her home, a two-story frame farmhouse at the far edge of her forty acres in east Tennessee. It had been her little piece of Heaven until Agnesia had entered its solitude. Truth to tell, after her husband's passing, Agnesia's whiny voice and wheezy laugh (whenever her twisted reading of scripture permitted her to do so) was a comfort among the old walls, like the murmur of broody chickens underfoot. It was especially so on hot summer evenings like tonight when Agnesia offered up the blessing with their supper and all Sephie could hear was the reverent cadence in her sister's voice, repeating the familiar worship words while the summer flies buzzed against the open screened windows.

Sephie smiled, looking forward to blessed biscuits and chicken and dumplings that Agnesia made just like their long-departed grandmother had. But as she entered the kitchen door, Agnesia was laying into somebody on the phone in the hall, and it certainly wasn't Pastor Woods.

"I don't give a care how important you think your little message is, missy. I told you she ain't here!"

"Agnesia, is that for me?" Sephie called out.

"Well, it's about time you got here. If you didn't spend half your life down in Dark Holler chasing after God-knows what, you'd be able to answer the phone yourself." She waved the cordless phone in the air but wouldn't walk it over to the kitchen where Sephie was leaning her walking stick in a corner by the back door. "Well, don't stand there dawdling. It's long distance, and it must be costing the child a fortune to call all this far."

Sighing, Sephie walked to the little gossip bench in the hall where Agnesia stood with the phone. The green upholstered mahogany chair with the two shelves for phone and phone book had belonged to Agnesia's mother-in-law. It had been the elder woman's single concession to technology in the 1940s. She had a phone line put into her small house up on a ridge two mountains over just so she could hear her husband's voice when his ship came back from Japan and the Philippines when WWII ended. Agnesia and her husband had inherited it when the old woman had died and now it graced a spot in Sephie's home where it was just a place to put a twenty-first century phone base and a slim personal book of numbers.

Taking the phone from Agnesia, Sephie frowned at her sister. "Don't you have something to stir in the kitchen?" Turning to the caller, she said, "Hello."

"Aunt Sephie!" The perky enthusiasm in the voice could only be her great-niece, who was operating a store in North Dakota.

"Mandy girl, how are you?" Sephie eased her bulk into the seat of the gossip bench. "Is it hot up there where you are?"

"Yeah, it got up to ninety-five today, but Riverbend doesn't have the humidity you have."

"Well, we just sit and drip. Thank the Powers this isn't the genteel South where polite women don't even perspire in their laced corsets."

Though the conversation was light, Sephie sensed something was off. "Are you doing okay?"

"I'm fine."

"Shop doing all right?"

"We're doing okay."

"Boyfriend trouble?"

Mandy laughed. "No, Aunt Sephie! You know I haven't looked at a guy since I met Laura."

Sephie grunted, grinning to herself. That had certainly rocked their conservative family. It had taken some careful maneuvering to keep Agnesia from finding out. It wasn't the old biddy's business anyway, and her great-niece Mandy had enough on her hands trying to smooth things with her mother, Lisa, who mourned the loss of the grand wedding she hoped one day to plan. When Mandy's dad, Greg, had called Sephie, looking for an herbal sleeping aid for Lisa, who hadn't stopped crying since Mandy had told her about Laura, Sephie had recommended chamomile tea or a stiff shot of bourbon. She also told her nephew that Lisa could still plan a wedding, only she'd have two brides. But Greg hadn't found the humor in her response or that reality. Sephie had speculated then that her late husband's family was perhaps just as tight-laced as her own.

"But something's up, Mandy," Sephie said, closing her eyes and trying to get a read on the place far to the north of her. "There's a disturbance in the field there. . . . That's why you called. What's going on?"

Chapter 2

Day 1: Riverbend, ND

Cellphone held to her ear, Mandy paced in front of the display in her store window. A large, yellow papier-mâché sun dominated the space. Below it was an assortment of books about summer solstice and Celtic tree divination. Spaced among them were three quartz crystals and two painted, clay masks of the Green Man and Green Lady.

Taking a deep breath, she started to explain. "I think we're dealing with something out of the ordinary."

"Of course it's out of the ordinary or you wouldn't be calling me," Aunt Sephie said.

Typical. Mandy grinned at her partner, Laura, wanting to share her response. But Laura, perched on a stool behind the glass counter, was studying cards she had laid out from the Daughters of the Moon tarot. It was a nuanced deck that was popular in the 80s among feminists, that required the user to note not only the cards' meanings but how each one of the round cards pointed to other cards. Laura absently pushed a stray curl behind her left ear, revealing a flash of silver and the soft rose quartz of a dangling earring, as her face creased in concentration. Mandy found that deck frustrating, preferring a more clear-cut reading with the ancient and time-proven Rider Waite deck. Granted, she did enjoy the imagery of some of the newer decks that the store carried. Tarot, after all, was very personal to the user.

"I just don't know how to explain what's going on here," Mandy said, returning to her great-aunt.

"What do you think it is?"

She took a deep breath, looking out the display window at the verdant color of the greenway outside that ran down to the Red River of the North. "I think we're dealing with a vampire."

There was a pause before her aunt replied. "Well, now. That sure is different."

Mandy laughed. "You're beginning to sound like a local. Seriously, I need your help. Our customers are getting desperate. We've tried everything. Garlic. Silver crosses. I drew the line at supplying hand-whittled wooden stakes, though someone did bring in a box of those for us to sell."

"That won't work."

"But the books all say—"

"You can't use regular magic or remedies where y'all are, child. The river runs north, right?"

"Yes, but—"

"And you get those Alaskan winters there with wind chills down to eighty below, right in the US, right?"

"Yes, but—"

"Mandy, my girl, y'all are dealing with contrary magic. You can't use regular remedies there."

"Then what can we do?"

There was another pause. "I'll need to gather some things. I could get them in the mail by—"

"Aunt Sephie, could you come instead? I need for you to see what's going on. We could get you a plane ticket."

"I couldn't get through security with what all I'd carry. They'd have drug dogs on me, thinking I was bringing in dope. Herbs are fragrant."

"Then I could fly down there and drive you up here."

"No, don't disrupt your routine. You got customers to tend to and try to calm down. It'd take me a day or so to gather what's needed and then, what — two, three days to drive up there?"

"That'll be almost a week, Aunt Sephie."

"Child, you never were patient. I'd always find you shaking all your holiday presents and trying to peel back the wrappings just to get a peek."

Running a hand through her buzz cut, Mandy resigned herself to the fact that she'd have to wait. "All right. But it's a long way for you to drive on your own. What if something happens to your car?"

"I got road side assistance. And I still can change a tire, even if my body will ache for three days after."

"Then you should make sure you keep that cellphone I gave you charged up."

It was Aunt Sephie's turn to chuckle. "I'll do that. And my old car still has a cigarette lighter I can put that fancy charger into."

"It's a smartphone. You can get Google directions on it and never get lost."

"What's the fun in that?" Sephie laughed again and promised to call tomorrow.

Pocketing the phone, Mandy announced as she joined Laura at the counter, "Aunt Sephie's coming."

"I got that," she said, then added. "But she isn't coming alone."

"Literally or figuratively?"

Laura looked up. "Both."

Chapter 3

Day 2: Dark Hollow, TN

"Be careful with that!" Sephie cautioned B.D. Travers. "I don't want any broken tinctures smelling up the backseat of my car."

"Yesum," the young African American man teased.

"Stop that! I don't work you that hard," she said, checking the list she'd written down after Mandy's call.

He grinned. "I'm not about to break any of these. I worked too hard learning how to make them," he said, stacking the box of well-wrapped bottles onto the dolly he had been using to transport Sephie's stock out of the hollow. He'd already toted up a load of boxes full of mason jars, two boxes of green and dried herbs, and a pile of dogwood limbs that had made him look askance at the old woman.

B.D. had been one of the college students who had helped her build her cabin and get it set up. He'd shown a natural interest and some rudimentary knowledge of wildcrafting and herb lore, and Sephie had tried to nurture that.

"How long you plan on being gone?"

"Don't know," she said.

"Won't the people in Dark Holler miss their Granny Woman?"

"They'll manage. I stocked 'em well. It's only the old people who still come to me anyway. I ship a lot up north to my great-niece. For some reason, they can't get enough herbs up there." Taking a distracted look around the room, Sephie added, "Lordy, I hope to get back home here before the snow flies. Do you know how cold it gets up there?"

"Yup, I looked it up," he said, moving to the portable fridge and disconnecting the propane from it. "My Creole ancestors probably won't even come when I drum, much less any loas I needed for help."

Sephie's head shot up, giving him a glare. "Be respectful. Loas, like angels and spirits, will come no matter where you are if you show respect. As for your ancestors, they're always with you."

"Yes, ma'am," he said, removing what little there was in the fridge — a bottle of gin, a Mason jar half full of lemonade, some cheese, and the hard end of a loaf of French bread. Putting the items on the table in front of Sephie, he spoofed, "A loaf of bread, a jug of wine, and cheese?"

Sephie laughed. "You know I can't tipple up at the house. My sister would have the preacher pray even harder for my soul than he already does."

"Then you better let me put this in your car." He picked up the hard end of the bread. "But I think the birds would appreciate this more than you would now." He tossed the end up in the air and caught it deftly in his hand. Then he headed outside to crumble it well away from the cabin.

"Don't forget to say blessings on that," Sephie called, following him to the porch. In truth, she just wanted to hear the young man sing. B.D.'s deep baritone started slowly as he crumbled up the bread, singing the first verse of "His Eye Is on the Sparrow." This was always a miracle to watch. Carefully, the young man tossed out a few bread crumbs about six feet in front of him close to the stream that ran along the path they had created in the hollow. His actions always left a few bits around his feet. B.D.'s voice was soft but powerful, drawing in the winged creatures. By the time he got to the chorus about singing because he's happy, there were about a dozen songbirds pecking on the ground, even up close to his hiking boots.

Sephie smiled. He was a modern era St. Francis, at least where birds were concerned. He didn't have as much luck with birds of the human variety, remembering her 60s slang. But Sephie had always said that he needed the right woman. Someday, he'd find one as deeply spiritual as he was. She just hoped that young lady didn't lure cats to interfere with his working with birds.

Reluctantly, B.D. backed away slowly and returned to the porch. "Sure you don't need a bird feeder in North Dakota?"

"I can take care of myself, thank you."

"What about that old station wagon of yours?"

"I keep it in tip-top shape. And I can still change a tire."

"I'm not saying you aren't capable, Miz Sephie. It's just a woman shouldn't be taking a trip all that way all by herself."

Sephie rounded on him, ready to verbally blast his overprotective butt into the creek.

He quickly held up his hands. "I'd tell my little sister that, and she's got a black belt in Karate. Besides, if I share driving, you can get there quicker to deal with whatever your niece says is troubling her town. I Googled it, and it's only nineteen hours. We'll be going through a lot of big cities, and I know you hate city driving. I can do that. I'll drive at night, too."

She squinted at him. "Why're you so eager to see the Frozen North? And it doesn't get that way until November."

He shrugged. "Adventure?" he squeaked out meekly.

Sephie chuckled. "Well, we both might be biting off more than we can chew. All right, then. Just be quick about getting your things together when we get up top. I'll probably need to repack what all you toted to my car anyway."

"Oh, no worries. I already put a bag in your car before I took to the path down here."

"Shoot," was all Sephie said before she started barking more orders for closing up the cabin for the summer.

Chapter 4

Day 2: Riverbend, ND

"They're on the road," Mandy announced as she brought two mugs of mint tea into the main store room.

"Told you," Laura said, turning her head toward her partner's voice as she placed candles by color into little triangular cubbies in a wooden display rack. "But who's the other person?"

"Did the Daughters tell you it was only one?" Mandy placed one mug on the glass counter and sat down on the stool behind it, sipping the hot liquid carefully.

"Yes, male. But who?"

"One of those college boys, she said."

"He's more than that, I bet. Do you honestly think your great-aunt would trust that old car and her life, much less all of those herbs and whatever else she's bringing, to some varsity type?"

"Jocks were good at building that cabin of hers, from what she told me a few years ago."

"Hmm. You've got me curious," Laura said, hurrying to finish her task. "We should ask the cards."

"No need. They'll be here tomorrow morning some time. Seems the guy will drive all night so they won't be stopping at motels. I'll call later to see where they are and how she's holding up."

"At least she's using her cellphone," Laura said, returning to her former pace of stocking candles.

"After I finish my tea, I'll go next door and see what I can do to make their rooms welcoming. You're really better at nesting than I am. I did change the sheets on one of the beds and put out fresh towels. I'll need to make up another bed."

"It was a good investment, buying that little house," Laura said. "Though I thought we'd be hosting guest adepts for workshops or seminars. Or at least a paying Airbnb client."

"Well, Aunt Sephie is an adept with a long lineage. Maybe we can coax her into doing some trainings while she's here helping us solve our problem."

Finishing her task, Laura crossed to the counter and picked up her mug of tea. She blew on it before tasting. "Needs more honey, honey," she teased and leaned to give Mandy a quick kiss. "I'll go walk through next door and see what the space tells me it needs to welcome your aunt and her companion. Did she say what the guy's name was?"

"Yeah. B.D. Travers."

"Initials. Very southern. Wonder if it's Billy Dean or Bobby Dan or something."

"Don't you go disparaging my southern roots, you Yankee," Mandy warned, only slightly teasing. "There's deep ancestry there."

Laura flashed her a bright smile. "No disparagement intended, my love. I'll be back in a jiff. And I'll even make up that extra bed."

As she slipped through the back, the bell above the front door jangled and two frightened young women burst in. "It's happened again," one of them said.

Chapter 5

Day 2: South of Indianapolis

"Of all the things you could've ordered, you got grilled cheese and tomato soup!" B.D. commented.

Sephie wrinkled her eyes at his plate, piled high with fried chicken, mashed potatoes, and greens. She fully expected him to get half a pie for dessert. "I see you aren't being frugal, with me paying the expenses."

"We are saving on motel rooms."

"Rooms? Who said you'd get your own?"

He grinned, grabbing a drumstick.

"You're enjoying driving Miss Daisy, aren't you?" she poked.

"Driving? I just got you through Louisville and Lexington and soon through Indianapolis. That's not driving much."

She tasted her soup, nodding her head, indicating that it met with approval. "Don't think I don't appreciate it."

"You never did tell me what you're going up north to deal with."

Sephie took a bite of a grilled cheese triangle. "Hmm," she remarked, chewing.

B.D. scrunched his face up, obviously wondering whether that grunt was in reference to the sandwich or his question.

The old woman swallowed. "Don't quite know, exactly. I'll need to ask. Maybe now's as good a time as any to check in with Mandy before she tries on the road and can't get us."

"Cellphones work along all major interstates. It's some kind of rule or something."

Sephie punched in the numbers of Mandy's cellphone and then spooned soup into her mouth while she waited.

Without preamble, "North Star," Mandy's voice answered. "Where are you?"

"How'd you know it was me?"

"Caller ID. Now where are you?"

"You can do that?"

"Yes, Aunt Sephie. Technology is our friend. So, where are you?"

"Near Indianapolis. B.D. will drive through there, and then I'll do a few more hours until it gets too dark to see."

"That's what headlights are for."

"Stop being a smarty-pants, young lady. So, tell me about your problem. I'm assuming it's the physical kind."

"As opposed to a psychic vampire? We can deal with those, I think. You just need to teach people how to shield."

"Well, it wouldn't hurt to apply a bit of that even for the physical kind. You salting your doorways?"

"Always. We have a ring of salt around the store and our rental next door. That's where you and B.D. will be staying. Laura and I fixed it up for you. Laura is better with that than I am. I just make sure your necessities are covered, and you're safe. She does the ambiance."

"How're your customers dealing with the problem?"

"They're scared."

"Are people being drained?"

"Not yet. We've had a rash of animal attacks, though. Cats, mostly."

"Cats? That's odd. Are you sure you're dealing with what you think you're dealing with?"

"I saw the wounds myself. And one of my customers took her limp cat to the vet. Vet didn't know what the problem was."

Sephie frowned at B.D., who was enjoying his meal but keeping an ear alert to whatever she said. "I'll call after B.D.

takes over for the night. We should be in around nine or ten in the morning."

"What route are you taking?"

"B.D., where we going next?"

The young man pulled out his cellphone and Sephie reached hers across the table so B.D. could tell Mandy the route. "Peoria, Waterloo, Minneapolis, Fargo, then on to Riverbend."

The old woman put the cellphone back to her ear. "You get that?"

"Yep. He sounds nice," Mandy said.

"He'd better be," Sephie cautioned. "See you in the morning."

When she'd placed her phone back into her giant handbag, Sephie looked at her tomato soup, thankful it was more orange with the milk in it than red. She was glad she hadn't ordered spaghetti with marinara.

"So, what are we dealing with?" B.D. prompted.

"Vampires," Sephie muttered, filling her mouth with sandwich before she had to explain further.

Chapter 6

Day 3: Riverbend, ND, midmorning

B.D. waited patiently, holding the box of pint Mason jars full of different dried teas as Sephie pushed open the door of North Star. Perched on top of the box was a bundle of mint wrapped in damp paper towels. The old woman's movement released the bell at the top of the door; its quiet tinkle caused the pretty brunette at the counter to raise her head from the book she was reading. She smiled, coming around the glass case toward them.

From the back, a muscular woman in a buzz cut rushed out to grab Sephie in a bear hug.

"Hey there, Mandy girl! Treat my old bones like fine china."

The young woman laughed and kissed her aunt on the cheek. She stepped around her to take the box from B.D.'s hands. "And this is B.D.?"

Sephie rescued the mint before Mandy stuffed the box under an arm and stretched out a hand to the young man. "I'm Mandy." She looked over her shoulder. "And that's Laura."

Sephie turned to her niece's partner. "Here's some chocolate mint. It tastes just like those peppermint patties."

Laura pinched off a leaf and ground it between her teeth. "Mmm. It does!"

"It's potent, so use a small sprig or a couple of leaves per cup. I had a bartender make me up a mojito with three or four of those leaves, and it blew my head off!"

Mandy squinted up at her aunt's traveling companion. "So, what's B.D. stand for? Billy Dean?"

It was an uncomfortable question no matter who asked, whether in the South or this far North. Sephie turned to him and raised an eyebrow, showing her obvious curiosity. He respected her reticence to ask him about it in all the time he'd known her. "Actually, it's Brian Dennehy."

"The alien from *Cocoon*?" Laura said.

"And those Jack Reed crime films? Wasn't he in *Silverado*?" Mandy offered.

"My mom was a fan. Don't tell me you never thought Denzel Washington or Dwayne Johnson were mighty fine?"

"Or Idris Elba," Laura said, a little dreamily.

B.D. wasn't surprised that she would know that heart throb.

"Or Chadwick Boseman," Mandy added.

That made B.D. grin. A Black Panther fan and obviously a film buff.

"I was more of a James Earl Jones and Morgan Freeman fan," Sephie confessed.

B.D. chuckled. "It's the voice, right?"

"How'd your father feel about you being named after a White actor?" Sephie wondered.

"I don't know. He died before I was born."

"Are you a seventh son?" the old woman asked.

"Nope. I've got six older sisters, though."

"Hmph," she grunted. "You're at least a son who never saw his father. Do you know what you can do?"

"What do you mean?"

"You can stop issues of blood."

"Say what?"

"My daddy was a seventh son who never saw his father," Sephie said. "He was a thrush doctor — thrush, what babies get in their mouths. And he could stop blood."

"How'd Great-Aunt Agnesia handle that?" Mandy asked. "Is that why she lives in the church?"

"Oh, it was all very Bible based, Mandy. My daddy had a

Bible verse to use for each of those healings. But I never knew what they were. It was all very secret."

"There's no way I'm a faith healer nor a root doctor," B.D. protested.

"You're on your way to becoming a root doctor, hanging out with me."

"No, you're an herb doctor. I'm no hoodoo man. Though my granddad was, I've been told. I don't do no bad stuff."

Sephie squinted at him. "We need to define terms. But first." She swung on Mandy. "Point me to the ladies'. It's been a long drive."

"I'll show you," Laura said, taking the box from Mandy and ushering the old woman into the back.

Mandy smiled at B.D. "I'll give you a hand." She moved to the door and then headed to the station wagon on the street. When B.D. swung open the rear door, she saw a box full of tiny bottles and vials. Reaching for that, B.D. warned, "Be careful. Miz Sephie'll have your hide if anything gets broken. Truth be told, so would I. We worked hard on those."

"How long have you known Sephie?"

Moving a box onto another one, B.D. lifted both as Mandy tended to the tincture box. "I helped her build her cabin in Dark Holler. That was — what? — five years ago. I was a freshman then and looking for summer cash. I came back every time she needed something done. Then last year as I was finishing up my folklore degree, I hung out more often, learning and helping with the wildcrafting."

"She has a lot to teach," Mandy said, opening the shop door. "How much of this is for the shop?"

"All of it. We just packed a bag apiece."

Mandy glanced at the station wagon packed full. "We'll use it."

"Was she kidding about vampires?"

The color drained from Mandy's face. It was evidently no joke.

Chapter 7

Day 3: Riverbend, ND

"Do you really think your aunt can help with the vampire problem?" Laura asked, squeezing the plastic bear to release the honey out of its head into her cup of hot mint tea that was sitting on the glass counter.

Stirring her own cup of tea with a spoon, Mandy quickly remarked, "Sure. You saw all that stuff we brought in."

"What's she planning on doing with all of that? I mean I see the tea and tinctures and maybe some of those brown paper bags of dried herbs, but all those tree limbs?"

"Maybe she plans on whittling her own vampire stakes."

Laura giggled then sobered. "We won't have to resort to staking anybody, will we?"

Mandy shrugged, then sipped her tea. "Lordy, Aunt Sephie was right. This mint kicks. I put in three leaves."

"She said only one or two." Laura tasted hers. "Very nice. Only one leaf." She took Mandy's cup from her hand. "I'll go water yours down from the kettle."

"Don't waste it," Mandy warned, following her.

Laura found another cup in the back room and poured off half from Mandy's mug. Then she filled it with more hot water and handed the mug back to her partner. On her way to the front, Laura peeked into the boxes that had been brought in and lined up on the floor. She leaned over the one nearest the doorway. Inside were sealed quart jars with a clear liquid in them. She lifted one and tilted it slightly. "Did she bring her own water?"

Mandy laughed. “No. I don’t think that’s water.”

Laura replaced the jar and straightened, screwing up her face in question.

Mandy put her arm around her partner and guided her back into the store. “I think it’s Cousin Lije’s shine.”

“What?” Laura’s eyes grew big. “She brought illegal whiskey across all those state lines? And B.D. was driving most of the time. What was she thinking?”

Settling into the stool behind the counter, Mandy explained, “She was thinking about tinctures.”

“But isn’t she a teetotaler? Isn’t her family Baptists or something?”

“Aunt Agnesia is. But I’m sure Sephie tipples a bit. She likes store liquor for that. Gin, mostly.”

“Then we’ll have to show her where to get some down the street. But why not buy vodka or gin for her tinctures?”

Mandy shrugged, studying her tea. Laura came around the counter and nudged her with her hip. “You don’t know, do you? You don’t know that’s what’s in those jars? Or that she uses it for her tinctures?”

“It definitely is Cousin Lije’s shine. I’ve seen it before at her cabin. But since she brought all those tinctures ready-made, I don’t know. I do know that there’s a tale around Cousin Lije’s family that only Aunt Sephie knows.”

Bracing her elbows on the counter with her cup of tea between her hands, Laura said, “I can’t wait to hear it.”

Chapter 8

Day 3: Riverbend, ND, late morning

It was a cozy, feminine room. The antique cast iron bedstead had been painted white. Over the mattress, a white comforter with medium-sized yellow flowers added bright color. A small vanity and a tall bureau, both painted white, faced the foot of the bed. A white wicker bedside table, holding a lamp with a cream silk shade that bore white fringe, had been placed beside the bed near the open window that was framed in long panels of white with yellow flowers. On the wall opposite the bed, a closet door stood open , as if welcoming the old woman's things.

Aunt Sephie smiled at those old-fashioned touches, as if Mandy or Laura were old enough to remember anything like what was in that room. She herself barely remembered her own grandmother's little house in coal country that had flour sack curtains and a handmade quilt. She had been thankful to have a bed to sleep in with her sister when they visited. There had been no indoor plumbing. She remembered running barefoot across the faded linoleum and out into the wooden porch on dewy summer mornings, stuffing those feet into tennis shoes, and rushing to the outhouse in the back. The amenities that Mandy — no, probably Laura — provided were the touches found in city homes in an era far older than the 1940s of Sephie's youth.

"You should get luggage with wheels," B.D. announced, hauling a very heavy, beat-up suitcase into the bright room.

Sephie pointed to the bed, and her companion heaved the

old case onto it.

"Nice room," B.D. pronounced.

The old woman walked to the single window and looked out onto the street. She pulled a curtain panel away from the sill and noticed a thin line of white crystals. She licked her forefinger, touched the white line, and then brought it to her tongue tentatively, recognizing its familiar taste — salt. In the center of the white line rested a sliver of black obsidian. Sephie nodded her approval.

Turning to B.D., she ordered, "Reach under the bed and see if there's anything there."

The young man knelt, pulled up the comforter, and stretched a hand under it. He pulled out a small cottage cheese container. When he saw what it contained, he scuttled backwards. "Somebody put a root under your bed!" he cried. "A hex."

Bending over the container, Sephie saw that it was a white chicken egg. She said, "Don't be hasty. It may not be a root working that's a hex. Could be a protection, like what's on the window sill." She straightened. "Shove it back under there and be careful not to break it."

When B.D. had completed the task and stood, he asked, "What makes you think it's a protection?"

"I don't think Mandy or Laura would let any harm come to me, if they could help it. I don't see how somebody could get in here and hex a place next door with both of them in and out of here for the past day or two. It's just a path I don't know. I don't get a bad feeling off of it." She squinted at B.D. "There's probably one under your bed, too. Now, don't you go messing with it until we find out what it is and how it's supposed to work."

He raised his eyebrows. "If you say so, but I don't trust it."

"You're an educated young man. Magic, like science, reveals its workings the more you know about it." Sephie reassured him. "Remember that pandemic we had not so long ago? Some people said that science was wrong. No, science wasn't wrong. We just hadn't caught up with all that there was to know about the disease. Our science just got more refined. Same with magic or any kind of working. Now, go get freshened up. I'm hungry. Let's see what they have to eat in this far north country."

Chapter 9

Day 3: Riverbend, ND, near noon

"Wanna help me carry back lunch?" Laura asked B.D. "Mandy usually does the heavy lifting, but I bet you'd like to see some of the town."

"We driving?" B.D. asked, not really wanting to get into a car again for a while.

"Nope. Just walking. It's not far, just a couple of blocks."

Outside on the sidewalk, B.D. asked, "What do people do for fun in town?"

"Drink." She smiled up at him, obviously waiting for a reaction. "A lot."

"You're kidding. I thought they only did that where I've been living. There's not much there. A drive-in theater and a couple of cafés. There's more to do at the college in the next town."

They had stopped at an intersection, and B.D. looked up at the signs. Third Avenue was the street they were walking along, and that ran parallel to the river and the long greenway. Here, other buildings cropped up on the other side of the road. The cross street was short and named Water Street. B.D. could read the far street sign and it said Fourth Avenue. He looked again at the greenway and back at the other avenue.

"Wait. What happened to the rest of your streets? Where are First and Second Avenues?"

"Flood took 'em."

"What?"

"Forty years ago, there was a big flood here. We put in a

massive dike system. Parts of it get assembled every spring to ward off the flood after the big thaw. Those streets became part of the greenway. The Fourth of July celebration is held down there."

"Well, that sounds like more than just drinking."

"It is. Lots of booths and bands." She paused. "And a beer garden." She pointed ahead. "You see the rest of this street?"

B.D. craned his head to look down the long street.

"There are three breweries on this street alone. Two across the river on the Minnesota side," she said, continuing down the sidewalk. "Every restaurant has a liquor license and usually does off sale — meaning you can buy a bottle of beer or wine and take it home. And you can get beer and wine in the grocery stores. But you have to get hard stuff at a liquor store."

"What about nightclubs? Places to go dancing?"

Laura shook her head. "Not down here. There used to be. You can hear some live music, but it's listening music. There are a couple of country bars on the edge of town out by the interstate on the west side where you can dance. And you can sometimes dance at the VFW across the river. But old folks go there. They do polkas and schottisches. The Norwegian schottische, not the Scottish or the Texas country schottische."

"Schottische. That's a new one. Sounds like as many variations as the two-step. Must be at least a dozen. Except the Cajun two-step is a heap easier."

"Cajun two-step? I didn't know they had one."

"Every grandmamma teaches her babies that as soon as they can walk. Then they learn the waltz."

"And you know both?"

"Yep, and a few more. I pick up real quick."

Laura grinned. "Mandy — God love her — and I do, too— But she can't keep rhythm worth a darn. She can play guitar great. That's the problem. She hears the melody and harmonies and counter-harmonies but not the beat. I wished I'd married a drummer."

B.D. laughed hard, catching his side, bending over. "Girl, you're gonna kill me."

"It's not that funny. I love to dance, but geez."

Sobering but still smiling, he said, "I hear you. I do. I miss the *fai do-dos* growing up."

"You're not from Tennessee like Sophie?"

"Lordy, no! I went to school there, and there's a cousin I stayed with, but my home's in Lafayette, Louisiana." His mouth formed the town's name so that it sounded like La-FY-ette.

Laura just shook her head. "And you're probably the farthest north as you ever could get."

"Life's funny like that."

They had stopped in front of a restaurant with tall windows in the front. Hanging overhead was a sign that looked like a pub sign found in England. This one, however, bore the tusked visage of a black wild boar, but no lettering. Laura paused. "Well, life is about to get quirkier." She reached for the door handle. Above the door, in dark gray letters across deep maroon paint, was written: THE W.H.

Chapter 10

Day 3: North Star, noonish

Aunt Sephie settled into the comfortable rocker Mandy had brought into the store and angled into a corner near the opening to the back room. The old woman had brought in the pale blue shawl she had started crocheting for Laura back home. Beginning the next row, Sephie crocheted while Mandy watched.

"Mama used to try to teach me to do that," Mandy said. "I just never could do it. Knitting neither."

"It's not hard once you learn right. Your mama learned from her mama. It was a different style."

"You hold your yarn different, and the hook."

Sephie smiled, looking at the way the yarn was wrapped around the little finger of her right hand and that she held the hook like a pencil. "Somebody told me it was the old German way. My people were English, Scottish, and Irish. I think there was some Welsh in there. But my mama thought she had ancestors who were Black Dutch. Those folks were Romani, but maybe they were a branch that settled in Germany. Maybe that's where the crochet style came from."

They were silent a while, then Mandy said, "It's very meditative. The way you do it."

"It is," Sephie said, "until my arthritis starts to cramp up my hands. So, I do a little at a time." She did a few more stitches and then said, "The egg under the bed. What path is that?"

"It's from a woman I know, a *curandera,* an Hispanic healer. I expect she'll be in here this week."

"How's it work?"

"It's supposed to absorb anything negative. Sometimes they pass it over the body to absorb the bad stuff."

"Raw egg?"

"Yep. So, don't break it. It's supposed to stay under the bed a week. I've had it under there a day already."

Sephie nodded. "You know good people. We'll need them before we're done. Tell me, what exactly are we combating here? Psychic vampire? Energy vampire? Spirit vampire? Or blood vampire?"

"We think it's the regular blood kind. It's been attacking cats. So, everybody's been watching their felines real close."

"Just cats?"

"Nobody's mentioned other animals . . . yet."

"Any humans?"

"Not in the past month when the cats started showing up lethargic with what looks like fang marks on their sides."

"What do the local vets say?" Sephie looked over at Mandy when she didn't answer right away. "You have talked to them, haven't you?"

"Medical people of all persuasions give us a wide berth," she said.

Sephie harrumphed, returning to her crocheting. "You have to change that. What have the pet owners said that the vets said?"

"Not much, just wondered whether the cats had crawled through something. But the owners see different vets all over town."

Sephie rested her crocheting in her ample lap. "And humans? Do you know what to look for with the other kinds of vampires?"

"Well. . . ." Mandy looked uncomfortable.

Returning to her handwork, Sephie announced, "We'll need to rectify that, too."

Chapter 11

Day 3: Watering Hole, noon

B.D. just stared, mouth gaping open. Palm ferns and a couple of gigantic ficus plants crowded the tiny foyer that led to the restaurant's inner door, making him feel as if he needed a machete. But it was when Laura opened the door to the main room of the spacious restaurant that B.D. wondered whether he'd stepped into the Twilight Zone. Afropop filled his ears — a mix of traditional drum beats and the beats of hip-hop. More plants hid among tables along with African *djembe* and tall village *ashiko* drums. A huge stuffed wart hog head stared out over the hostess desk, which was unmanned at the moment. A few steps further inside revealed a massive, stuffed water buffalo head looking down over the ornately carved wooden bar shelves and the bar itself with its brass monkey spittoons on each end. Bright Kenta cloth wall hangings, photographs of Victoria Falls and village markets, and posters of old Tarzan movies were plastered over every inch of the walls.

If that wasn't dramatic enough, a balding, walrus-mustached, portly man in his 60s at least, came rushing toward him, his arms open wide. He sported jeans, a chambray short-sleeved shirt, and a fly-fishing, multi-pocketed vest that was supposed to be a safari vest, B.D. guessed.

"Welcome to the Watering Hole!" his bombastic tones greeted them, turning every head toward him except those of the servers who were dressed as he was. He pulled Laura into a bear hug, released her, and extended his big paw to B.D., who shook it in a state of shock. The big man pulled him closer and said quietly nearer B.D.'s face, "Need a job? I could use you in here."

B.D.'s look questioned Laura while he struggled to release his hand. He wondered if that was a racist remark or whether the place needed young help.

"I don't think he'll be here very long, Bill," Laura explained. "He drove Mandy's great-aunt up from Tennessee last night."

"Shared the driving," B.D. corrected. "Miz Sephie's not helpless."

"That's no Tennessee accent, big city or little," Bill judged, then turned to the back of the restaurant where the open grill was preparing steaks and burgers. "Sugar! Come meet this young man!" A short blonde woman walked forward, wiping her hands on a long white apron. Her smile was warm and genuine, but life lines around her eyes clearly showed that she was only about ten years younger than their host.

"This is Sugar Daniels, my wife," the big man said, wrapping his arm around the petite woman. "Actually, it's Dr. Daniels. She kept her maiden name. She's a therapist."

B.D. raised an eyebrow, wondering if this bigger-than-life character needed at-home counseling.

"This is Bill Schneider," Laura explained. "He and Sugar do a lot of local theater here."

B.D. nodded, relieved but still wary. "I'm B.D. Travers. And I just went to school in Tennessee. I'm from Louisiana."

"Is he here to help with the bat problem?" Sugar asked.

"Bat problem?" B.D. wondered aloud.

Laura cleared her throat. "Aunt Sephie brought up some new remedies," she offered in explanation.

"One of the regulars talked about electronic deterrents," Sugar went on. "He said he knows a man who knows a man."

"They tried that with pigeons down here, but it didn't do any good," Bill countered, releasing Sugar. "They just clustered on buildings out of range of the things."

"Bats aren't all bad," B.D. suggested. "They eat mosquitoes."

"The city sprays for mosquitoes," Bill said.

"It's the cats I'm worried about. We can't let them roam anymore," Sugar said.

"You mean the bats are attacking your cats?"

Laura cleared her throat again, drawing B.D.'s attention. She had that look on her face that a mother gets who wants her child to stop talking. He realized then that they really weren't talking about bats.

Turning to Sugar, Laura moved the conversation in another direction. "Mandy called in an order. Do you have that ready?"

Sugar's face brightened. "Sure do. Come on back while I bag it up for you."

Bill reached behind him, pulled a paper menu from the bar top, and offered it to B.D. "We offer exotic food and comfort food. Take it with you. Study it for future orders."

B.D. scanned the offerings, noticing meatloaf and fried chicken, but also wild boar, ostrich, shark steaks, and kangaroo. His eyes flashed up to Bill's, wondering where the older man had developed such tastes. Then he considered his people, who ate crawdads and alligator. "Are you a veteran? Did you spend time in Africa?" he asked the older man.

"No, I was stationed in Dayton, Ohio, for my stint in the Air Force. I was a mechanic." He beamed as he surveyed his restaurant. "Always wanted to go there, though. So, I brought it here."

B.D. noticed Sugar and Laura carrying trays made from the bottoms of a couple of cardboard boxes. In them were several white paper bags. B.D. relieved Sugar of her burden, and they said their glad-to-meet-you's. When they were out on the street, B.D. asked Laura a question that had been chased out by all the talk of dancing and the experience at The W.H. "Why'd you tell me all about where to find liquor in this town?"

"I wondered whether you were such a big drinker that you needed to bring all that illegal whiskey Sephie had you carry in."

"What whiskey? Illegal? Wha—"

Chapter 12

Day 3: North Star, early afternoon

"Miz Sephie, I've got a bone to pick with you!" B.D. announced when he'd crossed the threshold of the North Star with his share of the lunch meals.

The old woman looked up from her crocheting as Mandy stepped to take the food he carried.

B.D. wouldn't relinquish his box, pulling it away from the younger woman. "Not until she explains why she had me driving illegal whiskey across state lines — and at night. If I'd gotten pulled over. . . . It's bad enough driving while Black but add driving with jars of moonshine in the back of the station wagon.—.and there's no trunk to lock it up in.—.and it's not even my station wagon."

Head down, Laura scooted around B.D. and headed for the back room with her box. Mandy followed quickly behind her.

Sophie returned to her handwork. "It was good enough for that blues man, it's good enough for you."

"What blues man?"

"That harmonica player. He was explaining why he ended up in Chicago. Charlie somebody."

B.D. sifted through all of the conversations they'd had over the years about music. At one time in her younger years, the old woman had done a bit of freelance writing, covering music, for the county newspaper. It was a good fit back then because she had distant cousins who played, and she could talk the arm off anybody. Finally, he understood her reference. "He only drove around Memphis," he said. "You had me crossing

— what? six state lines. How much were we hauling?"

"Only a dozen quarts. I didn't have time to get more. That was all I had in the cabin."

"Where'd you get the stuff? You know it'll make you go blind."

Coming to the end of a row, Sephie pulled a long loop in her work and then anchored the crochet hook in the garment. She hefted herself out of the rocking chair. "You're cranky when you're hungry. Bring that lot into the back room. What did you get, anyway?"

Following her into the back, he put his box of white bags on the long table where they had been making tea. "I doubt this'll be typical North Country fare," he said. "The restaurant was . . . unique." He turned to Mandy, "What did you order?"

"A bit of this and that." She reached into a bag and handed her aunt a sandwich wrapped in white butcher paper. "Go sit back down out front. I'll bring some lemonade in, and a bowl of soup and some sweet potato fries." She turned to B.D., handing him a sandwich. "Grab a folding chair over there and take it out front."

B.D. went to a corner and picked up a brown metal chair while Laura poured soup into paper cups, sticking a plastic spoon into each. "Why do you have so many chairs? You hold meetings or something?"

"Classes, really. Sometimes a celebration in the winter time when we can't get out on the greenway."

Laura handed Mandy a cup of soup as she followed him out front.

When they had all gathered in the store with glasses of homemade lemonade, Sephie asked. "So, what are we eating?"

Mandy announced, settling next to Laura onto one of the two stools behind the counter, "Aunt Sephie, you've got a kangaroo burger and some of Bill's special Mock Turtle Soup."

"You want me to eat Roo?" Sephie asked.

"You never minded eating Piglet back at your sister's church barbeque that you wanted me to sing at?" B.D. countered.

"All day gospel sing and dinner on the ground. Not a barbeque." She lifted the hamburger bun to look at the burger. "You sang pretty."

"Sing?" Mandy perked up.

Laura grinned. "He dances, too. Cajun two-step, waltz. And more."

B.D. stared at both eager faces, feeling like the prize stud bull. He dipped into his soup and tasted it, astonished. "This is Mock Turtle Soup?"

"Yep."

"But it tastes like the real thing."

"Well, Bill says it's Mock Turtle . . . beef . . . because he can't guarantee getting any turtle meat. Sometimes a friend bags a monster from the river or one of the many lakes around here and brings it to him. They're huge. Not those tiny green things you think they are."

"River turtles. We got 'em back home. Big as hogs." Sipping some more, he pronounced, "Bill and Sugar are mighty fine cooks. But somebody has to do something about that music. He needs some blues in there to soothe the stomach."

"I hear ya," Mandy said. "What he's playing is called Afrobeats. Here, let me put on something. Tell me what you think." From behind her, she found a CD case, opened it, and slid the disc into a player. The store was filled with intricate guitar and plucked African string instrument music with a definite blues beat, enhanced by a variety of hand drums.

"Good stuff. Who is that?" B.D. asked.

Mandy read the CD case "Ali Farka Toure."

B.D. shook his head. "Who would ever have thought I'd be introduced to great Afropop in the frozen north!"

"Life is always full of surprises," Sephie said. "Roo tastes like beef."

B.D. challenged Sephie but without the anger of before. "Now, tell us. Where did you get illegal whiskey and why'd you bring it?"

Sephie took a drink from her lemonade glass. "It's quite a tale, and I guess it's time to tell it. But you're beat from driving all night, and this food will make you sleepy. Later, after you take a nap."

B.D. shrugged. He knew he never could get anything out of Sephie until she was ready to speak. For the moment, the Mock Turtle soup occupied his taste buds and his heart, making him suddenly homesick.

Chapter 13

Day 3: North Star, afternoon

Placing the last bottle of goldenseal tincture onto the top shelf of an old wooden display case Mandy had secured onto a scarf-covered card table near the rocker, Sephie smiled at the handiwork of last Fall's harvest. It looked professional on the rack and the blue designs of the scarf added a homey touch she liked. She had carefully dried the roots of the herbs and then made up the tinctures this past Spring. She had used a mixture of distilled water and the precious moonshine she had brought with her. Cousin Lije's brew was hard for most people to handle, but it preserved the medicine better than commercial liquor. Besides, finding store spirits was hard back home in a dry county. She would have had to travel two counties over to get it. Lije always delivered and was even able to transact his business with her right under Agnesia's sin-aware nose.

"I'm glad you brought goldenseal. We can't get any quality tinctures from our suppliers," Laura said from behind the counter.

"They have some," Mandy added, picking up the empty carton beside the card table. "But, geez, the price of goldenseal has skyrocketed over the past couple of years. One supplier is selling a small amber bottle the same size as yours for two hundred, seventy-five dollars."

Sephie whipped her head around toward her niece. "And I thought selling this for twenty dollars a bottle was pricey."

"For the cure-all for everything? They'll pay and shake your hand for taking their money," Mandy said before heading into the back room with the cardboard carton.

"Well, I'm glad I brought all my stock, then. There's more back there." Sephie took a step away to look at all of the bottles of tinctures. Not only did the rack contain goldenseal but also echinacea, ginger, ginseng, chamomile, and feverfew. Enough for headaches, energy, tummy soothing, and immune boosting. Sephie stood by her herbs, but she wondered whether Lije's liquor might be the best healer. It could surely make you sleep.

The bell atop the door jingled, drawing the old woman away from her pride. A white-haired frail woman rushed in holding a very fat, gray and white, long-haired cat. The animal's head and hind quarters were poured over the little woman's thin arms. "It got Precious! I found her limp like this in the garden. Look at her! I thought she'd OD'd on catnip."

Sephie and Laura stepped toward the woman, but Laura reached the animal first and placed it on the glass counter. "Poor Puss," Sephie crooned, moving in finally to stroke her hand across the animal's back and head. She sniffed her own hand. "She has gotten into catnip, for sure. But it makes them sleep for only a little while after they get all crazy."

Laura interjected, "Miz Lucy, this is Mandy's Aunt Sephie. She's a wise woman."

"Can you help her?" the old woman pleaded.

Sephie pushed open each of the cat's eyes and saw an unnatural look in them. "This isn't catnip. She's been drugged. Did she eat anything outside?"

"I don't think so. But she must've gotten into something."

Sephie made a thorough examination of the animal's ears and paws and then began to go through the fur. Concealed by the long hair were three long scratches. They had smooth edges so it wasn't barbed wire or a broken fence railing. It was as if some kind of talon had raked across the cat's side. "I think you need to take . . . Precious, did you say her name was? Take Precious to the vet."

"But how? I can't drive and hold her. She needs comfort now."

"I agree," Sephie said. "My car is right out front. But I'll need someone to help me navigate."

"I'll drive," Laura said.

Sephie reached into her faded jean's pocket and handed Laura the keys. Then she picked up Precious and rushed out the door with Miz Lucy trailing behind. "Precious doesn't know you. Let me take her. Precious, can you hear me?"

When they got to the car, Laura gently pushed Miz Lucy into the back seat and Sephie put the limp cat into the old woman's arms. As Laura and Sephie climbed in front, they both asked in unison, "Which vet?" Sephie raised an eyebrow and bit her tongue on the old jinx about speaking at the same time.

"Riverbend," Miz Lucy said, as Laura started the car and whipped it out of the parking space. The old station wagon leaped forward, forcing the young woman to slam on the brakes, looking shaken.

"Should have warned you. She's got some pep."

Chapter 14

Day 3: North Star, midafternoon

B.D.'s yawn was wide and loud as he trudged into the shop from the back door. It was loud enough to draw Mandy from the front to crane her head around the door frame to see what beast was lurking among Aunt Sephie's herbs and moonshine. "I thought you were sleeping."

"I was," B.D. said. "But who can sleep when the sun's shining?" He followed her into the main shop and hoisted his lanky frame onto a stool beside the counter. "Where is everybody?"

Mandy resumed her perch behind the counter and turned another page of the wholesale catalog she had been perusing. "They're at the vet."

"The vet?"

"A customer's cat was attacked by the vampire. Poor old darling got so upset."

"Say what? A vampire that feeds off cats? Is that why we're here?"

"Didn't Aunt Sephie tell you? It's serious business. Our clientèle has been complaining of cat attacks for weeks. It looks like a vampire. Everyone's jumpy."

"But cats? Not people?"

"People could be next."

B.D. shrugged, not convinced. "I suppose."

"Aunt Sephie needed to see for herself. We've tried garlic and putting mirrors up. But that hasn't protected the poor cats."

"Well, Sephie sure brought enough stuff to fight anything."

Mandy straightened. "She did bring me some stock I can't get anywhere else." The young woman gestured toward the display case of tinctures. "She'd promised to ship all that to me. I'm glad she didn't, because it's too precious to risk breaking."

"I guess she felt the same about all that moonshine I've been driving across way too many state lines."

Mandy looked at the man's sports watch on her left wrist and grinned. It was close to 3:00 p.m. She leaned closer to B.D. "Want to try a sip? It's four o'clock where you just came from."

"We'll go blind with that stuff."

"You ever have it?"

He hesitated. "Well, no."

"But you're curious, right?"

"I don't know about this, Miss Mandy."

Not waiting for his agreement, Mandy slipped into the back room, with B.D. following. She quickly found the box with the illegal whiskey in it and pulled out a jar. On the long white table, Mandy found two small juice glasses. Taking the lot, she brought it back to the counter and resumed her seat on the stool. Gripping the jar lid, she tried to twist the ring off. After three attempts, she reluctantly handed it to B.D. "You got bigger hands," she admitted. "It's not because you're a man."

B.D. chuckled. "No worries. I won't hold it against you." With a mighty twist, the ring was loosened, and he set the canning jar back on the counter.

Mandy pulled a Leatherman knife out of her pocket and found a bottle opener to pop off the inner lid on the jar. She sniffed the contents and jerked her head away. "It's potent," she announced. Carefully, she poured two inches into each glass and put the lid and ring back on the jar. Grinning, she raised her glass to B.D. "Welcome to North Dakota," she said.

Reluctantly, B.D. picked up his glass and clinked it against Mandy's. Looking skeptical, he took a sip as did Mandy.

"It's smooth," the young woman announced. "Like good vodka. It doesn't have much flavor."

"Guess it's not drunk for its taste," B.D. said and downed the rest in his glass. This time, he drew in a deep breath. "That'll open your sinuses, though."

Mandy grinned and downed hers. "One more," she said.

"No, no." Then, he also grinned and held out his glass.

Mandy poured two measures again, and this time after sealing the jar, she placed it on a low shelf in behind her out of sight of customers. Instead of chugging the shots, she and B.D. both lingered over the liquor.

"So, what brought you all the way from Louisiana to Tennessee? Laura said you went to school there?"

B.D. nodded. "You'd think you could study folklore in a state so rich in its own, but it really wasn't more than what Grammy and my aunties used to tell me. So, I went up North to my cousin's where he said that the college had a professor who knew not only all of the stories of haints and curses, but every single mountain ballad hidden in those Appalachian foothills. And Miz Sephie, well, she showed me a whole other history behind the lore. I wrote my honors thesis on the herbs mentioned in the old stories and folk ballads."

"I guess you must know all hundred million verses of 'Barbara Allen.'"

"There're only fifteen, but there are many variations and many other murder ballads."

"What other songs do you know?"

B.D. chuckled. "I was born singing. In my family, you had to or be disowned. I learned gospel first and some Cajun dance tunes in French — waltzes mainly. I was a sponge."

"Do you play an instrument?"

He shook his head. "Never learned. Too busy singing and

dancing, I guess."

"You're not going to be idle here," Mandy said, taking another sip of the liquor. "You'll be singing and dancing."

"I will?" Hearing a car door slam, B.D. looked out the window to see Laura and Sephie getting out of the car. He tossed down the last of his glass. "Better drink up before we get caught."

Mandy didn't even glance toward the door. She gulped down the last bit and grabbed B.D.'s glass and stored them both on the shelf behind her.

When the bell finally tinkled and the women entered, Mandy realized that they *were* caught. Sephie always had a sixth sense about any trouble she'd ever gotten into. Or was it guilt she never could hide on her face?

The old woman walked in with an eyebrow raised. "The mice have been playing."

Chapter 15

Day 3: North Star, afternoon

Laura frowned at Sephie. This was no time to start parental type scolding. "It's worse than we thought," she said as she hurried around the old woman and squeezed behind B.D. She spotted the canning jar of liquid on the shelf behind Mandy but continued her report. "Poor Precious never twitched a whisker and never shed a single hair at the vet. With all those fear smells there, she should have been bald. You remember me telling you about how my Persian used to shed all over me when I'd take her for her shots when I was living at home."

Mandy stood to offer the stool to Laura, who shook her head in sympathy. "Will the cat be all right?"

"The vet was stumped, but figured someone had poisoned her."

"It wasn't blood loss like we thought before?" Mandy asked.

Sephie stepped to the counter. "I told that vet to swab those scratches. I think that's where the poison or drug was introduced."

"Our customers said their cats were lethargic and some listed to one side when they walked," Laura explained.

"You ever have to pill a cat for travel?" B.D. asked. "I did for a college friend of mine who was moving back home. Gave the cat a tranquilizer. When I saw that poor thing stumble down the stairs to the front door, I thought I'd poisoned it. Its eyes were all wrong. I swore I'd never do it again."

"That's what this looked like to me," Sephie said. "The eyes were like you said. All wrong."

"Is the vet keeping the cat overnight?" Mandy asked.

"Yes, and running a lot of tests," Laura explained.

Sephie moved over to her rocker and eased herself down. "You said the cat attacks were all over town."

"Yes, I think so," Laura responded.

"You got a city map," Sephie asked, "and a list of customers with addresses, a data . . . something?"

"A database," Mandy offered. "We've got a mailing list."

"There are maps in the phone book," Laura said. "I'll photocopy them for you."

"And I'll print off that list," Mandy offered. "Then we'll highlight who has had cat attacks. There might be a pattern there."

Laura and Mandy hurried into the back room and up the stairs to their little apartment. There was only one big room, the bedroom, and bathroom. Off in one corner was a desk with a desktop computer and printer.

"Was the shine good?" Laura asked her partner as she leaned over to open a desk drawer to search for the phone book. They rarely used the book, since most of their frequently used numbers were in their cellphones.

Mandy grinned as she sat down in the office chair. "Smooth."

"Not a drop more. You don't know what that stuff'll do to you."

Mandy dropped a kiss on the side of Laura's neck bent tantalizingly close to her. All the talk of vampires made Laura flinch automatically.

"No worries," Mandy said, trying to recapture the romantic mood. "I've got shine in my genes."

Laura looked at her wife's blue jeans, wondering what she was talking about.

"DNA," Mandy said. "Geez. Forget a butch trying to be romantic." Turning back to the computer, she added. "I do come from a long line of moonshiners."

Finally finding the phone book under a jumble of papers, Laura said, “Yeah, I want to hear about that. Your Aunt Sephie promised us a story.”

Chapter 16

Day 3: North Star, late afternoon

"Thorkleson, Iola," Sephie called out from her copy of the customer mailing list she had.

"Yes," Mandy said. "An old gray tiger cat."

Sephie gave the address and marked the name and address with yellow highlighter.

Mandy told B.D. "Riverside area. Map Three." B.D. and Mandy found the street and estimated where the house number was on it. Using a marker, B.D. slashed it with a big red X.

"Joyce Simonson," Laura said, coming in the front door from outside where she had been calling customers who had complained of attacked cats and who had only given PO boxes for their addresses. She stated the address, and Mandy and B.D. went to work marking it on one of the maps. "That's the last," Laura said.

"So, what do we have?" Sephie said. "All over the city, as you thought?"

Mandy spread out the maps across the counter. "Well," she announced. "Yes, a cross section of the town north to south."

B.D. compared the long line of maps to the smaller inset map of the city limits of Riverbend. "Hey, every one of these is along the river. Not exactly on the river bank because of all of this open space between the river and the streets."

"There aren't any buildings directly on the river any more after the big flood in the late nineteen-nineties. That area is all greenway, park land. It's a buffer area between the river and the permanent flood walls. It allows the river to flood without hurting the city."

"How often does it flood?" B.D. asked

"Every year," Mandy explained. "Some years more than others. Depends on the snow pack and how quick the thaw is. When the thaw comes, the river thaws, sure. But we get a lot of overland flooding that goes into the river. It starts way south of us and by the time it gets here, there's a lot of water."

Sephie leaned back in the rocker. "When did you first start hearing about the cat attacks?" she asked.

"After the flood in early May," Laura said. "It was a pretty high one this year."

B.D. was perplexed. "Think something living by the river is getting at those cats? Never thought vampires were interested in cats, really."

"Maybe it's a bat," Mandy said.

"Bats? Is that why you think it's a vampire?" Sephie said and gave a hearty laugh.

"I never said that," Laura argued. "Precious was drugged."

B.D. interjected. "Vampire bats, the only ones that drink blood, live in tropical countries. They couldn't survive in the frozen north. We got a rare one once in bayou country, blown in on a hurricane. Shoot, if we were back home, I'd worry more about gators, but they'd just eat the cat whole."

"You don't think something came up out of the river, do you?" Laura said, her voice shaking slightly.

"The Riverbend Monster," B.D. announced, grinning, coining a new folk legend. Then his smile shrank as he asked, seeing some flaw in his statement. "But why cats? Why not dogs or small children?"

"Hush your mouth!" Sephie cautioned. "There's something afoot here. Something not normal."

Chapter 17

Day 3: North Star, late afternoon

B.D. frowned over the books on vampires that Mandy had unpacked from the day's merchandise shipment.

"You have the expertise in folklore," she had said. "Tell us if anything in there applies to our little monster."

He had spent a good hour gleaning what he could from the writings of an occultist who had made the talk show rounds and another by an historian. The books detailed the lives of famous vampires from Europe, including a vampire from England. It was more than the normal Vlad the Impaler tale. The vampires, however, were the typical neck-biting blood suckers who preyed on women and weak men. None had turned to animals or even started out with them. And none slashed their victims as this Dakota vampire did.

A loud caw drew B.D. from his frustrating study. Another caw followed, then another, and another. He stepped toward the display window to look out. Black birds — crows — gathered on top of the unlit street lamps. One, two, three, four on one. Another four on the next. Five more fluttered down into a big shrub in the greenway between. And three more settled down into the grass below. B.D. opened the front door slowly so not to let the little bell ring. He stepped out to look up and down the street. Nowhere else had birds gathered. Their calls across from him were distracting, as if a brood of church ladies had gathered to scold him about some rule infraction. Above, a loud throaty drum made B.D. look up. A much bigger black bird circled the crows below. Its wingspan was double that of the crows and its tail was broader and pointed. It was a solitary raven.

B.D. counted the crows again. Sixteen in total sitting in almost a circle, with the one big raven overhead. B.D. sucked in a breath in awe. Sixteen, the sacred number. The circle of birds and the lone bird above. It looked like the sacred staff of protection of the herbalist of Osanyin gathered here in front of him — all this way from his people's practice. Osanyin, the orisha of healing, the knower of roots and herbs, the diviner of healing knowledge. Why was he honoring B.D. when Sephie was the sacred healer?

He stood in awe for several minutes, absorbing the message that Osanyin was near. Then, as if a silent call had been passed among them, the birds shot upwards and away toward the river, the sudden explosion of wings startling B.D. causing him to bow to their divine message. Humbly, he turned back into the shop.

"Been singing birds down again?" Sephie asked, waddling from the window to settle back into her rocker.

B.D.'s throat constricted. There were no words for what he had witnessed. How could he respond to Sephie? He stared at the old woman, who had picked up her yarn and was concentrating on her crocheting again. Had Osanyin's sacred staff appeared to him because he was a man and Sephie was a woman? In the orisha's eyes, women were not meant to be healers.

Seeking answers, his attention went to Mandy, who was placing new books onto the back shelves, totally oblivious to what had happened outside. B.D. looked at the books scattered on the counter where he had been studying. There was an explanation . . . somewhere. There had to be. Then his mind filled with images of ceremonies he'd witnessed. He was reminded that medicines could be made to cure or curse.

Laura, returning from the back room where she had taken an empty box, came into B.D.'s field of vision. She stopped abruptly, staring at him. Finally, Laura stepped toward him and softly asked, "What's happened?"

Mandy turned to look over her shoulder and recognized something was amiss. "Laura?" She turned full around. "B.D.?"

Sephie looked up then.

Laura took B.D. by the arm and pulled him toward the stool where he had been working at the counter. She gave him a little shove, and he plopped onto the seat.

B.D.'s brain sifted through prayers and songs to find understanding. He needed Papa Mamoud, the old griot from back home. He was his people's storyteller and keeper of history. He had been the one who had filled his head with so many tales as a boy that he wanted to learn them all and every old song. Papa Mamoud would know the right tale to explain this and the proper song to sing to honor Osanyin, and Papa Mamoud would know why he had been chosen to witness the message outside.

The sound of a fruit jar lid being unscrewed disturbed his confusion. A small glass was placed in his hand.

"Drink this," Mandy said. "All of it."

B.D. stared at the glass in his hand. He felt the weight of it. He blinked. raising the glass, he swallowed the clear liquid. The fire hit his throat and slid down his esophagus, burning all the way. He coughed, and his vision cleared. B.D. looked around at all three women who were now gathered around the counter.

"Cousin Lije's shine works wonders," Sephie said. Providing a proper motherly scowl, she added, "But I suppose you and Mandy already know about that."

To turn attention away from himself and the spectacle he felt he had made, B.D. prompted Sephie, "You promised to tell your tale about the moonshine, Miz Sephie."

"Maybe you should tell us what just happened to you," she countered.

He shook his head. "Later. I need to ponder it."

"Well, then," Sephie conceded. "I guess you all deserve to hear Lije's story. If nothing else but to make sure you little mice don't go playing in his wares. It's strictly medicinal."

Chapter 18

Day 3: North Star, late afternoon

Nestled back in her rocker, Sephie picked up the blue shawl she had been crocheting. She put in another row before beginning as if she needed those soothing movements to gather her thoughts.

"I come from a long line of moonshiners. Mandy girl, I'm sure you remember your granddad telling a few tales about my dad. His dad used to go hunting with my dad."

From behind the counter again with Laura, she replied, "Just the one about how he'd had to row out to an island in the river to give your dad food and then had to sink the rowboat every night. He was hiding out from the revenuers, wasn't he?"

Sephie chuckled. "I remember that story. He would have been eight or nine years old. And frankly the revenuers were all over those hills well past Prohibition." She shook her head. "My daddy and his younger brothers made shine nonstop and taught their sons, too. I think one of the younger generation went straight and got their works certified back in the nineties. They sell Tennessee moonshine legally in some liquor stores down there."

She took a deep breath and then added a few more stitches. "What y'all have to remember is that making moonshine was a way of life in Dark Holler. It caused some pretty strange ways of doing things among family members. As I said before, Daddy and his brothers all made shine. One of his brothers had a son called Lije, short for Elijah, and he was known as Black Lije, part by his appearance and part by his way of living. There never was a meaner son of a gun than he was. He'd shoot you between the eyes if you looked at him funny. It's a wonder he married and had a houseful of children. It was said he beat his wife if she didn't do what he said. His whole family feared him and hated him. His wife nearly lived in the church because she never wanted to be home when he was there, especially if he'd been drinking, which was most of the time. She went to all the services, even the Bible classes and prayer services. She got all her daughters to go with her. She called on the sick and served on every committee she could be on.

"When Black Lije died, they buried him up on the ridge by the river. Yet, something strange happened to his grave. About six months after he was buried and the grass had grown back, his grave sank. Just fell right down into the ground. His family was concerned so they dug up the grave, but his coffin was never found. Folks around those parts said the Devil got him and took him down to Hell, coffin and all." She shrugged. "I figured maybe it was more an act of God, flooding the river and maybe undercutting the bank. But there was no big open hole under the bank where the grave was. It could've been something else. That whole area is full of caves and such. Maybe one of those floods fed an underground river and it undercut where the grave was and the coffin just dropped down into that. The ground was always shifting up there anyway."

The room had grown unnaturally quiet. Sephie raised her head to see her listeners staring with wide eyes.

"I'm telling y'all this because you can't always believe the old tales. More often than not, there's a natural explanation to everything, though I won't deny the Almighty's hand in a lot of things I can't explain. There's lots of tales around moonshine. Sometimes it's to scare people away from trying to find the family's still. Sometimes it's just to keep youngun's like you from tippling their wares."

"So, was it one of Black Lije's son's who made the moonshine you have?" Mandy asked.

"That's Cousin Red Lije's brew." Sephie returned to the shawl, pressing out her work to see if she hadn't missed a stitch. She nodded, approving of her work. "Well, technically, it's Black Lije's grandson's brew. Same recipe. Just a tad cleaner production. He makes it in his basement."

"Why did you bring it?" Laura asked.

"I use it in my tinctures because it's so pure. I like it better than store vodka. That always tastes like chemicals. Somehow Red Lije's has a softer taste." She chuckled. "Though it still packs a kick." She paused and then added. "I thought it might help us deal with vampires. I'm going to infuse some with dogwood bark." She then raised her head and admonished. "And don't you go sipping that when it's done. Who knows what that'd do to your brain?"

Mandy commented, "I wondered why you brought all those tree branches."

"Dogwood. B.D. can make stakes from them if we have to."

"But why dogwood? Was it just readily available?"

Sephie put her crocheting down in frustration. "Mandy, didn't your folks ever teach you any mountain lore? The dogwood tree is holy. It was supposed to be the tree that Jesus was crucified on. The tree was cursed by God so that it would never grow to be a big tree like an oak and used to crucify anyone again. The flowers have four petals with a cut in them that has a brown stain. They represent Christ's wounds. And the yellow stamens in the middle form a crown like the Crown of Thorns Jesus wore. The tree has properties as well. You can use the bark like quinine for malaria and like willow bark for headaches and fever. Sometimes, you can put it into a poultice for wounds."

"Then why can't you drink it in moonshine?"

"Well," Sephie muttered, fussing with the shawl. "We need it for the vampires."

Chapter 19

Day 3: Watering Hole, early evening

When B.D. passed through the foyer jungle at the Watering Hole this time, he was prepared for what he saw, but still had to brace himself for the Afrorap he heard. At six o'clock in the evening, the restaurant had a handful of couples at as many tables, not a real dinner crowd, and they were all talking loudly. A few college students were at the bar. B.D. figured the place might fill up later in the evening though he had no idea what the eating habits of these northerners were. He picked up a menu from the hostess on his way in and went to the bar where he waved off a drink from the bartender.

A robust thump to his back jolted him from his perusal of the international delicacies the Watering Hole offered.

"Good to see you back." Bill beamed at him. "Ordering dinner?"

"Yeah, for everybody again. I want to try some new dishes. Props to your turtle soup, by the way."

Bill leaned in as he took a seat on the stool next to B.D. "It was real turtle this time. Can't always claim that."

"So, what do Miss Mandy and Miss Laura like?"

Looking over his shoulder, Bill pointed to a pasta dish. "That's Laura's secret desire. Lobster and shrimp mac and cheese." He pointed to a photo of prime rib. "That's Mandy's weakness, but it's pricey. Otherwise, you could just get her a bison burger."

B.D. whistled at the cost of the prime rib. "Probably worth every penny if the turtle soup is any indication. But the bison burger will have to be what my wallet can afford."

"Mandy's aunt is from the South, right?"

B.D. nodded.

Bill pointed to the wild boar plate. "It's actually grilled, not something people do with pork, though Southerners like to fry any kind of pork. She might like that with mashed potatoes and white gravy and some real greens on the side."

"Greens with vinegar?"

"But of course. Now, what about you? What strikes your fancy?"

"You know, I'd like your goat stew."

Bill grinned. "You're a man an after my own heart! I'll go tell Sugar and then maybe we can hoist one together."

"Before you go," B.D. began and pulled a thumb drive from his pocket, offering it to the older man. "Miss Mandy sent over this drive with music on it. Want to slip that into your computer?"

"Anything that would embarrass me?"

"Would Miss Mandy do that?"

Grinning again, Bill handed it to the barman, telling him to boot it up. "I'll go get your food going."

After a few minutes, the drive uploaded and the shrill Afrorap was silenced, the restaurant was filled with soothing guitar and softer French lyrics from Ali Farka Toure. Mandy had burned the entire album she had of that artist and one from Boubacar Traore. The music was a mix of jazz and blues with the exotics of Africa. Its effects were immediate on the patrons. The din of loud talking diminished. Couples smiled across their meals at each other. One twosome in a booth moved their desserts closer, their bodies following. The college students waved a greeting at the bartender, tossed down some bills, and left. B.D. overheard them tell the hostess that they'd be back with dates later.

Coming out of the kitchen, Bill stopped in the restaurant and stood in awe, his arms open as if receiving blessings from heaven. Still beaming, he took his seat beside B.D. "What is this, and why haven't I heard it before?"

"It's Ali Farka Toure. I never heard him before, either. But I like him."

"Me, too. I need more." He spun around to look at his patrons. "They like it, too."

"You might get an older crowd in here because of it. But they'll linger."

"Don't mind that. I just want them to be happy and come back."

"Your food is great. Music always makes food more pleasant."

"Well, let me buy you a drink, my friend," Bill announced.

B.D. shook his head. "I had my share of drink today. But you could buy me a Coke."

"Been tippling with Mandy? She likes aged Scotch." Bill told the bartender to bring the soft drink and had him pull a draft of one of the local brews.

"Never cared for that myself," B.D. admitted. "We drink lager and wine where I come from, maybe a little rum."

"We get a good lager from a brewery down the street. Most people want ales, though. When we order, the brewery guys just roll the kegs down here." Bill sipped the beer placed before him. "They also make a really good root beer. We keep it on tap for the kids."

B.D. took a long draught of his drink. "This tastes like soft drinks from the South."

Bill smiled, but remained silent for a minute. Then, he confessed. "Soft drink formulas are made for the water in the city where the company is located. That's why most soft drinks taste better in the South. Restaurants use a mix, a syrup, and it's mixed with water in the dispenser that adds the CO2 to make it fizzy. The taste of the local water is what makes colas, in particular, taste different in different parts of the country.

The local water here is very hard. I run ours through a special filtration system that softens the water. You get a better tasting drink. It also makes our cola-based cocktails taste better."

"Are you going to have to shoot me?" B.D. asked. "You're revealing trade secrets."

Bill shrugged. "People can try to do what we do here. But it won't be the Watering Hole, no matter what they do."

B.D. smiled. "I guess you're right." He paused and then asked. "So, what's your take on the cat attacks?"

"People shouldn't let their cats roam, especially at night. No telling what they could get into. Sugar and I keep ours strictly inside, along with our wee Chihuahua. We get eagles and owls down here along the river. They can swoop down on a cat or small dog and carry them off. Haven't heard of it happening in years, but they still could."

"So, there are stories about things like that? Any folklore about animals getting taken or—" He hesitated. "Or vampires?"

Bill laughed. "You should talk to Ole Swenson. He's about a hundred years old. Shoot, he was ancient when Sugar was a little girl. He knows a bunch of Scandinavian tales."

"Stories about things happening here?"

"Here and in the old country. He came over from Norway when he was a baby."

B.D. asked with more eagerness than perhaps the conversation warranted, but this was his specialty. "Where can I find him? What nursing home?"

Again, Bill laughed. "Ole in a nursing home? He'll be out at the VFW tomorrow night. He comes to listen to the live band and drink without his family counting how many. There's a dance there every Thursday night."

"That's an odd night for a dance."

"Everybody used to get paid on Thursdays, and all the stores stayed open late. The VFW never changed their schedule."

"Can anyone go?"

"Sure. They need the money from the cover charge. Take everybody with you. They'll enjoy the music."

At that moment, Sugar showed up with a big bag of takeout boxes. "Good to see you, young man. You come back, now."

Chapter 20

Day 3: North Star, evening

The glass cleaner clung to the counter waiting as Laura paused to say, "So, Bill thinks it's some raptor nesting along the river after the flood?" She applied a paper towel to the glass, then interrupted herself again. "And it's only cats who are put out at night that are affected?"

"Seems logical," B.D. said.

Laura applied the paper towel again to finish the job.

"But it doesn't explain the drugged state of the cats," Sephie said, returning to her crocheting after dinner.

"Maybe the birds got into something poisonous," Mandy suggested.

Laura gave her wife an are-you-crazy look. "And wouldn't that affect the birds? And why would it eventually wear off?"

A silence filled the shop, only broken by the tinkle of the bell at the door. Two teenage girls came in.

"Do you have that new witch romance novel in yet?" one of them asked.

"Not yet," Laura explained. "It's on back order. But the company did send some pagan mysteries and a new book on Summer Solstice rites." She moved the girls to a tall, revolving book rack.

They selected two mysteries and the ritual book, pooling their cash to pay for it all. Grinning, they rushed out, eager to dive into their new reads.

"I didn't know you sold novels. I didn't know there were real witch books," B.D. said.

"Oh, yes," Laura said, settling back behind the counter. "Pagan novels have been around for decades, but they were mostly written by people who never practiced or who used secondhand knowledge. I get these from a respected New Age publisher. That's also where we get our tarot decks and all of the non-fiction books."

"We have other suppliers for essential oils, candles, and ritual tools," Mandy added.

"There's a big need here?" B.D. asked.

"Yes. There are a couple of other stores in Fargo, but they sell only candles and incense," Mandy said. "Books can be found at book stores, but it's hit or miss. And they don't sell the novels or some of the more sophisticated non-fiction that's geared for the mature practitioner. We are a one-stop shop."

"And you deal with local troubles like the one you're currently dealing with," Sephie stated.

"Well, before this, we only dealt with curious teenagers and some older adepts. The only workings we provided expertise and tools for were mainly love spells, which are more psychological than any real magic," Laura admitted.

"We have protections resources, too," Mandy added, "as you have seen."

"We do so appreciate the new line of tinctures you brought," Laura said.

Sephie smiled. "I have a few salves that might be helpful. Arnica salve and some calendula. I think I brought the comfrey lavender salve."

"Did you just clean out your entire stock for us?"

"Pretty much, as far as I could tell," B.D. said.

"Won't your neighbors need your wares?" Mandy asked.

Making a few more stitches in silence, Sephie considered. "I think they're well supplied until next year." She worked her hands some more. "I have been curious to find what herbs you have here and if they're the same. I might consider doing some wildcrafting later in the summer. But I'll need to get this young'un," she said, pointing at B.D. with her crochet hook, "back home to his folks before too long."

"Don't worry about me, Miz Sephie. I'm learning alongside of you. I might even have an idea for a graduate thesis, if I can find a university that has a Master's in folklore."

"What idea do you have in your head?" Sephie peered at him like a doubtful mother.

"Bill told me about this ancient guy who came over from Norway ages ago who still knows all the old tales," B.D. said. "I thought I'd go listen to what he has to say tomorrow night." He looked eagerly at Laura and Mandy. "He'll be at the dance at the VFW. I thought maybe I could talk to him between some dances. Ya'll want to come?"

Laura grinned, then looked at Mandy to gauge her reaction.

"A live band, I'm told," B.D. added to sweeten the invite.

"Sure," Mandy said. She turned to her aunt. "How about you coming, too, Aunt Sephie? You can get a proper gin and tonic there."

A sly smile crossed the old woman's lips.

Chapter 21

Day 4: North Star, Thursday morning

B.D. juggled a plate piled high with bacon in one hand and one with a stack of fried eggs in the other as Laura opened the back door of the shop. "Miz Sephie is bringing the fried taters and the biscuits," he announced as he strode into the back room and placed his burdens on the cluttered portable table where they made coffee and tea. "Ya'll make some coffee in that fancy machine of yours." He pointed to the K-cup machine as he laid out napkins and plasticware. "You stocked our kitchen and fridge, but ya'll got nothing over here. Do you eat take-out every day?"

"Food smells fill the shop," Laura explained as she poured a mug of water into the machine and closed the lid onto a cup of flavored coffee. "We have vegetarians who are regulars. A cloud of bacon smell would chase them out before they put a foot across the threshold."

A thump against the back door drew Mandy from the stairs she was descending, spurring her to help her great-aunt in with her full plates.

"You should get that young'un to make us all some jambalaya," Sephie said as she entered. "I've done my cooking for the week."

"Jambalaya?" Laura brightened. "The real deal?"

B.D. grinned. "Grammy's recipe. It's sort of magical. It turns out, no matter what meat or seafood you can find. It's actually a mix of gumbo and jambalaya. It was great for feeding a lot of hungry mouths in the bayou. But you have to have four ingredients or it ain't worth a darn. The Holy Trinity and Andouille sausage."

"Holy Trinity?" Mandy asked, setting up folding chairs for them.

"Onions, celery, and green pepper. We put it in everything. In French cooking, it's mirepoix — onions, celery, and carrots."

"I don't know where you can find the sausage. I suppose it's spicy," Laura said.

"You might find it at Anderson's," Mandy suggested. "It's a butcher shop. They do all sorts of sausage, and it's the place all the hunters bring their deer to make jerky and deer sausage. We can check them out tomorrow if you want."

B.D. grinned. "And then we can get the proper meats for the pot, too." He fixed a plate and sat himself down to enjoy it.

"We'll be too busy today. We have to get ready for that dance tonight." Mandy cast an impish grin at her wife.

"You can make your own coffee," Laura said. "It doesn't take me all day to get ready."

"Just that long to decide what to wear."

"Amanda Branscombe, you're evil! If you'd take me out more often, it wouldn't be such a monumental decision."

"Armilda," Sephie corrected as she eased her bulk into a metal chair and balanced her plate on her knees.

Laura swung her attention to her wife's great-aunt while Mandy shrank into her seat. "Ar . . . what?"

"Armilda," the old woman repeated. "She was named after her great-great-grandmother, who came from England."

Laura twisted her body toward her mate. "And I suppose the name on our marriage license is false then? Is that why you never let me have it framed?"

"No, you keep important documents in a safety deposit box, not on your bedroom wall."

"So, are we legally married or not?"

"We are. Believe me." Mandy glanced at her aunt, who'd opened up this can of worms, and wondered how she could put them all back in. "The license has my full name on it. I just told the magistrate to use Mandy because that was what everyone called me."

"And all this time, I thought you were Amanda." Her fury was building. "You led me to believe that! What other secrets are you holding back?"

"Now, children," Sephie said calmly. "Truth is always good no matter how uncomfortable it is in the telling. Now, what are we going to do about the cats?"

Laura harrumphed, turning back to look at the food on her plate, obviously not finding it appealing. "I'll call all the people we identified with cats or small dogs from the mailing list," she said, "and tell them to keep their animals inside at night." Rising, she added, "In fact, I'll start that right now." She put her untouched plate on the only free space on the table and fled to the display room.

"I feel guilty about dragging you all this way, Aunt Sephie, when it's just something natural."

B.D. raised an eyebrow at her words, remembering the bird gathering yesterday.

It was Sephie's turn to harrumph as she slathered butter onto a biscuit half. "One answer doesn't mean there aren't more questions. This is an odd place."

She tasted her handiwork and nodded. "It's always tricky baking in a strange oven." She looked at Mandy. "Go take Laura's plate in to her and make up."

When Mandy rose, the old woman added. "Secrets are doors that can allow other things to creep in. We can't risk that now."

Chapter 22

Day 4: VFW, Thursday evening

"One, two, three, hop. One, two, three, hop," Laura chanted to B.D. as they rounded the wooden dance floor in skater position. "You got it. Now, the crossover. One, two, three, hop." Laura slid in front of her partner and then slid back beside him. "Keep the count. Now, we'll swing. Hop, hop, hop, hop. Back to the count."

They traversed the room just like the elderly couples on the floor. One sneaked up beside them. The gentleman said. "Just learning?"

"He's a quick study," Laura explained.

"Try this next." The man and his white-haired, tightly-permed wife moved to the inside of the circle of dancers. After the steps and hop, instead of swinging each other or moving his lady back and forth in front of him, he dropped to one knee and she skipped around him. Surprisingly, he rose to pick up the count without missing a beat.

"I don't think I'd be able to do that at his age," B.D. said. "But if I tried now, I think Mandy will give me the evil eye."

Laura laughed as the band ended the song.

"I'll go ask the band to play a slow two-step or a waltz," B.D. said. "It's my turn to teach you. We'll do the Cajun styles. Easy peasy, but different."

"What do you want to drink?" Laura asked.

"Beer's fine. Whatever is the local brew."

Laura put her hands on her hips and frowned like an impatient mother.

"Oh, I forgot. There's a ton of local brews. You choose."

As B.D. headed for the bandstand, Laura made her way back to the table where Mandy talked with her aunt, who sipped a gin and tonic. Laura waved at a waitress before she trailed her fingers across Mandy's shoulders and took her seat beside her wife. "Aunt Sephie, you need to get out there, too. If the locals can see you can dance, you might get yourself a boyfriend."

Sephie almost choked on her drink. "I don't need a boyfriend."

"Girlfriend, then," Laura teased.

"I don't need entanglements. I came here to do service. Besides, I'm too old to think of moonlight and romance." She snorted. "Shoot, I don't even think I remember what to do."

Mandy really did choke on her beer on that confession, causing the waitress, who had appeared unannounced, to pound her hard on the back.

"Honey, I thought you were old enough to drink," the heavily-made up, middle-aged woman said in a deep voice.

Mandy squinted up at her. "Charleen, what are you doing working here?" Mandy emphasized the CH in her name.

"I'm incognito."

"That's obvious."

"They won't let me take tips to sing like I do on campus or in the Cities. And from what little they're paying me, I decided to wait tables before and after. So, what'll you have?"

Laura spoke up. "Do you have any Grain Belt?"

Charleen scrunched up her face. "What do you want that old brand for?"

"It's a regional staple, isn't it?"

"Well, if you like beer of that era. It's a bit hoppy for my tastes. I'm a lager gal."

"It's for our friend."

At that moment, B.D. approached the table. "The band's taking a break. They'll play a waltz when they get back on stage," he told Laura. "There's a singer who'll do a couple of tunes in the meantime."

"Oooh. You're a tall drink of water," Charleen said, offering her manicured and ring-endowed fingers. "They call me Charleen."

B.D. tentatively shook her hand.

"That's B.D.," Laura introduced. "And this is Mandy's Great-Aunt Sephie. They came up from Tennessee."

"He's getting the Grain Belt, right?" Charleen asked the others at the table and turned back to B.D. "Uh-huh. I'll be back in a jiff."

Off she strode on red platform stilettoes that matched her nails and lips, and accented the snug, black-sequined number behind her bar apron.

B.D. slowly sank into an available chair. "That was—"

"Miss Charleen EverBright, one of the best singers in drag in the area," Mandy explained. "She does have an amazing repertoire. I guess it's country tonight."

"Do they know she/he's—"

"Obviously," Laura said. "She's in demand."

"But the VFW?"

"She's a veteran. Been to Afghanistan, Bosnia. Did some peacekeeping in Africa."

"But not as Charleen, surely."

Mandy glanced down at her beer. "No, as Charles Evenson. He lost his partner over there."

B.D. turned to look at the bar. Charleen put a pilsner glass on a tray and disappeared behind the counter. She popped up within seconds to place a frosty can next to it. Catching B.D.'s eye, she kissed the air, before sidling around the heavy wooden bar counter and strutting straight for B.D. As she placed the beer and the glass in front of him, she said, "I'll do 'Tennessee Whiskey' for you, baby, but in a soul version. The keyboard player knows my style. It's not what they're all used to here."

Laura suddenly burst out laughing.

"What? You don't like country music?" Charleen demanded, feisty hand on her hip.

Laura shook her head. "It's just these two—" She pointed to B.D. and Mandy. "Have had way too much Tennessee Whiskey since they got here."

"Say what?" Charleen leaned across the table to get close to Laura's face. In a stage whisper, she asked, "You brought moon up here?"

"Shhhh." B.D. and Mandy both said, looking around furtively.

"Is it as smooth as they say?"

"This was," B.D. admitted.

Charleen straightened to cast an accusing look at Sephie. "Your doing, I suppose."

The old woman shrugged. "I'm not responsible for the curiosity of youth."

"But it's yours."

"Not for drinking."

"Oh, I guess you use it for liniment then."

"Sometimes. Mainly, it binds tinctures. And I had another use in mind for the troubles here."

Charleen looked confused.

"There's been a rash of attacks on cats down along the river," Mandy explained. "Turns out it's probably just an eagle or owl."

"Then I better make sure Sir Pussalot doesn't go wandering." Charleen turned and added, "I might come calling tomorrow to do some tippling."

B.D. could only gawk at the big drag queen as she strode away to whip off her apron, toss it onto the dance floor, and take a thigh-revealing large step onto the bandstand.

Charleen grabbed a microphone and greeted her audience like the pro she was.

Chapter 23

Day 4: Greenway, Thursday evening

The branch high in the cottonwood tree creaked with the added weight of the presence that huddled there. It waited, watching, obscured by the thick summer's growth of leaves and darkness, blending with its own ebony color. Its black cloak fluttered once or twice as the breeze lifted it, threatening to reveal the figure there. The creature pulled the cloth tighter around its bulk, its taloned fingers digging into the fabric, securing it fast. A hunger gnawed deep inside the being. The evening's wander had produced nothing easy. The creature snarled, echoing the profound unrest within. It was time to look for something more robust, pumping with life, and food.

Soon, it would be time to walk.

Chapter 24

Day 4: VFW, Thursday evening

"I have a special song for some very special new friends of mine from the South," Charleen announced and then bowed low. She watched the keyboard player as he began his organ introduction.

Those few initial notes spurred the drummer to slip on stage and take up the hypnotic beat as Charleen launched into a slow, soulful delivery. While she sang, two older couples moved to the dance floor and began slow dancing.

B.D. tapped rhythms on the table, trying to figure out the timing and realized it really didn't fit because of that haunting strong downbeat. Suddenly, he remembered an old man who danced a variation of Cajun two-step that might fit. B.D. turned to Laura. "Sorry, Miss Laura, I promised you a dance, but this one's for Miz Sephie." He reached across the table for Sephie's hand.

Reluctantly, the old woman eased herself out of her chair and took B.D.'s hand. When in dance position, B.D told Sephie, "It's a two-step in three to the side. Follow my lead." Catching the beat, he started the old woman off, counting. "Quick, quick, slow to the side, then shift weight to the other side." Before they had gone very far, Sephie started to smile as she fell into the rhythm and the sentiment of the song.

B.D. noticed a middle-aged couple come on the dance floor. They started out with a couple of back steps, moving into nightclub two-step. He hadn't seen that since some young tourists had come down to a festival in the park in Lafayette where a country band was playing. B.D. had been mystified by the cross steps and turns that showcased the female follow. A lot of other dances did that, allowing the lead to just do time steps in place. The only exception he had seen was in salsa, which allowed the lead to do some fancy styling while the follow did fancy turns and her own styling. He'd gotten the couple to show him the steps, but there never was anyone to practice with, and he figured he'd probably forgotten most of what he'd learned anyway.

B.D. put Sephie into a couple of turns and then moved her into skater or sweetheart position for more moves around the floor. When he turned her back into closed position, he saw that she was in tears.

"Oh, Miz Sephie, I didn't mean to make you cry," B.D. said, clutching her shoulders to look at her face.

She waved him off. "Too much talk of romance tonight," she said as the band ended the tune.

Arm around her shoulders, B.D. ushered her off the dance floor, pulling her close. He did love the cranky old woman.

"That was a song for all the sentimental lovers everywhere," Charleen said. "Now a song for all of us who love our country."

By this time, the band had resumed their places on the stage. Charleen and the band burst into Toby Keith's "Made in America," quickly drawing all the dancers who'd had enough sitting.

While B.D. and Sephie refreshed themselves with their drinks at the table, Laura nudged Mandy while covertly pointing to an ancient old man in a corner table far from the band speakers. "How can he sleep with all this music?" she remarked.

Mandy only shrugged, but B.D. twisted his body to look behind him at the man, remembering that an old Norwegian storyteller might be here. However, he couldn't just walk up to him. Back in Tennessee, he'd always gotten an introduction by someone to talk to a folklore source. They had mostly been musicians who were always eager to show off their tunes to young ears. There were always stories attached to how they'd learned the songs, or events that spurred the writing of the tunes, or even odd happenings that occurred when they'd played them. But a few had been just good storytellers who could spin a yarn so laced with mountainisms that the telling was more exciting than the tale itself.

As B.D. sat, trying to figure out who could introduce him, Charleen ended her song and headed to the bar for a drink. She soon sashayed back to their table with a blue-colored cocktail with a straw and kabob of fruit sticking out of it.

"Looks like you brought dessert," Sephie commented.

"Almost," Charleen said, pulling up a chair beside the old woman and sitting down elegantly but revealing a lot of thigh. "Except it kicks like a mule. It makes a Long Island Tea seem like buttermilk."

"Don't knock buttermilk. It's good for the soul on a hot day."

"I suppose it has its place."

B.D. leaned across the table. "Miss Charleen," he began.

"What is it, Pretty Boy?" she said putting her red lips around the straw and taking a long sip. As she swallowed, she closed one eye, and it wasn't in a flirty way. "Like a mule," she repeated, flashing both eyes wide.

"Miss, Charleen, do you know that elderly gentleman in the corner?" He asked tilting his head in the old man's direction.

The drag queen scanned the crowd until she found the focus of B.D.'s question. "That's Ole Swenson. He's been around for ages."

"I heard he knows some good stories, folklore, from both here and the Old Country."

"He does," Charleen confirmed. "But he won't just tell anybody."

"Do you think you could introduce me?"

"Why are you interested?"

Mandy interrupted. "He's got a degree in folklore. So, it's a special interest. Says he knows a lot of the old ballads."

"I just wanted to find out what the tales are here," B.D. explained.

Charleen picked off a pineapple spear and chewed on it. "He's the man to ask. But, you're a stranger. Who knows what he'll tell you?" Pausing just a minute, she rose. "Let's see what this font of knowledge has to say to you." Charleen picked up her drink. "I'll sit with you for a bit. He'll feel more comfortable." Using her glass, she gestured toward the glass in front of B.D. "Take your beer. And bring the can. He'll recognize that."

They crossed the dance floor. Charleen placed one hand on the old man's nearest shoulder and gently shook him. He startled awake and focused on B.D. "*Draugr*!" he yelled, trying to scramble out of his chair. "Get away! *Draugr*!"

Charleen returned her hand to the old man's shoulder and moved her coiffed head so that her face filled his vision. "Ole, it's Charles. Remember me?"

He blinked. "Charlie? You come to entertain the troops?"

"I have. But you missed my first set. I'll be on again later." She glanced at B.D. "This is my good friend, B.D. He wanted to meet you."

The old man leaned closer to study B.D., recognizing him for a man. "You one of the troops?"

Charleen straightened as she waited for his response.

"No, sir. I never had the privilege of serving. But my dad did in the first Gulf War. And my granddad in Korea, and my great-gran in Germany during World War II."

"Why not? You ain't one of them pacifists, are you?"

"He's been educating himself, Ole," Charleen explained.

The old man reached for his beer bottle and drained the last of it.

Charleen picked up the bottle. "Let me get you another. Why don't you ask the young man to sit down?"

Ole gestured to a chair in front of him. "Educating yourself? What in? Fancy computer stuff?"

As B.D. sat down, he said, "No, sir. I've been learning about old ways. Old songs and old stories."

"Whatever for?"

"So they'll be preserved. I learned all I could back home in Louisiana, so I went on up to Tennessee to see what songs and stories they had. I'm up here visiting, and I thought I'd learn about the people here."

Chapter 25

Day 4: VFW, Thursday evening

Sephie watched the old man from across the room. His body language showed fear and then hostility and then contempt softened by something. She thought it was probably respect for Charleen since he hadn't seemed to freak when she was in his face. Sephie hoped B.D. found a good source of song or story in the old man. He had always been good at ferreting out tale-tellers around Dark Hollow. Somehow, he charmed the old timers into talking. She grunted a laugh. He probably sang a song they all knew. That was always a good introduction even among the most racist rednecks in those hills. They eventually respected his skill if not him as a person. Shoot, a few of them were secret Charlie Pride fans.

Sephie tasted the second gin and tonic Mandy placed before her. The young people needed a night out. B.D. had won their loyalty in a short time, and he hadn't even opened that golden voice of his. She wondered if Nat King Cole and Barry White were looking down at him, envious of such melodic vocal cords. The quality of B.D.'s voice was closer to Nat's than Barry's but equally as enticing — if he'd ever sing a soul love song and not those murder ballads and coal mine disaster laments he was so fond of. Sephie wondered if he'd proclaimed himself the repository of Appalachian tragedy songs like some character out of that book *Fahrenheit 451* Mandy had insisted she read when the girl had been in school.

Sephie took another sip of her drink. It tasted off, somehow, different from the first sip she had just taken. Setting the glass down, she felt a growing oppressiveness creep upon her, filling her with a distinctive unease that soon shifted into dread. She closed her eyes, hoping to zone in on where that came from. She only shivered when nothing came. Then she searched for B.D. and the old man, who was now laughing as Charleen returned with more beers.

Closer to her, Mandy and Laura were whispering about something and Laura giggled. Sephie smiled but soon felt a deep sadness coming from somewhere in the room. She scanned again, eyes open, trying to look at every old face in the club and all of the staff. Face upon face, enjoying the music or sharing jokes or sitting oblivious to everyone else as if glad to be among people. A couple of folks were having some sort of private tiff but not of consequence, probably about someone's eyes straying. Close to the back door that led to the parking lot, a pair of eyes caught hers — dark and burning in a shadowed face that seemed youthful but ancient both at once. Awareness flashed in those eyes. Two men passed in front of the figure, heading toward the bar. When Sephie looked again, he was gone. Suddenly, she felt extremely hungry, as if she hadn't eaten in hours.

Pushing that encounter toward the back of her brain, Sephie leaned toward Mandy. "Could you order me a Coke? Do they have anything to eat?"

"Are you feeling all right, Aunt Sephie?"

"I need to eat something." She turned to Laura. "Could you go with me to the Ladies'?"

Laura rushed to the old woman's side and helped her stand as Sephie gripped the edge of the table, steadying herself. Laura wrapped the other woman's arm through hers and guided her across the floor to the restroom. Inside, Sephie splashed water on her face and dried it with paper towels Laura handed her.

"Are you okay?" The question came again.

"I will be," Sephie said. "Just wait here for me." She shuffled to a stall, sat down while she used the facility, and tried to think of what protections to use. All that came to mind that was handy was salt. When she was at the sink again, washing her hands, she said, "Have Mandy order me something salty. Chips, popcorn, pickles. Anything salty. And sugar. The Coke."

When they had returned to their seats, Mandy had a soft drink on the table and a paper plate with a soft pretzel, encrusted with salt. As Sephie sat down, she smiled at Mandy. "I always knew you had the gift. You read my mind."

Concerned, Mandy explained. "I only saw you like this once before. You're a feisty woman and when you get this drained, there's something not normal happening. You asked for salt the last time."

Sephie tore off a piece of the warm pretzel and chewed, as if she were taking communion of some sort. "Same situation," she explained before washing it down with the sweet drink.

"But that was an energy eater," Mandy blurted out.

Looking her young great-niece in the eye, Sephie said, "We've got more beasties at work here than a hungry eagle or owl."

Chapter 26

Day 4: VFW, Thursday evening

"What was that you called me?" B.D. asked after the old man had taken a large drink from the cold beer Charleen had brought. "I've been called a lot of things doing my research by some folks who don't like my kind."

"What kind? Young smart-ass college boys?"

Surprised, B.D. offered him a genuine smile and a laugh.

"Aw, I was sleeping. The music's good and the beer. I dozed off. When Charlie here woke me and I took a look at you, well, what was I to expect?" He gestured at B.D.'s hand holding his glass. "You got a man's hands. Didn't see no claws."

"Claws?"

"Yes, sir, no claws."

"Why would I have claws?"

"*Draugrs* have claws and faces like the night, so they blend in."

"What's a *draugr*? Tell me about it."

"My nana used to tell me stories about 'em. She heard about 'em from her nana who was from Iceland. A *draugr* haunts graveyards."

"What is it?"

"They're dark figures. Said to have been alive." He drank again. "Once." He stared hard at B.D., as if waiting for a reaction. When none came, he continued. "But they torment the living, walking the night, lashing out with their claws at those that disturb them."

"Why are they wandering? Are they looking for something?"

Ole leaned back in his chair. "Who can say? No one's ever asked. Though some said they guarded the grave goods of the dead, the treasure buried with the dead long ago."

"Do you think there are *draugr* around today? Here?"

"Could be."

B.D. wondered about the claws. "I've been hearing about cats being clawed here. Cats from homes along the river. Do you think the *draugr* could be responsible?"

Ole leaned forward. "If they're walking and clawing cats, something's stirred 'em up. No one'll be safe now." He eased back into the chair. "But if something's along the river, it's not a *draugr*. All the graveyards are far from the river because of the regular flooding." He raised his beer to take another drink but stopped. "Nana's sister said they sometimes walked far and wide and could change shape as they wanted." He took a sip from his bottle, then added. "She said that there were other things along water. Her husband was from the Orkneys. That's somewhere in the North Sea between Sweden and Scotland. The Finn Folk, she called them, like the folks from Finland. The Finn Folk live in the shadows along water. Seas, mostly. Sometimes rivers. But not lakes or ponds or even wells where the water's still. They somehow thrive on the energy of flowing water. But the *nakki* lurk in deep water of ponds and lakes and wells. They're supposed to lure children to drown. Nana warned us away from deep water and foolish skinny dipping with that tale."

"Would they harm cats?"

The old man laughed as if B.D. were addled. "Not unless the cats were taking the fish! Finn Folk protect their fishing rights, sometimes climbing into boats with greedy fishermen who take too many. They toss the fish back or cut nets."

B.D. frowned. None of this fit. "What other kinds of folk did your nana tell you about?"

"Oh, she had tales about all sorts of creatures. The *huldre*. That was Nana's warning about being lured by girls. The *tontu* and the *nisse* — kinda like house elves. And giants and trolls, of course. And the *nattmara* that brings bad dreams. And there's a *fossgrimmen*, who plays the fiddle, and the *stromkarlen* that does, too. *Pesta* who bring disease. The *vittra* that own their own cattle but live underground. And then there are Finnish creatures like the Finn Folk, the *hiisi*, who are henchmen of Lempo, the god of evil, and the *haltija*, the *peikko*, the *keiju*, the *lenninkäinen*, and the. . . ."

The old man droned on and on with more Finish creatures and then Norwegian and Swedish. B.D. felt like the dog in the cartoon whose master was jabbering at him in gibberish as he waited patiently for the one word he knew: treat.

Chapter 27

Day 4: VFW, Thursday evening

Sephie looked up as dazed B.D. stumbled back to the table. "You drink too much beer, son?"

He shook his head. "My brain hurts. It's too full of creatures with names I'll never pronounce, much less remember."

The old woman chuckled. "Sounds like a good resource for you."

"Miz Sephie, you know storytellers back home. They string out a tale, adding as many embellishments as they can to add to the spooky atmosphere to make sure you go away scared. But Ole?" Again, he shook his head. "There are so many creatures he knows about, and yet I came away with nothing."

"What were you really looking for?"

"I was thinking about the cats."

Mandy interrupted. "So, you thought there might be a creature from the local culture at work here."

"Sometimes creatures are used to scare kids into behaving. That comes in the storytelling," B.D. defended, "like Miz Sephie's tale of Black Lije."

"I could have told you that there aren't any Scandinavian vampires," Laura said. "We never heard about things that would get us in the night. Except ghosts. Everybody has stories about ghosts."

"So why did you think you were dealing with vampires then?" B.D. countered.

"Scratches. And lethargic cats," Laura defended.

"It'll be interesting to see what the vet's test results show," Sephie mused. "But we're stirring up something."

B.D. turned to the old woman. “What do you mean?”

“Aunt Sephie encountered an energy vampire tonight,” Mandy explained.

“Why would we stir up anything?”

“Could be because we’re new,” the old woman said. “Different energy frequency.” She turned to Mandy. “Did you ever run into an energy vampire here before?”

Her niece shook her head. “Not in the time we’ve been here.”

“And you?” Sephie turned to Laura.

“I never knew what one was until tonight. I mean I’d read about them.”

“Wait,” B.D. interrupted. “You mean there was an energy sucker here? Tonight?”

Sephie nodded solemnly. “He’s a handsome one, too. From the brief glimpse I got of him. A real charmer.” She drank the last of her soft drink. “And I don’t think he’s from here, either.” She turned to Mandy. “I think your floods here leave a lot on your banks.”

Chapter 28

Day 5: North Star, Friday afternoon

"Where has B.D. squirreled himself off to?" Laura asked when Mandy brought in a cup of mint tea and set it on the counter.

"He must still be putting the Anderson's haul away."

"Did he find everything he needed?" Sephie asked, squinting at her stitches, making sure the patterns of the pineapples she was crocheting were uniform.

"Seems so."

"But you got back — what? Over an hour ago?"

Mandy stepped up onto the stool rung and eased herself down on the wooden seat. "We can hope he's cooking us up something or we'll have to call in an order from Bill."

"He'll be sending out a search party, since we didn't order yesterday. That breakfast was huge and we had a few leftover nibbles before we went out dancing," Laura said.

"You mean you went out dancing," Mandy corrected.

The shop bell above the door sounded as Miss Lucy wandered in. "I wanted to let you know what the vet said about those scratches on Precious."

Mandy rose from her stool and went to the back room to retrieve a folding chair as Laura met the old woman. "How is Precious?"

Miss Lucy laughed. "Oh, she's all right now. She's been sitting by the window watching birds most of the time. I know the poor thing wants to go out, but really she shouldn't."

"No, you'll need to keep her inside for a while." Taking the old woman by the arm, Laura guided her to the chair.

"What did the vet say?" Sephie asked, putting down her crocheting.

"Well, there was catnip all over Precious' fur and deep in those scratches. But somehow, they found valerian in the wounds. A lot of it. Where she got into that, I have no clue. There's catnip in my back yard, but no one around that I know of grows valerian. It doesn't grow wild here."

"Valerian." Sephie repeated. "Cats do like it. But you have to be careful because too much will sedate a cat after it's done all that rolling around."

Miss Lucy turned to Sephie. "That's how Precious acts with catnip. She just rolls around in it and then takes a nap. But a short one. You can always rouse her from her nap. But not this time. She just laid there like a stone."

Sephie nodded. "You been feeling all right yourself, Lucy?"

She laughed. "I'm fit as a fiddle. Though going to the store sometimes tuckers me out."

"You need to get that grandson of yours to help you, now that school's out," Laura said.

"Any particular store you like to shop at?" Sephie asked. "Any one down here?"

"You are new here," Miss Lucy said. "The grocery stores are all west of town near the big mall. The only thing along the river here is that foreign place. Oh, and the Farmer's Market on Saturday."

"You have to go tomorrow, Aunt Sephie," Laura said. "There's music and all kinds of produce and honey."

Sephie smiled indulgently. "What's this foreign place?"

Standing above Miss Lucy, Laura gave Sephie a shake of her head as a warning. "Miss Lucy, let's get you a bit of mint tea to take home with you. On the house."

The old woman stood with a hand from Laura and went to the rack of packaged teas on display. From a hook, Laura pulled off a small plastic bag containing five tea bags and pressed it into Lucy's hand. "Thanks for stopping by, Miss Lucy."

"You're gonna run your business into the ground giving away product," Sephie said after the old woman was gone.

Mandy explained. "We grow it out back and dry it ourselves."

"It's good for business to be kind," Laura said.

Sephie smiled. "That's true enough."

Some clamoring at the back door drew Mandy from her seat into the back room. "What is that wonderful smell?" she asked.

B.D.'s voice boomed out. "Wait and see. I'll bring it out. Now go sit down."

Chapter 29

Day 5: North Star, Friday afternoon

"Gotcha!" Bill boomed out from the open door of the shop. Everyone looked up from the bowls that were demanding their gastronomic attention. A look from face to face showed first surprise and then guilt from Mandy and Laura. "Now, who's been tempting your taste buds?" Moving to the counter, he stuck his ponderous nose over Laura's bowl and took a deep whiff. "Exotic. You been frequenting the halal market café? Did you send B.D. in to get your order?"

"Exotic it's not, Mr. Bill," B.D. said, rising from the folding chair he'd brought in. "It's just cooking from home. My grammy's jambalaya. Sit yourself down, and I'll get you a taste." He slipped into the back room with Bill in his wake. B.D. put a ladle of rice into a paper bowl and then covered it with the meat stew.

Bill took the bowl from him before he had a chance to offer it. He sniffed again. Spying a plastic spoon on the table, he picked it up, dipped it into the dish, and lifted up bits and pieces as if searching for something he'd lost. "Where'd you get okra?"

"It's frozen. The grocery store had two packages. I asked a clerk there, and he said they get requests for okra and greens from people from the airbase. These were in the storage from the back freezer."

Finally moving his spoon to his mouth, Bill tasted the aromatic stew. He closed his eyes in delight and then opened them wide as he bit into the spicy sausage. After he swallowed, he said, "It packs a kick."

"Oh, this is mild. We usually add some hot sauce to it. But I couldn't find anything but tabasco. It's just not the same. And I couldn't find any filé powder."

"Look in the little box on top of Cousin Lije's jars." Aunt Sephie called out.

"That woman can hear a gnat fart," B.D. whispered to Bill before he searched the box in the corner above the moonshine. Inside was a half pint fruit jar labeled Sassafras. B.D. held the jar up to examine the contents. Inside was a fine powder. He unscrewed the lid and sniffed it. Then he tapped out a bit into the lid and stuck his finger to it and then to his tongue. It was indeed filé powder. "Miz Sephie, when did y'all make this?"

"This spring when you were homesick. It was going to be a Christmas present. I don't use it, but I know how to make it."

B.D. took a clean spoon and sprinkled a little over Bill's bowl. "Taste the difference."

Bill dug in and nodded. "Sure does make a difference."

B.D. added another ladle to his own bowl and sprinkled filé powder over it, too.

Shaking his spoon at B.D., Bill offered, "Come cook for me. My customers would love this."

The young man laughed. "Now, how y'all gonna convince your customers it's African?"

"Well, it is sort of, isn't it? It's Creole."

"Some jambalaya is Cajun, Mr. Bill. Big difference." Then B.D. grinned a little sheepishly. "This one is Creole because it's got tomatoes in it, and we layer the cooking. We don't dump it like the Cajuns do. It does have my grammy's twist of adding gumbo okra to it." Seeing Bill's eyes sort of glass over, B.D. admitted. "Totally confusing you, aren't I? There's history in everything. Especially in food. Lots of stories and folklore."

Bill seemed to have another wild idea. "Maybe we could have Africa in America special nights. And offer soul food, too. And stories and music."

B.D. laughed. “Eat your jambalaya before it gets cold. I hear your cold winter up here is intolerable. I don’t think this Louisiana son would like it here then.” He turned to re-enter the main shop. “But I might give you the recipe if you name it after my grammy. Now, what was this hal-whatever place you mentioned?”

“Halal. It’s run by the Somalis,” he said following B.D. into the shop. “They’re Muslim and only eat special meat. Halal meat. It’s kind of like being kosher, I’m told. They have a market and a little café inside. Lots of goat meat.”

B.D. gestured to his empty chair while Mandy rose from her stool to take her bowl into the back room. Bill sat and continued. “I got their recipe for goat stew and only buy goat from them.”

“Why would they let you use their recipe?” B.D. asked.

“Their café is really small, and they mostly serve men who come to visit around midday to share news. Women aren’t really welcome. They’ll sell their meat to anyone, but there’s not much of a market for goat outside of their community. They wanted us to advertise for them by showing where we got our goat. It’s right there on my menu. And we take orders if our customers want some meat. We’ve placed a few extra orders with ours. Not many.”

Sephie interrupted. “Laura, why didn’t you want to talk about that in front of Miz Lucy? It’s harmless enough.”

“A lot of people don’t understand them. They look different and they worship differently. And the spicy smells from the café are unusual.”

Sephie grunted. “The world is full of people not like other people.”

“True dat,” B.D. said. “I thought that was what Ole was reacting to last night when he saw me.”

“You talk to old Ole?” Bill asked.

“He knows a lot, but it was all so. . . .” He paused and then smiled. “So foreign to me. So different from what I’ve heard. Back home we got French mixed in with everything and bayou ways of explaining. Even up in the Tennessee hills there were odd stories, but I could understand them. I'm not sure yet just what Ole was talking about. Still don't know if there's a vampire."

"Vampire?" Bill laughed. "Not here in the frozen North. I thought you were wondering about cat attacks."

"So far," Sephie said ominously.

Chapter 30

Day 5: North Star, Friday late afternoon

The fragrance from the roses at the narrow side yard of the North Star bathed Sephie in a brief euphoria. The small single blooms were more aromatic than the big double Gertrude Jekyll English roses she had back home. Her sister Agnesia loved the flamboyance of the bush beauties as she did the lush peonies with their own different but just as heady fragrance. Sephie smiled. There was a sort of green justice in these little bloomers that Mandy had gotten from one of their customers' farm fields and planted in the small yard in front of the store's only display window. Laura had told her that the hardy bushes had taken root and spread to fill that small space and well into the side yard. Not only were they fragrant, but they also produced an abundance of rosehips to dry for tea.

Voices drew Sephie from her rose admiration. On the sidewalk in front of the shop, two elderly women walked arm in arm. The younger and plumper one was dressed in a blue-flowered summer dress, adorned with large red beads and red clip-on earrings. A white, straw sunhat was pinned to her tightly permed hair with a large red-topped hat pin. The hat matched her wedge sandals, which she wore with nylons several shades darker than the color of her bare arms. The thinner, frailer woman was lost in the fabric of her tan linen suit and white blouse, with only black sensible shoes with equally black tights to complete her look. They turned into the narrow walk to the three low steps in front.

"Can you make the stairs, Sister? They aren't very high," the woman in the summer dress said to her companion.

Stepping away from the rose bushes, Sephie moved toward the pair to offer assistance if the frail woman fell. But her aid was unnecessary since B.D. met them at the threshold and took the thin woman's elbow. As Sephie joined him, he said, "I was just coming to get you. Your sister called and—"

"And wants to know when we're coming home," Sephie finished for him. "It's only been a week. You'd think she and the preacher would be happy I'm not there to interrupt their private prayer meetings."

"Maybe they can't find anyone else to try to pray into heaven like they do you," he offered.

The old woman grunted. "I swear, though, every time I think about her, she's up in my business."

"Well, you better call her back."

"Later," Sephie said as she moved further inside to remove her crocheting from her rocker and help the frail woman into it.

Laura came from the back room with a cup of herbal tea. "Sister Evangeline! Are you all right? Maybe you need this more than I do."

Sephie pulled the extra folding chair B.D. had been using nearer to the rocker and sat down beside the frail woman. "What kind is it?" she asked Laura about the tea.

"Ginsing and anise."

Sephie shook her head. "Make some mint or chamomile, please." She turned to the woman beside her. "Sister Evangeline, my name is Sephie. I'm Mandy's great-aunt. What seems to be the trouble?"

The stout woman spoke before her companion could answer. "She's been feeling poorly for a few days. Ever since she started her night vigil and novena to help the patients at the guest home."

"Guest home?" Sephie repeated.

"St. Gertrude's." Laura explained. "It's a nursing home along the river for retired nuns on the far north side of town."

"Isn't St. Gertrude the patron of cats and travelers?" B.D. asked.

The frail woman smiled up at B.D. "You know your saints, young man. Did you have a Catholic education?"

"Yes, ma'am."

"So, you've been feeling poorly," Sephie prompted, trying to bring them all back to the woman's health. "Tired?"

"Well, yes," she said. "But I've been praying for five nights now so it's no wonder."

"You haven't been sleeping through the night?"

"We're Benedictines. We keep the hours so we sleep for short periods and then rise to pray and work. I've been doing that for nearly all my life."

"Tell me about the reason for your praying."

Before she could answer, the stout woman interrupted again. "She's praying a novena because the residents aren't sleeping."

"Do they keep the hours, too, even though they're in a nursing home?" B. D. asked.

"Old habits," she said, then offered a thin laugh at her own pun.

Sephie opened her mouth to ask another question but B.D. interrupted.

"Do you know why the residents aren't sleeping?" he asked.

Sephie twisted her head to grimace up at him.

"There's a disturbance," the nun said.

"A spiritual disturbance," the stout woman stated, folding her arms across her ample bosom.

"Spiritual," Sephie repeated.

"The residents complain of bad dreams. One said she saw a dark figure walking the greenway in back of the guest home. Another said she heard something clawing at the windows at night." The nun looked up at B.D. "On the third floor."

"So, you've been praying for the residents to sleep well," Sephie offered.

"Yes, and—"

"And to rid the place of the evil that's befallen it," the stout woman stated.

"I'm not afraid," Sister Evangeline said.

"Have you been praying in the chapel?"

She shook her head.

"In your room?"

She shook her head again.

"Outside on the back terrace," the stout woman said. "They found her there this morning on the cold stones, prostrate. She could barely walk when they revived her."

"Were you asleep? Or did you faint? Or fall?" Sephie asked.

The old woman slowly raised her shoulders in a shrug. "I don't know. I know I wouldn't have broken my vigil by sleeping."

Laura entered the room again and offered a steaming cup of mint tea to the nun. "Be careful. It's very hot. I put a big spoonful of honey in it, too."

With the cup cradled in both hands, Sister Evangeline blew on its contents and took a tentative sip. She nodded. "It's good. Thank you."

"They also found a big scratch on her arm," the nun's companion said. "That's when they called me."

"Are you a relative?" Sephie asked.

"I'm her baby sister."

Sephie nodded. "Sit back and sip your tea." Frowning, she rose and scraped her chair toward the nun's sister. "Take a load off. It looks like you've got enough burdens on your shoulders."

Sephie raised a finger at B.D. and twitched it toward the back room.

Chapter 31

Day 5: North Star, Friday late afternoon

"What creature could've attacked her?" B.D. said, following Sephie into the back room.

"Don't know." The old woman pulled a quart of Cousin Lije's remedy from a box and held it out at arm's length for B.D. to take. Then she rummaged inside another box and pulled out a pint jar of what once might have been white flowers but had dried to beige and tan. When she'd straightened, she pushed it into B.D.'s other hand. Then she went to the corner where the long branches of dogwood stood. Selecting one, she moved toward the lunch table where she motioned for B.D. to put the two glass jars down.

Shoving the branch toward him, she ordered, "Shave off some of the inner bark into one of those paper bowls."

B.D. leaned the branch against the table and pulled out his pocketknife. After opening the blade, he cut off a bit of outer bark near one of the ends and then shaved the white center into the bowl.

Sephie unscrewed the pint jar lid and then did the same to the quart jar. Taking a plastic spoon, she measured out three spoons of the dried flowers and put them into the quart of liquor.

"That's enough," she said to B.D. when she'd glanced at the bowl. She dumped the shavings into the quart jar, too. After screwing the lid back on, she shook the contents thoroughly. "Put that branch back and bring in another chair."

Taking a couple of napkins and the paper bowl, she returned to the main room. When B.D. had unfolded the chair beside the rocker, she sat and put the bowl, the napkins, and the quart jar on the floor in front of her.

"Sister Evangeline, could you show me the scratch?"

The nun handed her tea mug to her sister and, with Sephie's help, proceeded to shrug off the left arm of her jacket. The blouse she wore had short sleeves, so her bandaged forearm was unencumbered.

Sephie carefully removed the tape securing the gauze bandage and pulled the covering away from the woman's injury. Three long scratches marked the nun's skin as if some creature with talons had tried to grab her arm. From the stain on the bandage, they were deep enough to have bled a bit. Sephie frowned. "Have you ever been scratched before during your prayers?"

The nun shook her head.

Sephie picked up the quart jar. After unscrewing the lid, she handed the jar to B.D. "Bless it with song."

The young man raised an eyebrow and looked from Sephie to Sister Evangeline, obviously uncertain.

"Whatever is appropriate," Sephie prompted.

He closed his eyes and paused before quietly beginning the chorus of "God Is Love." The lyrics were like a Catholic namaste, and B.D.'s rich baritone as he repeated the chorus not only blessed the contents of the jar but created a quiet holiness in the room. On the fourth chorus, his voice softened, and he ended the hymn. After opening his eyes, he handed the jar to Sephie, who gave him a small smile of approval.

"Father Rivers', right?' Sister Evaneline asked.

"Yes ma'am. I know a few of his. And some Joe Wise songs. And a lot of old gospel tunes and—" he paused briefly. "And some others."

Sephie suppressed a smile as she poured some of the mixture into the paper bowl. Those other songs dealt with his other bayou religious practices, of which Sister Evangeline would not approve. After putting the jar on the floor again, she dipped a napkin into the bowl and pressed it to one of the scratches on the nun's arm.

Sister Evangeline hissed. "It didn't hurt like that when the paramedic cleaned it this morning."

"I know," Sephie said, dipping the napkin into the bowl again. "This is an old mountain remedy my people have used for generations for wounds, especially spiritual ones."

"What is it?" Evangeline's sister asked, as Sephie applied the napkin to the second scratch.

"Christ's holy tree," Sephie said. "Dogwood." She dipped the napkin again and pressed it to the third scratch. After she had handed the bowl to B.D., she secured the bandage over the three wounds once more and helped the nun put her arm through her jacket's sleeve.

Turning to Laura, she offered the jar and asked, "Could you put some of this into a smaller container please? About a half-pint or so."

Laura took the quart jar and escaped into the back room.

"I want you to sponge the wound with the contents of the jar I'll give you at least morning and night. Every few hours would be better. And from now on, pray in the chapel or your room. It's safer."

"What about the evil that's in the guest home?" the nun's sister asked. "Is she safe there?"

"Yes. Whatever got to her was outside. She probably was in ecstasy while praying and didn't feel a thing." Sephie turned to Sister Evangeline again. "Would you like us to have a look at the guest home tomorrow to get a feel of it? We can also sit vigil outside at night and see what's out there."

The nun's sister asked, suddenly suspicious, "Who would come? You and that young man? Or more?"

"Just B.D. and me. We don't want to disrupt your residents' routine."

Sister Evangeline looked down a little sheepishly and then raised her head. “Our priest can always bless the building,” she said. “But we have to know what’s there and where it is.”

“So, that was why you came here today? To find people who could read a house?”

“Oh, no,” Evangeline’s sister said quickly. “It was to get the candles we ordered. A case of white jar candles and one of blue ones for Our Lady. With the evil at St. Gertrude’s, we wanted to have enough for additional prayers.”

“They haven’t come in yet,” Laura said as she entered the room and handed a half-pint jelly jar to the nun. “I expect them any time. Mandy will deliver them when they get here.”

Evangeline’s sister said quickly, “No, we’ll arrange for someone— No, I’ll pick them up.”

Laura’s face tensed. There was more being said in those words.

“I could deliver them,” B.D. offered. “The folks would know me after our visit tomorrow. That is, if they wouldn’t mind having a man who wasn’t your priest on the premises.”

“We aren’t a closed order,” Sister Evangeline said and reached across Sephie to touch B.D.’s hand. “A good Catholic is always welcome.”

Sephie leaned back in her chair. She couldn’t suppress a harrumph, suspecting who they did restrict on the premises.

Chapter 32

Day 6: St. Gertrude's Guest Home, Saturday early afternoon

In the distance, ancient cottonwood trees rooted along the river framed the three-story building like tall green accents in a giant flower arrangement. They were only visible from the massive porch that wrapped around the irregular angles of the stone foundation of the building and connected with the stone flood wall. That wall stretched in one direction to the northernmost bridge in the city and in the other to the bridge in the heart of downtown and finally to the last bridge in the south end. In between the wall and the river was the extensive greenway that could be accessed at the bridges and at other strategic points. During floods, steel panels could be constructed across the bridges and at the smaller access points. St. Gertrude's Guest Home had witnessed over a hundred years of ebbing and receding of the river's waters that passed through the city northward to Canada, losing its destructive energy in those last miles.

On this warm, sunny day, Sephie squinted up at the historic building, finding it inconceivable that devastating flooding was such a part of the city's history. But buildings, like people, witness and endure.

"Reminds me of a convent in the bayou back home," B.D. said, craning his neck to see the sun glinting off the brass cross at the top of the roof. "Except it'd be surrounded by cypress and Spanish moss."

Sephie swung her neck to the side to gaze at him. "Was it haunted?"

"Now, why would you ask a thing like that?" B.D. challenged her, looking her square in the face.

"Just wondered if you could sense evil like the nun's sister said was here."

Turning his attention to the front door, he answered, "Don't feel anything here. It's just old."

Harrumphing, she moved toward the entrance and inside, with B.D. following. By the time they had reached the small, cherrywood desk at the end of the foyer, their vision had adjusted to the dimmer light. A very young woman, who may have been just out of her teens, rose from a chair behind the desk. She had on the same tan suit and white blouse that Sister Evangeline had worn.

"Welcome. Please sign the guestbook," she said, offering them a smile. "Who do you wish to visit? I'll find the room number for you."

"We're here to see Sister Evangeline."

"Sister," the young woman squeaked out, looking from Sephie to B.D. She looked flustered as if this was not in the script she had memorized. "Oh—," she began and glanced down a long hallway to her right and back to them. "I—"

Noticing a business phone on the desk next to a laminated list of numbers, the guestbook, and a cup of pens, Sephie suggested, "Perhaps you could call Sister Evangeline?"

"Oh," she said again and sat down. Picking up the phone receiver, she ran her finger down the laminated list. After she had punched in four digits, she said, "Mother Evangeline, you have two guests out here." She flicked her eyes up at B.D. nervously and then stared at the phone's buttons. "One's a man. And he's not a priest." The young woman listened and then her face turned bright red. Carefully replacing the receiver, she said softly, not looking up, "Mother Evangeline will be out shortly."

A door opened down the long corridor, and Sister Evangeline hurried toward them with her hand extended toward

Sephie. Grabbing Sephie's hand in both of hers, she said, "I hope you didn't wait long."

"Not long at all," Sephie said.

The nun shook B.D.'s hand as well and added, "Your voice should grace our mass tomorrow. Perhaps with a communion song. You said you know Joe Wise."

B.D. grinned. "'Take Our Bread'?"

Sister Evangeline smiled. "A perfect choice."

The nun turned to the young woman at the desk who was now back on her feet. "These are my new friends." She stared hard at the girl. "From out of town."

Sephie extended her hand to the young woman, who gave her a limp handshake. "My name is Sephronia, and this is B.D."

"He'll be making a delivery here in a few days," Sister Evangeline added. "He'll just put the box on the desk and be on his way."

The young woman nodded meekly.

"Shall we go into my office?"

Sephie hesitated and turned to B.D. "You were going to inspect the grounds, weren't you?"

He gave Sephie a questioning look but only nodded. "Yes, ma'am."

When he turned to leave, Evangeline said. "We have mass at seven-thirty for our early risers and at four for those who want to enjoy mass with their visitors." Taking Sephie by the arm, she ushered her into a spacious office and closed the door.

They soon settled into mahogany leather arm chairs in a corner sitting area surrounded by bookcases on two sides and in front of a low table with a tea service on it. Sister Evangeline poured the brew from a delicate china pot decorated with hand painted pink roses into two matching cups. "You'll have to forgive our young sister. She may truly be Isidora the Simple after her namesake, though that saint was humble and was only accused of being simple. God forgive me. I'm not being uncharitable. Something happened to her when she was a wee thing that has made her who she is. She sees the world in wonder and curiosity but anything that diverts from her routine also derails her mouth and her manners."

"But surely you have men who visit here. And repairmen."

"Yes, but the only men who come to see me are priests."

Sephie nodded, understanding the single-minded thinking. "Bless her heart," she said, taking the cup of tea the nun offered her. She took a sip of the reddish brew. It was a tart rose hip tea. "Very nice." She took another sip and then said, "You didn't tell us you were the Mother Superior here. I had a sense your sister would have wanted us to know your position."

Mother Evangeline leaned back in her chair to sip her tea. "She doesn't know yet. And, yes, she would. She'd think it elevates me or perhaps herself. It's just more work and responsibility."

Leaning back also, Sephie asked, "How could you keep such a thing from her?"

"Our past Mother was transferred to Arizona because of her health two weeks ago. It was a sudden decision by the Mother House. Mother Rosula was delicate and really shouldn't have been posted here. She has crippling arthritis that was aggravated by our winters. We begged her to request a transfer, but she was obedient."

"Stubborn."

Mother Evangeline chuckled. "Yes, that, too. We finally had to have her doctor write a letter recommending her to be transferred to a dry climate. She's happy working with retired nuns in Tucson and from her last letter, she is now teaching tai chi and chair yoga to them."

"We are called to be where we're needed the most."

Evangeline nodded. "And are you called to be here, as well?"

Sephie smiled. "I'm visiting my great-niece," she said innocently and paused. "But she did ask me to come."

"Ah." The nun sipped her tea and waited.

"You seem to have more energy today," Sephie said, diverting the conversation.

Bending and straightening her left arm, she admitted, "It no longer hurts. And, yes, I feel like my old self. Your Christ tree is working."

"And prayer," Sephie reminded.

"You're not one of us," Evangeline remarked softly before taking another sip of tea.

"No. My people are deep water Baptists of varying denominations. There might be a holy-roller—" she paused and then clarified. "A Pentecostal — thrown into the mix. My sister back in Tennessee lives in the church. I think for her it's as much an addiction as the moonshine our uncles and cousins make."

Evangeline nodded. "I read a paper on that years ago when I was a novice. The Church wanted us to make sure our choice was love of God and not love of the trappings of the Church. I think my sister Ophelia needs to learn that lesson."

It was Sephie's turn to say, "Ah," and take a sip of tea.

"So, do you follow your family's leaning?"

Sephie shrugged. "I believe there's a Hand bigger than mine at work in all things. I can't deny that when I look at the beauty and power of nature." She smiled. "And I see the work of love in people."

"Does your great-niece share your belief?"

Sephie grunted out a laugh. "I have no idea what that child believes. Besides, she's my great-niece by marriage. My husband's family was just as dysfunctional as mine, but they hid it behind being proper. Mine was, and still is, backwoods country and dysfunctional in your face. All I know is Mandy loves deeply and faithfully."

Evangeline placed her cup on the table and remarked, “That’s a great gift.” Reaching for the pot, she asked, “More tea?”

Sephie shook her head and drained her cup, returning it to the table as well. “I suppose we should read your guest house now and try to find that evil your sister said was here.”

“I really think that that task will be fruitless. There have been nuns living here for a century, with mass said twice on Sunday and the rosary prayed every night. Whatever evil Ophelia thinks she found here is in her own narrow thinking.”

Sephie stood, closed her eyes, and extended her arms, palms facing away from her. She opened to the energies of the room. After five seconds, she opened her eyes and relaxed her arms. “This is a good room.” She turned to Evangeline. “You do good work here.”

The nun tilted her head, giving a modest nod, and rose also. Extending her hand toward the door, she added, “Shall we?”

Chapter 33

Day 6: The Watering Hole, Saturday late afternoon

"Not a blessed thing," Sephie said, taking a bite out of her burger. "What is this, anyway?"

"Camel." B.D. answered, relishing his own sandwich.

"What?"

"Camel. Bill says there's a place in South Dakota that raises them for meat."

"Why?"

"It's good, isn't it?"

"Just like cow. So, why not raise cattle?"

"Less acreage to feed, I gather."

Putting the burger down, Sephie continued before more culinary questions arose. "I didn't find a thing amiss inside the guest house and you didn't find anything outside. Then what in the world attacked Mother Evangeline?"

B.D. shrugged. "Guess we'll find out tonight. You did get permission for us to encamp on that big porch?"

"Of course, I did! I'm not a ninny, though you may think I am at this age sometimes. I'm still sharp as a tack." She went in for another bite of cloven-hoofed meat.

"Front or back? Or do we split up?"

"Back. That's where Mother Evangeline was attacked. Something seems to be coming from the river side."

"Well, it must have flown over the floodwall to get to the cats. I still think it's bird-related."

"Maybe."

B.D. put his burger back on his plate. "But nothing normal."

"You called birds again?"

He shook his head. "Didn't need to. It's just a feeling." Frowning, he only said, "I wish Papa Mamoud was here."

"Maybe you should call him."

Shaking his head again, he only said, "No phone out in the bayou." Then he added, "And he'd only tell me to sing and pray."

"Maybe you should."

Taking a deep breath, he stared at his plate and pushed its half-eaten contents aside. "Osanyin's messengers appeared to me."

After taking a sip of her soft drink, Sephie asked, "Isn't he the orisha of healing?"

"Yep. He should've appeared to you."

Sephie harrumphed. "I'd offend him. I wouldn't know what's proper to do. After all, my spirits come from another country. Just as old. Just as wise. But different."

"Have you had messages from them since we got here?"

The old woman shook her head and gave a shrug of dismissal. "I haven't asked, either." She leaned back in the booth and squinted at her companion. "What we're dealing with here, I think, is unique to this place."

B.D. also leaned against the back of his own booth. But his action was more in defeat than in confrontation, as Sephie's action seemed to project. "I picked that old man's brain, and I got a litany of beings and allusions to their abilities but nothing resembled what we've seen."

"Perhaps we haven't seen all that this creature can do." Leaning slowly across the table, Sephie added. "And I think there's more than one being."

"But all the incidents have the same MO: the creature claws and kind of sedates its victims. But nothing else is done. Now, because the cats are kept inside, it's found humans."

"One human."

"It'll find us tonight."

"Let's hope so." Sephie saw Bill come toward them and raised her hand.

"What can I get you, young lady?"

"Chocolate. Anything."

Not even pausing to think, he immediately offered, "Kilimanjaro Kake — we spell it with two Ks, of course. A giant wedge of chocolate cake, raspberry filling, covered in chocolate ganache."

"Bring it." Then she added. "And two forks." Turning to B.D. after Bill ambled off to the kitchen, she said, "Might as well sin boldly before we go sit vigil tonight."

Chapter 34

Day 6: St. Gertrude's Guest Home, Saturday near midnight

Sephie pulled the blanket tighter around her body against the night chill. Around 10 p.m, they had set up two camp chairs side by side on the stones of the back porch of St. Gerrude's Guest Home. Between them sat a thermos of coffee and two paper cups.

"You can take a nap if you want," Sephie said. "Nothing's happened in two hours."

"I'm your second pair of eyes," B.D. said. "I'm not closing them until I have to." He looked up at the night sky. Most of the stars were still visible despite the lights from the town. "I wonder what you'd see out on a country road here."

Sephie swung her attention to B.D., wondering what in the world he was talking about. Realizing it was the sky, she retorted, "Same as you saw in Dark Holler and in Lafayette."

"I just wondered if it'd be different. It sure does get dark later here than back home."

"We *are* farther north."

B.D. threw off his blanket. "I think I'll take a turn around the porch."

"Give me a holler if you see anything."

After B.D. disappeared around the corner of the building, Sephie tossed her own blanket off. Slowly, she lifted her body out of the chair and stretched. The slight chill and the inactivity made her body stiffen and her right hip ache, causing her to shuffle for a few steps before she got everything working to her satisfaction. She made her way to the edge of the porch and leaned on the cold stones to look out toward the river. There seemed to be some small winged things flying among the cottonwoods.

"Psst."

Sephie thought she heard a noise.

"Psst. Psst. Sephie." It was B.D. whispering.

Sephie looked to her left. B.D. stood at the corner of the building, motioning for her to come to him.

"What the—?" she muttered, but moved in his direction.

When she was beside him, he put his hands on her shoulders and turned her toward the building. Then he pointed up at the roof eaves. In her ear, he whispered, "Just watch." Reaching into his pocket, he pulled out a coin and tossed it up at the eaves. When it hit the wood, there was a high-pitched squeak and out flew a small dark shape. It fluttered around the windows in an erratic pattern, and then seemed to understand where it was supposed to go and headed straight for the cottonwoods. "Bats."

Sephie stepped away from B.D. and looked at him. "So, that was what was scratching at the windows." She turned to look at the trees by the river. "What are they feeding on down there?"

"Mosquitoes, I think," he said, turning toward the river, too. "That's why we haven't been eaten alive out here. Laura did say that the city sprays for them but never gets them all, especially by the river."

"Makes sense. And for me, I'm glad they're going to eat their fill."

As they laughed quietly, Sephie spotted a movement on the ground skirting the trees. As it moved, something like wings flapped behind it. "What's that?" she said, pointing.

B.D. didn't wait. He rushed around her to the small opening between the porch and the floodwall and jumped through, hitting the ground hard and rolling. Once on his feet, he sprinted toward the figure. In seconds, he was lost in the darkness beneath the cottonwoods. Then, Sephie heard a cry and saw two figures rushing down the greenway toward the bridge before they were enveloped by the night. Sephie fretted as she waited, pacing the length of the back porch several times. After a few minutes, she saw a lone figure walk slowly back across the greenway. As it neared the opening in the floodwall, she realized it was B.D.

Looking up at her, he shook his head and then slipped through the opening and made his way around to the front steps. Sephie met him as he came around the side of the porch.

"Damn kid in a black cape," B.D. grumbled.

"A cape?"

"Yep."

"What was he doing down there?"

"Haven't a clue. I grabbed him. Before he wriggled out of my grasp, he said he didn't mean any harm and something about a newspaper article."

"Newspaper article! Well, that's the last thing we need."

Chapter 35

Day 7: North Star, Sunday early afternoon

"Get me yesterday's newspaper," Sephie demanded as she entered the shop from the back room with a mug of coffee that she'd brought from her kitchen next door.

"Well, good morning to you," Mandy said, sarcastically, from a stepladder as she nailed sun emblems to one wall.

"It's past morning," the old woman muttered.

"Have a nice lay-in?"

"I'll have you know we didn't get back here until seven a.m." She eased herself into the rocker. "And nary a thing to show for it, except that the guest home has bats."

"That's a good thing," Laura answered, popping up from behind the counter with a cardboard box. "Bats eat insects. They're badly maligned." Running a utility knife across the packing tape, she unfolded the lid and pulled out a clear glass vessel filled with sky blue candle wax. "These look great and seemed to have survived shipping. Aunt Sephie, you can ask B.D. to deliver these to St. Gertrude's."

"Ask him yourself. He's going to be singing for mass this afternoon. I'm sure he'll grace us with his presence before he goes. Now, can you get me a newspaper or not?"

"You're out of luck for yesterday's news," Mandy said, stepping down from the ladder and folding it up. "The Riverbend Times is really good about picking up old copies when they deliver the new ones." She passed by her aunt as the old woman pronounced, "We'll have to go to the morgue then."

Stopped in her tracks, Mandy asked, “Say what?”

“The morgue. At the newspaper. Where you go to read old issues.”

“Well, I’m sure they have one, but it’d be easier to access online. Let me put this away, and I’ll show you. You can do it from your phone.”

“My phone?”

“Well, maybe *my* phone,” Mandy said. “I’ve got a smartphone.”

“Smartphone? Is it smarter than mine? Or anyone else’s?”

When Mandy had put the ladder in the back room, she retrieved her phone from a shelf behind the counter. Within seconds, she’d Googled the newspaper and got a search box. “What are you looking for?”

“I don’t know,” Sephie said.” That’s why I wanted to look at a real newspaper.”

“Well, there might be a way to search by date, but it’s easier if you knew what to look for.”

“All I know is B.D. chased a kid in a cape last night who was hanging out along the river. When he got his hands on him, the kid said something about a newspaper story.”

Mandy frowned. “How about ‘cape’?” She tapped in the word and hit the magnifying glass icon. She shook her head. “A kid in a cape,” she mused. “Maybe vampire. Let’s try that.” Once again, she did a search. “Nothing.”

“You know,” Laura began. “The daily runs actual news stories. Nothing sensational. There’s a weekly rag that runs all sorts of stories based on conspiracy theories and rumor.”

“Riverbend’s own National Enquirer,” Sephie commented.

“Those stories are pretty much nonsense, but their music and art coverage is top-notch. I’ll run down to the coffeeshop and get a copy. It comes out on Fridays.”

When she had rushed out the door, Sephie asked, "How can a town this size have a tabloid? There can't be that much gossip. And surely they don't send their reporters all over the country."

Mandy laughed and took a seat on the stool behind the counter. "This whole state doesn't have enough of anything juicy to keep a tabloid in business. That's why their entertainment section is so good. We have plenty of that in spades. Everybody reads the paper for those stories and their entertainment calendar."

Sephie grunted.

"You have to realize that their reporters are all volunteers. It was started about fifty years ago by a couple of college students. They wrote all the content, and, eventually, their friends began to write for them because they could get comp tickets to concerts for their pre-show publicity. It's a free magazine that gets its revenue from ad sales. Only the editor and graphic designer ever see any money. Today, college kids apply for non-paying, but full-credit, internships. It's a win-win for everybody. And a couple of those volunteer entertainment journalists went on to write for big city dailies and magazines. And a couple became published novelists."

"Well, I'll be. All because of a tabloid."

"Experience is experience, I guess. Sometimes being in a small town offers opportunities that you can't get in a huge one."

Sephie nodded. "Kind of like B.D. singing for mass, and he hasn't been here a week."

"Once word gets around about that voice of his, he'll sing at every church in town and then be asked to solo at the university. You watch."

At that moment, Laura rushed in out of breath. "I started thinking on the way. If a kid saw something about the cats or a vampire, we need to find out exactly what else the reporter might have found out. No matter how far-fetched. So, I ran all the way there and back."

She passed Sephie a copy. "This is this week's issue." She handed another to Mandy. "That's last week's, and they just happened to have a stray issue from the week before. Let's see what's there."

Sephie started paging through the half-sheet, magazine-like newspaper. It was printed on regular newspaper stock, and all the photos were in black and white as you'd expect. The front page boasted a photo of a well-known blues musician, leaning against a vintage Cadillac with tail fins, with his hand on the tuning keys of his electric guitar he had stood on its rounded end. The headlines around the photo announced his return to Riverbend for a concert. Sephie quickly paged to the article about the musician and scanned the first couple of paragraphs, deeming that it was good. From the two-page spread, she could see the reporter had gotten an interview because it was full of quotes and other photos.

Turning back to the front of the paper, she began searching the headlines, looking for something odd. There was a political article about water conservation and another about a gun rights issue. There was a memoir piece that looked like a regular column, a food section with pictures of odd vegetables and recipes for church casseroles that they called hot dishes, a column about car repair questions, and even an all-natural beauty column. There were several pages of music and movie reviews, a three-page events calendar, and a couple of opinion pieces about a government cover up of UFOs and how computer usage was the gateway to identity theft. And, of course, every page had lots of ads for anything and everything.

Sephie put the paper down. "Nothing. You two have any luck?"

"Oh, sorry," Laura said, looking up from the paper she had spread on the counter. "I got distracted by this natural beauty column. But I didn't find anything odd yet."

Mandy turned another page of her newspaper. "Wait. Here's something. Is Riverbend Safe at Night?" She paused as she scanned through the first sentence. "No. It's about women's safety." Looking further over the two open pages, she turned another page. Then she laughed. "This has to be it. Dakota Dracula!" She read a bit silently and then read it out loud. "Residents have been experiencing strange events during the long summer nights in Riverbend. Small pets have been viciously attacked and shadowy, dark figures have been spotted lurking along the river." She paused while she silently read more, then looked up. "The reporter interviewed cat owners; one or two of them are our customers, and he even found some — quote eyewitnesses unquote — who saw a figure in the trees in the greenway. Someone talked about seeing a huge raptor that they thought was bigger than a South American condor hunkered on a limb of one of those ancient cottonwoods. And somebody else swears she was attacked at night in her own bedroom by a presence and felt drained the next morning." She returned to the article to read further silently, then burst out laughing, "Oh, come on!"

"What?" Laura asked.

"Somebody saw a rock troll, and someone else saw something called a *draugr*, and somebody swears they saw *hiisi*, running all over the greenway at night. *Hiisi*, whatever in the world is that?"

"The henchmen of the evil god Lempo."

Startled, everyone turned to the doorway of the back room.

B.D. yawned loudly. "They're Finnish. Who saw them?"

"Some eyewitness in the paper," Sephie growled. "What are you doing up?"

"I'm hungry. Besides I don't want to keep musician's hours. I can't help you if I do. And, I need time to get cleaned up for church and practice. Where'd that eyewitness see the *hiisi*?"

"Somewhere on the greenway," Mandy said and handed the newspaper to B.D., who immediately was lost in the wild speculations of the writer.

After reading a bit, he turned to front page. "This is last week's paper," he pronounced. "It's a weekly, right?"

"Yeah, so?" Mandy challenged.

"I had a friend at the college who worked on a weekly. He had to get his stories in about four days or more before they went to press. This means that people were seeing all sorts of strange creatures along the river for at least three weeks, well before we got here."

"That's why I called Aunt Sephie," Mandy explained as if to someone who was incredibly dense.

"This article says the activity started after the greenway dried up following the annual flooding back last month and that no one ever saw this after a flood before."

"From what you've told me, Laura, the water comes not only from the towns and cities south of here but also from runoff from the farms along the river."

"Could have stirred up something," Sephie said, "and it decided to come ashore here."

"But why?" Mandy asked.

"Could be where we are," Laura suggested. "We have not only the Red River here that flows north, but there are more large streams and rivers that feed into the Red before it reaches Riverbend. North of us is just farmland with less runoff from snowmelt flowing into the river."

"We need to find out what's upriver," Sephie said.

"Let's think about that after we eat," Mandy said, pulling out her phone. "B.D. is fading away before our eyes. I'll call in an order to the Watering Hole. What do you all want?"

"Surprise me," B.D. said. "I haven't been disappointed yet. I'm going to shower and shave. Let me know when the food gets here."

After he left, Sephie asked, "You got a crock pot?"

Mandy looked at Laura, who said, "I think we got one as a wedding present. It's probably still in the box. I just never figured out how to layer everything."

"Go find it. You can't keep spending all your money on restaurant food. Mandy girl, after we eat, let's go to the store and get a roast and a chicken. Those are easy to cook ahead."

"I don't know," Mandy began, "Bill came looking for us when B.D. made jambalaya."

Sephie squinted at her. "Do you have a backroom arrangement with him?"

Mandy again glanced at Laura and then looked down, guilt clearly on her face.

"We do," Laura admitted. "Bill uses us as his testers. He's always coming up with new dishes, and we try them out. In between those, we get our orders for half price. It works out, since neither Mandy nor I are very good cooks."

"It really has helped us out. We may own the buildings — well, we're paying mortgages — but we're just a small business and things can get lean," Mandy admitted.

"And we give Bill and Sugar free tarot and astrology readings. And they both get a fifty percent discount on merchandise."

Sephie smiled. "I wondered how you can live like you do. After all, I haven't seen your store bustling with people since I got here."

"It gets busier when we have events, and with Summer Solstice this weekend, you'll see a difference. We're hosting a big outdoor event Saturday on the greenway with vendors and drumming and ritual. There'll be people coming from all of the little towns around. We drew about hundred people last year. The event goes well into the evening, and we have permission this year to drum all night in tents beforehand. We start with a sunrise ritual."

“Sounds like a music festival,” Sephie commented.

“Or a country fair in England,” Laura said. “It’s an experience.”

Something, however, bothered Sephie. “Will it be safe with what’s out there?’

“We’ll have a community police presence because some of the vendors will be there overnight,” Mandy said. Again, she glanced at Laura before adding. “And we put wards on the space when we set up that we only lift in the evening when everyone leaves. I think you’ll feel them.”

Sephie only nodded, still musing about their creature problem.

Chapter 36

Day 8: North Star, Monday evening

"You don't have to help me close up," Laura said, after ushering out the last customer and locking the front door. She turned the open/closed sign to Closed and turned to watch Sephie straightening her display of tinctures and salves.

"No trouble, sweetie," the old woman said. "You weren't kidding when you said business would pick up."

"And it's only Monday of Solstice week." Laura began re-shelving books that had been pulled out by customers. "I'm really glad you brought your herbal remedies with you. I think you'll be sold out by next week."

"People have need everywhere. I've been meaning to get you and Mandy well stocked. I brought everything I had made up, and I have the makings for more here." Finishing, she put her hands on her back and turned to Laura. "But I'm weary and need to lay this old body down."

"You might need a sip of your cousin's remedy before bed." The young woman put her arm around Sephie and walked her through the back room toward the door.

"No. I never touch the stuff. I'll just take some ibuprofen. My arthritis is kicking up."

"Could be rain coming," Laura said, opening the back door and turning on the outside light. "Watch your step going down those stairs."

Sephie eased down the steps, right foot first, extending her hip to take pressure off it since it had been a bit achier than normal. She winced as she moved her other foot. The old woman knew it could be rain or maybe it was all of the standing on her feet that day as she helped in the store. Back home, she'd forage for herbs a while and then sit and sip a gin and lemonade. Then she'd putter in her cabin and sit and sip some more. It was a routine she knew. The only real challenge was the long trek up and down the mountain. By the end of the day when she'd reached her house and Agnesia, the liquor would have eased whatever wear and tear she'd put her body through. Here, she hadn't sipped regularly and perhaps she should.

When she had reached the steps at the back of the little house next door, Laura switched off the yard light. Sephie took a few minutes to look up at the night sky. There were few stars visible, making her surmise that perhaps rain was indeed coming in. If so, she wondered if the river creatures would welcome that — *hiisi* or raptor or vampire.

A rustle in the shrubbery that masked the two properties from the dirt alley behind drew Sephie's attention. Only a small, wooden gate in back of the shop allowed access there and an old rusty iron one blocked a graveled area from the alley. The hairs on the back of her neck rose, prompting a shiver across her shoulders. She couldn't make out anything, not even shapes, in the wall of darkness. Another rustle in front of the back gate caused Sephie to jerk her head in that direction. *If it's that kid in a cape, I'll tan his hide and go toe-to-toe with social services for it*, she thought. She took a few tentative steps toward the last rustle. As she neared the wooden gate, a slim figure came into view, wearing a long coat and a hat, heading toward town. Even in shadow, the attire seemed antiquated, like a figure from a 40s film noir movie.

"Who are you? What do you want?" she challenged as she gripped the gate, suddenly feeling weak.

The figure stopped, turned slightly, uncovered its head, and offered her a deep bow, sweeping the hat in a grand gesture.

Suddenly the yard light came on, causing Sephie to blink and turn in that direction. When she looked back, there was no one in the alley.

Mandy opened the back door with a baseball bat in her hand. “Aunt Sephie? Are you all right?”

“There was someone lurking in the alley.”

Mandy rushed down the steps, across the yard, and out the little gate. Sephie followed, and they both looked up and down the dark lane. Nothing was there.

Turning back, Sephie said, “I couldn’t see clearly. It was a man or as tall as a man in what could have been a trench coat and a fedora.”

“Like Laura’s granddad used to wear to church?”

“I have no idea what Laura’s granddad wore to church, but it looked like something out of an old movie. And he had the cheek to do a sweeping bow.”

“Maybe it was an actor from the theater company here. They’re doing a summer show, and Bill says they come into the Watering Hole after rehearsal at night.”

“Are they doing Mickey Spillane?”

“I have no clue. But I could ask Bill to take you over to the theater tomorrow night and you can ask around.”

Sephie harrumphed. “Actors. Kids in capes. Finnish demons. Giant raptors. I could have enjoyed a quiet summer in my little cabin watching lightning bugs. You don’t even have lightning bugs here.”

Mandy put her arm around Sephie and walked her to the door of the little house. “But it’s not boring here, is it?”

Once more Sephie harrumphed.

Chapter 37

Day 9: The Old Garage Theatre, Tuesday evening

Like St. Gertrude's, the theater building was over a hundred years old, faced with the cream-colored brick well-known during that era in eastern North Dakota. Two large doors that originally opened to allow vehicles inside bore a new coat of paint a few shades darker than the light brick. A small door painted that same color led to the box office and the room where popcorn was made and other refreshments were offered. No one was there when Sephie and Bill entered, but voices from the interior drew them further inside. Though technically only one story, the space within was probably closer to a story and a half. The high ceiling could have competed in height with any gymnasium, but surrounding it on three sides were banks of windows.

Bill pointed up at them. "They used to open, I'm told, to let the exhaust fumes out and offer more light inside."

Sephie twisted her neck to look at the double doors. "Couldn't they just open those doors?"

"Sure, but in winter it would freeze everything. So, they'd keep a wood stove going in the back and crack the windows open up top."

"Who told you all that?"

"Ole Swenson, of course. His great-great-granddaughter roped him into telling stories here one summer for a children's workshop. He decided to give a history lesson, complete with resident ghost."

"A ghost?"

"Yep, supposed to be an old man in overalls carrying an old-fashioned oil can."

"I wonder what he was going to grease."

Bill laughed. "The building is on the historical register. When the theater company bought the building thirty years ago after the Flood, there was concern that they'd destroy the architecture. But they did a good job with preserving the outside and most of the inside." He pointed to stairs that ran up each side of the far wall in behind a stage platform and the rows of red theater seats facing it. "See those stairs? They go to the dressing rooms. That space was just a long ledge that was used to store tires and automotive parts. They just enclosed all that into one long dressing room and costume shop. When sets are built, they always extend out to cover the stairways so the actors can go back and forth to change during a show. They'll start construction for the set in a day or two for the big summer melodrama."

"Aren't those supposed to be done outdoors?"

Bill nodded. "They'll do small cuttings from the show throughout the summer, but the full extravaganza will start this weekend and run through the end of July."

"Have you ever trod the boards yourself, as they say?" Sephie asked.

"Well," Bill grinned. "I have a time or two."

"I bet with that mustache of yours you were cast as the villain."

"Or the congenial uncle. I just love it! You ought to try it."

"Not me," Sephie said. "I have enough trouble remembering what I ate for breakfast, much less a whole script." As she followed Bill down toward the stage, she thought about breakfast and realized it was the last time she'd eaten. At that moment, her stomach produced a very loud growl.

Bill chuckled. "I think you're right about your memory. When was the last time you ate?"

"Breakfast. The shop's been inundated with customers. It's taken three of us to handle it all."

"Three? Who's laying down on the job?"

"B.D. He's gotten booked singing all over the city. He's been off practicing."

"Singing?" Bill looked thoughtful. "He must be good."

"Oh, he is." Then she grabbed Bill's arm and turned him to look at her. "Don't get it into your head to get him singing at your place."

"Why not? If he's that good—"

"He didn't come up here to become a chanteuse."

Again, Bill chuckled. "We'd have to put him in a dress and a wig to do that."

"What?"

"I think you mean a lounge singer."

"Whatever," she said, turning back toward the stage. "I don't know how long we'll be here, anyway."

"Then I'd better book him while I still can."

Sephie harrumphed. Secretly, she was happy others recognized B.D.'s talent. In truth, she missed his spiritual insights. Mandy and Laura had book knowledge, but B.D. had been raised by elders who had dipped his baby toes into matters of Spirit that she would never fully understand. The busyness of the last few days had kept her from fretting too much about his newfound fame.

She sighed, suddenly feeling very old and weary. She needed to eat or at least sit down. She'd come to ask the theater group a few questions about midnight marauding and to give them a piece of her mind. At this moment, all of her steam had escaped, leaving her exhausted. When she'd reached the first row of seats, she sidled around Bill to rest her bones in the red velveteen of the end seat. She chided herself for not taking better care of herself. She'd been alone long enough to realize that she was the only one in charge of her health. The weariness continued, clouding her thinking and even blurring her vision.

She looked up at Bill, who was waving at someone. He had moved down to the far edge of the stage toward a half dozen people with scripts and pencils in their hands. He was laughing and shaking hands, finally pointing back to Sephie.

The old woman suddenly felt cold in the air conditioning of the theater. She shivered, wishing she'd brought that shawl she'd finally finished for Laura. She'd given it to her that morning, hadn't she? Or had she only thought about doing it? She certainly hadn't done much sitting in the past two days. Did she really finish it? Where was that shawl? Where had she seen it last? In her rocker? She looked around her as if to see if she'd brought her hook and yarn with her. An iciness filled her. She looked up to see the dark eyes of a handsome young man that seemed to blaze into hers. Waves of coldness radiated off him as if she'd set foot into a morgue. He was dressed in a dark suit, a black shirt that was open down his hairless chest, a dark printed vest, a long black Western duster coat, and a black fedora. He was a mix of 40s gumshoe and riverboat gambler.

"Good evening, my dear," he said in a soft voice, laced with something foreign but familiar, reminding her of old television shows. As she sifted her mind for the fragment of memory, she thought of old westerns and mysteries and finally comedies. That was it! A voice that had coined a phrase: "You got some 'splaining to do." The voice was Cuban.

Sephie looked up again and the figure was gone. Muddle-headed, she searched around her seat for him and finally found the strange man talking with Bill and the other actors. Something was terribly wrong. She needed to get out of the theater. Hoisting herself out of her chair with great effort, Sephie struggled toward the box office, holding onto the theater seats as she walked. She crossed the open space and made it through the office until she pushed open the door to the warm summer evening. Once outside, she leaned against the heated bricks of the building and took in several deep breaths.

This was one reason she needed B.D. with her. He would have sensed something was amiss well before they even entered the theater. Shoot, she should have sensed something was wrong, herself. But B.D. had a right to his own life. Why had he come, anyway? She wasn't that helpless. She could have driven by herself. *He should be back home with his own family in the bayou, not here where he's a novelty.* She should tell him tonight he needed to go home. She'd book the flight herself tomorrow — as soon as Mandy helped her do that on the computer. But for now, he needed to get as far away from this place as he could and she should, too — at least as far away from this building.

Pushing her body away from the bricks, Sephie shuffled a few steps and wondered just how far she could get on foot. Discarding that idea, she searched for Bill's car. There it was! His reliable Toyota, new but not ostentatious. It suited him. She'd thought so when he'd come by the shop to pick her up. She shuffled toward the passenger side and tried the door. It was unlocked.

"Trusting soul," she muttered before she swung the door open to get in and found her purse on the floor. "Or dumb as a post."

She pulled the black bag onto the seat and immediately searched for her wallet. Finding it, she saw that her driver's license was there, as well as her one credit card and the thirteen dollars she had. She also stuck her finger into a small slit and pulled out her emergency twenty-dollar bill.

Relieved, she replaced her wallet and rummaged inside to find a small packet of salt she'd put in from one of the places she and B.D. had stopped to eat on the way up there. She ripped it open and poured the contents into her hand. Concentrating, she closed her eyes and asked for a blessing of protection to remove all negativity connected to her. She then sprinkled the salt over her head, over her shoulders, down her backside, and then over her front. She even lifted up one foot at a time and passed the last few crystals of salt over the bottoms of her shoes. Only then did she pick up her handbag and settle into the passenger seat.

Once inside, she shut the door in spite of the heat and took a few more deep breaths. Her mind was slowly beginning to clear. She concentrated again and drew upon the last of her energy and raised power to create a mirror ball in her mind that covered the entire car. Raising her arms in an arc as far as she could in the small car, she muttered, “Let there be a circle of protection within this space for all that drive or ride in this car. Let all harm sent toward it be reflected and returned to the sender. It has no place here.”

Dropping her arms into her lap, Sephie leaned back in her seat and closed her eyes.

Chapter 38

Day 9: The Old Garage Theatre, Tuesday evening

Knocking awoke her. Sephie was stiff and overly warm. She opened her eyes to find Bill pecking at the car window with his left forefinger. Squinting up at him, she wondered what he'd gotten into a bother about. Sephie reached for the window crank and realized that she needed to push a button for the power window. She pushed but the button did nothing. Frustrated, she was about to crack open the door when Bill jerked it open. "What's gotten your boxers in a knot?" she grumbled.

"Are you all right?" Bill asked anxiously.

"Of course, I'm all right."

"I looked around and you were gone."

"Are you finished jawing with your theater cronies?"

"Well, I — Don't you want to come in and talk to them? You sure had a bee in your bonnet before we got here."

"Well, I found the Midnight Marauder. Get in," she ordered. "And take me to that restaurant of yours. I need food and maybe a stiff drink."

Bill shut the door and rushed around to the driver's side. "You had me worried."

"No need. Just feed me."

In only a few minutes and one traffic light, Bill turned the car into the alley behind the Watering Hole and parked. He immediately offered Sephie a hand getting out. She fussed, even though she appreciated the help. Her mind had cleared, but she was still weak. Once inside, Sephie settled into a booth in the bar area where she watched the foot traffic in the waning light outside through the big front windows. Bill brought her a little loaf of bread and butter and set a cocktail with a lime in it in front of her. She sniffed it, took a sip, and looked up at him. "How'd you know?"

"Thought you might be a gin and tonic gal. That or maybe some kind of vodka cocktail."

"Why?" she said before taking a big gulp. She applied her energy to slicing herself a piece of bread.

"My granny always said a lady should never have alcohol on her breath. It's a genteel quality."

Sephie grunted, buttering the bread and finally stuffing it into her mouth.

"Do you want some soup or something heartier?"

"Pasta, mac and cheese, something heavy," she said. "I need to ground."

Bill escaped to the kitchen while Sephie contended herself with the bread.

When half of the loaf was gone, the old woman noticed a small group of people walk past the restaurant, seeming to head for the front door. Within a minute, the inner door opened and the group entered. Over the top of the booth, she recognized B.D.'s head. They proceeded toward the bar and filled the empty bar stools. B.D. swiveled in his stool to look over the rest of the patrons and spotted Sephie. He stepped away from the group and slid into the booth seat in front of the old woman.

"You all right?"

"I will be." She swallowed the last of the gin and tonic. "How was your rehearsal?"

"It was great. I'll be doing two services this Sunday. I'll do the afternoon service for guests at St. Gertrude's again. Before that, I'll do one at a big Lutheran church near the university in the morning. Mother Evangeline arranged those, and they'll be easy. She's called a lot of people to come out to the rehearsal. I was asked to sing 'Free at Last' from that play *Big River* for a showcase at the university and 'Ole Man River' for a melodrama that the community theater is doing." He frowned. "I don't know that I can sing that kind of music."

Sephie's eyes widened at the mention of melodrama. She grabbed B.D.'s arm with her right hand. "Stay away from the theater. It's too dangerous."

B.D.'s hand covered hers. "It's okay, Miz Sephie. I will." He studied her face. "Something's happened."

She nodded, released his arm, and leaned back against the booth.

"Related to what's been happening here?"

"There's an energy vampire in this town."

"And he's at the local theater?"

"He's also been lurking around the alley in back of the shop."

At that moment, Bill appeared with a bowl of pasta covered in meat and cheese. A large soup spoon stuck out of the bowl. "Lutheran funeral hot dish," he pronounced. "I don't know of anything heavier or more satisfying. I keep it on the menu all the time. I've seen hockey players scarf down copious amounts of that before a game. I feed it to college kids who come in late from barhopping every other place in town. It also is just plain good." He clapped B.D. on the back. "You want some?"

The young man hesitated and then said, "Sure, but make it a half bowl please."

"You want another G and T, Miss Sephie?"

She shook her head. "It's time for a soft drink."

"How about you, son?"

"Actually, could you get me a cup of hot water with the juice of a whole lemon, and float about a finger of bourbon on top? It's for my vocal chords."

"Sure thing." He started to leave for the kitchen but paused, giving Sephie a wary look. "Could we talk later about you singing here? I'll gladly pay."

"That does it!" Sephie said, tossing her napkin on the table. "Now, you've hooked him. Singing for church is one thing. But now that there's a dollar in it, he'll never go home." She turned to B.D. "You do want to go home to see your family, don't you?"

"Well, sure, Miz Sephie. But this'll be my summer job. I can go home for Christmas when it's warm back home."

As Bill fled the battle, Sephie kept up the argument. "How long do you think we're gonna stay here, anyway?"

"I suspect we'll be here until you have to get back to do your fall wildcrafting, which I'll help you with. Then I'll go home for Christmas and then we can bring all that back up here next spring."

"Oh, so you think you'll have a recurring gig here in Riverbend?"

He grinned. "I think Mandy and Laura won't want to let you stay away for long. Besides, there's way too much juju going on here that needs to be dealt with."

"Oh, bother," she muttered and paid attention to her hot dish, ignoring the spoon and attacking it with a fork. The flavors were familiar but different. No canned tomato sauce over pasta and meat. Tomatoes, yes, and something else. She passed the big spoon to B.D. "Taste this. What am I tasting besides meat, tomatoes, pasta, and cheese?"

B.D. dipped into the dish and chewed on what he found. "Well, there's onion and celery." He chewed some more and then he raised an eyebrow. "Anise! I think there's Italian sausage in this besides hamburger." He moved to take another bite, but Sephie moved her bowl away. "Wait for your own. I need every calorie of this."

"So, you got zapped by an energy vampire?" he said, leaning away from her food.

She nodded. "Got me good. The third time I encountered him. First was at the dance."

"Mandy mentioned you were feeling peaked."

"Then that Midnight Marauder on Monday. He was lurking out in the alley and arrogantly bowed to me when he got found out. Then now. I should have shielded better."

"Anyone else affected?"

She shook her head. "Didn't seem so. Bill was even talking to the guy and nothing."

B.D. frowned. "He's targeting you, probably because he can read your special energy. I should've been with you. He'd be no match for the both of us."

"He seems to find me when you're not around." She stopped trying to eat and rested against the booth back again. "Doesn't mean you wouldn't be affected, too. He's feeding on energy. He's fed when there's been others around. Is it just feeding, or to make me weak?"

"I'll cancel my singing gigs."

Sephie reached across the table and took both of his hands into hers. "No. You have a right to use your talents." She gave him a grumpy frown, which she knew he'd know was fake. "And to get paid for it."

"But I came up here to help you. I got sidetracked."

"And I thank you." She released his hands and smiled. "We do make a good team. We can still help this town, but we need to rethink how we're doing it. There still is so much we don't know."

Bill arrived with a tray that held the hot dish, a soft drink, a cup with the mixture B.D. wanted, and two glasses of water.

Sephie pointed to B.D. "And you can give him the bill since he's going to be a man of means."

"I'll take that out of your first gig check," Bill said.

Chapter 39

Day 10: North Star, Wednesday midmorning

"Good morning! What a glorious day the Lord has made!" the small Black man said as he closed the shop door to step further inside. He wore a dark suit and a sky-blue shirt open at his throat. Around his neck was a long chain made of large gold links from which an equally large plain gold cross was suspended. In his hands, he grasped a bundle of flyers.

Laura looked up from the till at the counter where she was arranging money to all face one direction. From a ladder at the back of the shop, Mandy paused in the placing of a large angel statue on top of a bookcase. She twisted her head toward the door. Aunt Sephie looked up from her crochet hook and yellow yarn where she was counting the stitches that she had chained to start a new shawl. The old woman put down her work and said, "Good morning, Reverend. What brings you to us today?"

He started passing out flyers. "I'm the Reverend Horatio Brown of the New Life Church of John the Baptist. I just wanted to invite you and your neighbors to a revival we're having."

Mandy, having made sure the fragile angel was secure on the bookcase, started to climb down the ladder. "We appreciate you coming in, but—"

Sephie rose, wincing with the effort. "I'm afraid I'm the closest thing to a Baptist here, Reverend."

He handed her a flyer. "We are a baptizing church," he said. "But we baptize with both water and fire."

Sephie smiled. "I understand that, too."

"Are you in pain?"

"Just arthritis. It'll feel better after it rains. If it ever does."

At that moment, B.D. entered with a plate of doughnuts.

"And you must be that singing young man I've been hearing about," the Reverend said, extending a hand to B.D., who moved the plate to his free hand and shook.

"I'm B.D. Travers, sir."

"We're in revival, and we're having a special healing service tonight. I know it's short notice, but would you come join us and maybe offer a song for the Lord?"

B.D. cast a wary eye toward Sephie, who nodded slowly. "I could."

"We'd be glad to join you," Sephie said. "B.D.'s sung for a couple of all day meetin's and dinners on the ground back home."

"And where's back home, young lady?"

Sephie winced. Every time anyone called her "young lady" she knew it wasn't because she was young. They might just be honest and say, "old woman." "Tennessee. But B.D.'s from Louisiana."

"What brings you this far north?"

Sephie glanced at Mandy who was off the ladder and on the floor. "A family visit."

The Reverend turned to B.D. "You work for this young lady?"

B.D.'s brow wrinkled into a frown. There was judgment in the question. "Miz Sephie's like family. We help each other," he said.

"Well, God bless you both. I look forward to seeing you tonight. Seven-thirty." He looked down at Sephie's legs. "We can pray for a healing for that arthritis of yours."

"Thank you, Reverend. But sometimes pain comes to offer a lesson. You have to be open to that, too."

"If it's God's will." He chuckled. "Yes, ma'am, you're a Baptist all right."

He left as abruptly as he'd come. Before Sephie sat back into her rocker, she grabbed a glazed doughnut off the plate B.D. held.

"Why do you want to go to a revival, Miz Sephie?" he asked.

"It's good energy to be in when you need to restore your own. All that singing and praying — and healing, in this case. It's all the same Spirit, the same energy, no matter what church or ritual it is."

"I suppose," he said.

"And it will be interesting to see if there are any requests for healing that aren't physical."

"What do you mean?"

"Soul problems. I still don't have a clear picture of the whole of what we're dealing with."

"Do you think this church will try to disrupt our Solstice Fair on Saturday?" Mandy asked.

"Might. Depends on the wards you place on the site," Sephie said.

"We've got our work cut out for us on Friday, then, when we set up," Laura said.

Chapter 40

Day 10: The New Life Church of John the Baptist, Wednesday night

The organ, pumping a throbbing rhythm, greeted B.D. and Sephie as they climbed the stone steps, flanked by two white stone columns, of the red brick church a few blocks from the North Star. Inside the white double doors, the congregation was already on its feet, clapping and singing along with the members of a large choir that was stepping right and left *en masse* to the beat at the front.

As B.D. and Sephie walked down the aisle, searching for an empty aisle seat, the old woman muttered, “My mama was right. You have to come early to get a back seat.”

Finding some space in the front pew, Sephie nodded and muttered thanks as an elderly Black couple made room for them. She and B.D. picked up the beat and clapped along. It was a modern contemporary gospel song that Sephie wasn’t familiar with. It had a catchy chorus, though, that she and B.D. soon learned.

When they finally sat down, Sephie leaned over to B.D. and said softly, “You know that one?”

He shook his head.

“What’re you going sing?”

“Don’t know. I’m waiting on Spirit.”

She patted his knee. “Good answer, son.”

Reverend Brown made some lively, welcoming remarks to the congregation and introduced the guest evangelist, the anointed Sister Blanche Wilson, who came down the aisle, dressed in white from a head wrap to her long flowing dress and shoes, singing. Though she was close to Sephie's age, her voice was powerful. She whipped up the people into a clapping frenzy. Shouts punctuated her song, which was interrupted periodically with exhortations to believe and be open to the holy ghost.

The service continued with more singing and preaching as the energy in the building built. Calls for healing were made and a stream of people came to the front asking for all manner of miracles. Sister Wilson talked with each one, passing the microphone to each person, making sure the entire congregation knew what was being healed. Then she prayed and placed a hand on the head of each. Behind the person being healed was a man or woman spotting, because invariably every single petitioner fell backward. If a woman was laid down, another woman from the congregation covered her legs with a cloth.

Almost all of the petitions for healing were for physical ailments: cancer, failing eyesight or hearing, arthritis, etc. Sephie began to wonder if this congregation had been protected in some way from the strange events in the city.

As the healing was winding down, Reverend Brown stepped away and bent over the front pew and asked B.D. "Brother, have you brought us a song tonight?"

He paused before saying, "I think so. I'll do your altar call."

"Hallelujah! What do you have mind?"

"Let me talk to your organist and choir."

"I'll introduce you."

B.D. slipped out into the aisle and followed the Reverend to the organist. There was some discussion and the organist waved the choir director over.

Sephie wondered what the three men were plotting. It was more than the title of the hymn and what key. They were all grinning, and the choir director was literally rocking up and down on his toes. The choir director then went over to the choir and tapped four men from different sections of the choir and brought them to shake hands with B.D. Then they all slipped out a door behind the altar area. The organist followed with a small keyboard in his hands.

A loud scream of praise distracted her. A person being healed was praising God and raising her hands. Then she started running across the open space in front of the altar, back and forth, giving praise for obvious healing to her legs.

The last few healings were more subdued. Reverend Brown took charge of the pulpit and began to preach about faith when no answers seemed to be coming. Sephie listened to his words. It was something she needed to hear. Patience was something she struggled with. She smiled as she listened, grateful for wisdom from unexpected sources. Not only was her energy being restored, but also her own faith in Spirit was boosted. Just as the preacher was winding down, B.D. and his new friends came out of the back room and gathered near the organ. The organist softly played a few chords to underscore the minister's message.

Reverend Brown smiled over at the organist and saw the group waiting. He turned back to the congregation. "Brothers and sisters—"

With a microphone in hand, B.D. interrupted by starting the opening lines of "Pass Me Not, O Gentle Savior." He moved toward the front of the choir, his four companions following, each with a microphone, who offered vocal backup. The hymn was slow and deeply felt, done in the fashion of the old gospel group the Swan Silvertones Sephie had heard years ago. B.D. built the energy as the other men, especially the high tenor, took on special parts. That vocal collaboration, though a song, was really preaching and drew people down to the altar, stream after stream of people, down on their knees covering every space, with some forming another row behind. When the song was over, the four men behind him continued to hum while the organist played. B.D. slipped away from them and sat back down beside Sephie. He looked overwhelmed.

Sephie took his hand into both of hers and held it. She understood how powerful the movement of Spirit could be in any context. He only sat still a moment before he headed up the aisle toward the front doors. Sephie got up and followed him outside, only to find him sitting midway down on the stone steps with his head in his hands. With effort she sat down beside him and waited.

"I've sung for mass and for weddings in my church. People are concentrating on the Eucharist or the bridal couple. I've sung for your Baptists, and it's like singing with old friends, trying to find a harmony or a contrapuntal falsetto. But this . . . this is where people's hearts are touched. To see them come down at your feet and cry in confession. . . ." He shook his head.

"You sing for ceremonies, too, where spirits are alive."

"Sure, but I'm singing the same thing with others and drumming. I've seen the orishas mount congregants and ride them, making them dance in a frenzy. But it's all an organic whole."

"And familiar."

Reluctantly, he nodded.

"You can't let your ego get in the way of your gift, son."

He turned his head toward her in question.

"You have a gift, but it's Spirit that's moving, not what you're doing. Sometimes, you have to step aside and let Spirit have its way."

The front doors behind them burst open and two White teenage girls came rushing out. "There's a boy with a demon in there!" one of them said. "He's — it's—"

The other girl grabbed her friend by the arm. "Let's get out of here," she urged and dragged her friend down the steps and onto the sidewalk, where they ran away as fast as they could.

Sephie braced a hand on B.D.'s shoulder and stood. "One man's demon is another man's mental illness or another's quirky habit. Let's go see what kind of demon this is."

B.D. rose and followed Sephie back into the building. The four backup singers were still delivering the chorus of "Pass Me Not" while the congregation was calling out for God's help. A few were speaking in tongues as they prayed. Amid that tumult, a young boy's voice was heard. "Take me, Jesus. Save me from this demon." Then his voice disintegrated into gibberish. Several men laid hands on him, but it didn't ease his agony. In spite of the agitation of the boy and the congregation, there was a dark depression in the church, a definite switch in atmosphere from when they had left.

About halfway down the aisle, B.D. said, "They need to change the song."

"You're right," Sephie said. "There should be a praise song now."

B.D literally ran down the aisle and up to the altar platform. There he talked to the organist and the choir director and finally to the four backup singers who drifted into that humming they had done before.

Sephie made her way back to her seat in the front pew. As she sat down, she saw the choir director cue the organist who made a very smooth transition from "Pass Me Not" to "Oh, Happy Day." B.D. grabbed a microphone and began slowly, building up speed and enthusiasm. The organist followed his lead while the choir, with the backup singers in their usual places, offered the power behind B.D.'s solo. Soon, the whole congregation was clapping and singing along, changing the entire feel of the church. Whatever had been let in and had taken hold of the service was not there now. Sephie looked at the teenager who'd been in such agony before. He now was merely crying at the altar as the men around him wiped their foreheads and eyes with white handkerchiefs.

Sephie twisted around to look at the back door, thinking she'd go let out the negative energy. Two ushers were already opening the doors, pressing a shoe down on the locking mechanism at the base of each one, securing them in place. She wondered if they were letting the demon or negative energy out. But the action seemed so routine and orchestrated that it was probably just a way to bring the night breeze inside since the AC didn't seem to be affecting the temperature in the church, with all of the singing and praying.

When the song had ended, Reverend Brown took the pulpit again and began praising God. B.D. slipped away and leaned over the pew at Sephie. "Let's go."

Sephie nodded and followed him outside and down the steps toward where they had parked the old woman's big station wagon. "Didn't want to stay for any congratulations?" she asked.

He shook his head, slowing his pace a bit. "I did what I was supposed to do."

Thinking deeply, Sephie shook her head. "Something sure took hold of that congregation."

"Do you think it happens often, or was it something I did?"

"Lordy, it wasn't you!" she said. They had reached her car so she fished out her keys, opened her door, and then tossed the keys to B.D. "You good enough to drive?"

"Sure."

Once they were inside, he started up the car. "Think we need some of Bill's Lutheran funeral hot dish?"

"Wouldn't hurt."

Chapter 41

Day 10: The Watering Hole, Wednesday evening

When Bill put two bowls of Lutheran funeral hot dish in front of Sephie and B.D., the young man asked, "Is this an authentic recipe?"

"Well," Bill said, obviously hesitant. "It's my mother's recipe."

"And she got it from the Lutheran Ladies Guild?" Sephie asked.

"Well, she was a Methodist. I don't know if my clientele would understand what it was if I said it was Methodist funeral hot dish. All funeral hot dishes do the same thing: they comfort. Doesn't matter what denomination."

B.D. chuckled. "Same way as gumbo and jambalaya."

"You still owe me your recipe."

"I told you what was in it, didn't I? It's never exact. You just toss in however amount you have and stretch the rest with rice."

Bill harrumphed and stalked off to the kitchen.

Turning his attention to Sephie, B.D. said, "So, was tonight worth the effort?"

She nodded.

"And that means. . . ."

Sephie began to count on her fingers. "First, we have an energy vampire who's targeting me. Don't know why. Next, we have some sort of raptor or creature that's attacking cats and Mother Evangeline, leaving behind some kind of poison that acts like a sedative. Then, we have some entity that was generated by or attracted to the healing service tonight."

"Do you think that boy was possessed?"

"Lord, no! What I saw was teenage guilt. Probably just had his first sexual encounter and was afraid what he'd done was written all over his face. No, there was something else. You felt it when you said they needed to change the song."

"Would a church like that, pumping out all that energy, attract negative beings? Could it be like sending out a beacon?"

Sephie screwed up her face in impatience. "Son, do your bayou ceremonies attract evil?"

"No, but—"

"Positive energy like that — and so much of it — repels evil. No, something hijacked that service after we got out of there."

"But what? That's not the work of a vampire. None of this is the work of a vampire. Well, except for the energy sucker."

"We gotta stop thinking there's a vampire here. That was just Mandy and Laura's explanation for it because of the cats. And that crazy tabloid reporter. No, we have multiple entities that we're dealing with. Some may be explainable, like a raptor attacking cats. But I never knew a raptor that had poison on its talons before. Infections, sure, from all the carrion and live kills." She looked down at her food and shoved it aside. "What I really want to know is why multiple entities decided to converge on Riverbend right at this moment."

"Maybe they've been here all along, and it took Mandy and Laura — and us — to notice them."

"Could be." Sephie leaned over her bowl again and dug a fork in.

"Each of us has different abilities and different levels of sensing," B.D. offered.

"And we all come from different spiritual paths." The old woman ate another forkful of hot dish. "It may be that combination that is allowing us to see. Then that means we all have to report what we sense and see."

"Well, that's calling the kettle black."

"What do you mean?" Sephie challenged.

"You didn't tell me there was an energy vampire after you."

"Well, I finally told you."

"When did you first sense him?"

"Thursday. At the dance. But neither you nor Mandy and Laura were hit. Just me. Don't know why." She then countered. "And what about you? I know you've been having feelings."

B.D. looked around uncomfortably as if he wanted to make sure no one overhead. "There was one thing."

"Only one?"

He nodded. "Osanyin's messengers. The birds, remember? Outside the shop. Sixteen birds with a big raven overhead. The exact configuration of the orisha Osanyin's sacred staff."

"Oh." Sephie leaned back in the booth finally understanding. "Those were the messengers. Why do you think they appeared to you?"

B.D. shrugged. "I don't know. A warning is all I can think of. But of what?"

"Indeed. And to appear to you so you could deliver the message. Hmm. Who needs to be warned? Who needs the healing? And what kind of healing?"

Chapter 42

Day 11: North Star, Thursday midmorning

"Planning on a camping trip?" Sephie asked as she and B.D. entered from the back door. Mandy looked up from the floor where she was returning a tent, a tarp, and a bag of stakes back into a long duffle. Beside it were two sleeping bags in their nylon carry bags and two longer duffles that looked like they contained tents, too.

"Getting ready for tomorrow night when we set up for Saturday's event. We'll drum in the tent all night. Others will be arriving to do that with us. Want to join us?"

"No thanks. My old bones can't handle sleeping rough anymore."

"How about you, B.D.?"

"It'd be pretty crowded in that itty-bitty tent," he said.

"It's a lot bigger than you think." She smiled. "It's an experience."

Moving further into the shop, Sephie immediately checked the display of her tinctures and salves. She had carefully replenished the lot as customers bought them, but she didn't know if more had been sold the evening before.

"How was the revival?" Laura asked, placing more candles on another display.

"It was enlightening," the old woman said.

Laura looked at B.D., seeking his opinion, too.

"It was — different," he said.

She laughed. "Now, you're sounding like a Nodak. When people here run into something unusual or controversial, instead of railing on about it, they always say, 'It sure was different.'"

B.D. emitted a laugh, the first one he'd had since last night.

"He sang pretty last night," Sephie said, settling into her rocker. "Great back up. Not only the choir, but they gave him a male quartet."

"They were amazing!" B.D. exclaimed. "This was the most professional gig I ever did, but we didn't really rehearse. They knew the hymn, and we only went through a verse and chorus with the organist just giving us pitches. Maybe they'd been a quartet brought in for the revival, but if so, why were they in the choir?"

"They were good," Sephie remarked, "but they were like young horses ready to run."

"Yeah. I sensed that. Their arrangement was so like the old Swan Silvertones."

"I heard that, too," the old woman agreed. "My daddy had a bunch of old seventy-eights of their work."

"But these guys — each one vied for the spotlight."

"Ego," Sephie muttered.

"There was power in what we were doing," B.D. admitted. "I've never seen that before. But this power—"

"Was misdirected," the old woman said. "When ego gets involved, it opens the door to darkness and that's what hijacked that service. They needed to be brought back to praise, and you did it."

B.D. sat down on the stool behind the counter. He swallowed hard before he said, "I had to get out of there. It was a perversion."

"Singing is a gift," Sephie reminded, "and you know its value. It doesn't come from you."

An uncomfortable silence filled the shop.

"Will you be around tomorrow?" Mandy asked B.D. as she entered the room. "We're going to need more muscle to help set up the booth and the tent and everything."

"I usually help Mandy with all that," Laura said, "but

I wanted to keep the shop open as long as I can. We'll have vendors coming in from all over, and they usually stop here first."

"Sure, I can help Friday. I only have rehearsals today: this afternoon with the university for the showcase number and later with the Lutheran choir," he said.

"How are you finding the Lutherans?" Laura asked.

"They're friendly enough. Reserved."

"That might just be what you need, son," Sephie said.

The tinkle of the bell over the front door caused all of them to turn toward the customer. A large, horse-faced woman with purple hair charged into the room like a battleship.

"Did my mojo oils come in?" she demanded.

Sephie watched Laura quickly join B.D. behind the counter as if to seek a barrier between herself and this formidable woman.

"No," Laura said, then clamped her jaw tight.

"It's been a month since I ordered them! What kind of a place do you run here?" The customer eyed all of the stock on the shelves around the counter. "You sure have enough angels and goods for all the wannabe lightworkers."

Mandy stepped beside her aunt's rocker and placed a hand on the high back.

"And you even have a resident granny," the woman said with a little laugh. The statement was delivered with a lightness that hid something menacing.

Sephie felt Mandy's hand slip down to her forearm. Her niece shouldn't be worried. The old woman wasn't going to rise to the taunt. She simply added another crochet stitch or two to the pattern she'd begun, glancing up periodically.

"Well, while I'm here, how much is booth space for your festival tomorrow? I've been too busy to come in."

"We're all full," Mandy said calmly.

"Full? There's a whole greenway down there. You could put up the whole town!"

"We have limited space granted by the Downtown Business Association. We have people coming in from both sides of the river. We sold out early."

Sephie raised her eyes to study the customer. Her assessment was that this was a cookbook practitioner, someone who bought a book of spells and then thought she knew it all. The woman appeared to be dabbling in dangerous magic, but there was no power in her. Placing a hand on Mandy's, she said, "I'm sure you could make room for one table for the lady."

Mandy turned her head to frown at her aunt, who just patted her hand again and smiled, mouthing one word: "Money." Raising an eyebrow and then lifting her shoulders in a sigh, Mandy finally turned to the customer and said, "I suppose we could put you on an end."

"Wha—" Laura began to sputter as everyone turned to her.

Sephie shook her head at Laura who again clamped her jaws tightly together.

"Since it will require us to redraw the festival booth plan at this late date, the booth fee will be two hundred and fifty dollars." She paused. "Cash."

The customer slapped the counter and emitted a "Ha!" in triumph. "I'll go to the bank and be right back." She turned and nearly ran out the front door.

"What in all that's holy are you doing?" Laura demanded both of Mandy and Sephie.

"What's she into?" Sephie asked.

"She thinks she's a Voodoo Queen," Laura spat out.

B.D. laughed out loud. "Her?" He shook his head.

"We told her we didn't handle her oils or Hand of Glory candles or the hoodoo dolls and such," Mandy explained.

"Why'd she think you had ordered them, then?"

"She just thought we'd order because she asked for them," Laura said.

"Why'd you want us to rent space to her?" Mandy asked.

"Keep your friends close but your enemies closer," the old woman said.

"How in the world are we going to put wards up with her inside them?" Laura asked.

"I'll help, my dear. B.D. and I will help. Won't you, son?"

He frowned. "I think I'm going to need both of those church services on Sunday. I might even have to go to confession."

Chapter 43

Day 12: The Greenway, Friday late evening

A light poncho wrapped around her, Sephie stood at the top of the rise, the flood wall behind her. B.D. had helped Mandy set up their dome tent and the two screen houses with rolldown tarp sides to guard against inclement weather. When her niece had spelled Laura at the shop after all of them had carried their wares to the screen houses, Sephie had helped Laura arrange the displays. She now saw Mandy, who had just closed the shop, join B.D. and Laura to help them move some of the displays to the center of their festival booths as clouds obscured the night stars. These activities were repeated by all of the other vendors in the makeshift festival village, lit by camp lanterns and several tiki torches.

A rumble of thunder caused Sephie to look up. Those torches would be extinguished soon if rain fell. As she viewed the sight, she smiled, carefully making her way down to the North Star booth area, which was on the north end of the circle, far away from the two portable toilets the city had set up on the south side just outside the vendors' encampment. A couple of small teardrop campers were parked near the outhouses.

"Everything ready for tomorrow?" Sephie asked.

"Yep," Mandy said. "We're going to call the group together to set the wards now." Picking up a round hand drum, Mandy took a suede-covered beater and began a steady rhythm.

Laura joined her, singing "Light in Our Hearts." It was a happy chant that set a tone, drawing the other vendors around the circle of the encampment. As people came forward, she moved into "Light Divine," a song about circling together on solstice eve.

B.D. had apparently learned it, because he sang a higher counterpoint over her basic chant, moving into harmony on the chant itself. Sephie smiled as she joined in. The other vendors also joined and brought other drums with them. The chant continued building energy until Mandy signaled the ending with a barrage of rapid drumbeats, a pause, and then three loud drumbeats spaced well apart.

Sephie noticed that the horse-faced woman wasn't among those gathered.

"Merry meet, my friends," Laura said. "We gather tonight on solstice eve to create a circle of protection before we open tomorrow for our festival and the blessed solstice rite."

As the drummers began a simple rhythm, a young man stepped into the middle of the circle of vendors. In one hand was a large sage smudge bundle, and a fireplace lighter was in the other. "We bless all those who are here with fire from this smudge," he said in a loud voice. "May we be cleansed." He lit the smudge, waited until the flame had caught, and then blew that out, letting the smoke rise. He approached Laura and smudged the front of her body and when she had turned, he smudged her back. Handing the smudge to her, she did the same with him.

Several others began to add shakers and bells to the drummers as someone began the chant, "Earth My Body." It covered the four elements: earth, fire, water, and air. The young man went around the circle and smudged each person.

When completed, he handed the smudge to Mandy.

A young woman came forward with a bowl of water and a handful of salt. "Creature of earth," she said, raising the hand with the salt. "Creature of water." She raised her other hand. Then she poured the salt into the water. "Behold. Creature of art. The great salt sea that flows within all of us. May it cleanse us."

The chant changed to "We All Come from the Mother," a song with imagery about oceans.

Again, Laura was approached first, accepting being sprinkled with the salt water front and behind. Then the young woman was blessed before she in turn blessed everyone else.

Once that was done, the bowl of water was given to Laura. She addressed the circle of people. "We now bless this space. May there be a circle of protection around this place. Ancient spirits of the water and land, who were here before us, we greet you and honor you. We seek peace with you and your blessing so we may share our knowledge and abilities as we welcome the Sun on the morrow and honor his work to ripen the harvests to come. Mother Earth, we hear you calling us."

A young woman began the chant, "Mother, I Feel You."

Laura raised a hand, circled it clockwise, and then turned around. She and Mandy headed toward the edge of the circle of vendors. B.D. motioned for Sephie to join him behind them. Everyone else followed behind as they all processed clockwise around the inside of the circle with Mandy wielding the smudge and Laura sprinkling the salt water. The chant picked up speed with more syncopated drumming. B.D. again added a counterpoint over the main chant, letting his creativity lend harmonies and appropriate words.

When they had all returned to where they had started, B.D. left the group and went to one of the North Star screened tents. He came out with a small bucket and tapped Sephie on the arm. "I need your help."

She looked down into the bucket and saw that it was filled with fine tan sand. The old woman followed him to the back edge of the circle of vendor stalls.

"This is where the public will enter tomorrow," he said. "We need to put a circle of this sand around the perimeter on the outside. Mandy and Laura blessed it, but it takes two to do it: male and female, young and old, they said. And we need your words."

"Mine?"

"I've added my words from both my traditions."

"You think that," she pointed to the bucket, "needs Baptist words?"

B.D. shook his head. "It needs whatever you use when you make your wares."

Sephie smiled. "Do you think Mandy and Laura know I'm an old pagan at heart?"

"You are, aren't you?"

Sephie chuckled. Closing her eyes, she plunged both hands into the fine sand. "Simple sand. Product of water and earth. Appropriate for blessing. Ancient sand. Join with the ancient spirits of this land to protect this encampment from all evil. We are here only to help and offer healing. And to enjoy each other's unique company. Bless us. And when we are done become a part of the land once again."

B.D. grinned. "Fine words, no matter the path."

They each took handfuls of sand. With B.D. leading, they threw the first sand to draw a line around the outside of the vendors' booths and tents, going clockwise. A firm but gentle hand stayed Sephie's reach for another handful. She looked up into the dark eyes of a native man who was of an indefinite age — obviously older than B.D., maybe older than Sephie.

"Like this," he said, taking a little sand in one hand and sidestepping as in a native circle dance. His movement urged Sephie and B.D. to sidle around the circle, sprinkling sand. As they went, the old man added a song of his own.

To Sephie, it felt right. The old man seemed not only to approve of all their New Age trappings but seemed to be a part of it. When they had finished, the old man led them back into the circle where he closed it by laying a line across the opening with the remaining sand.

Sephie frowned. "But — but I'm not staying."

The old man grinned. "Guess you are now." Quickly, he slipped into the circle of vendors and stood behind a young woman with long dark hair and dressed in an ankle-length, dark green loose gown. She was keeping time with a rattle.

Sephie looked up at the flood wall, imagining the store left unattended and her soft comfortable bed in the little house unslept in. She turned to B.D., hoping he had an answer.

He just put his arm around her and said, “We’ll make you comfortable.”

Chapter 44

Day 13: The Greenway, Saturday wee hours of the morning

Stretched out on a cot and covered by a warm blanket in one of the screened tents, Sephie was awakened by the crack of thunder and the sound of drops of rain. She had been lulled to sleep around midnight with chanting and drumming, punctuated by a loud whoop once in a while. B.D., in the same tent as she, had added to the drumming for a while with a *djembe* Mandy had loaned him. He'd told her as she settled down in the tent that the rhythms were similar to the African drumming he'd done in bayou ceremonies.

Now, as the rain started, B.D. got up out of his cot to make sure all of the outside tarp walls were secure.

"Sure glad Mandy had these cots," Sephie said. "Do you think they both'll stay dry in the tent?"

"We laid down extra ground cloths," he said, picking up the *djembe* and placing it on top of one of the display tables. "We also folded up the corners so that rain wouldn't wick down the sides." Returning to his bed to take off his shoes, he paused to raise his head to listen. "It's a gentle rain. No wind."

In the distance, there was more thunder. Even through those rumbles, the pervasive sound of the drums came from different sections of the encampment. This time, the rhythms were soothing, comforting.

As Sephie pulled her blanket tighter around herself, she listened to the mixture of raindrops on the screen tent's roof and drumbeats as the rhythms were passed from drum to drum in different parts of the enclave, changing ever so slightly, sometimes one drummer offering a drum call and another doing a response, but always coming back together, in sync, comforting with the knowledge of the presence of each one during the night. The pulse soothed Sephie in her cot, lulling her to sleep.

Chapter 45

Day 13: The Greenway, Saturday morning

"Looks like you made it through the night," the native gentleman Sephie had met the night before greeted her as she left the screened tent. In the bright light of the clear morning, she noticed the wisps of gray in his hair that he had tied back with a piece of rawhide underneath a black Stetson. He was indeed far older than she first thought, nearer her age or more, but he carried it well. His face, handsome enough, showed living and perhaps hardship. It was so different from her late husband's, which had borne the smoothness of more affluent living than her people had experienced and possibly an innocence that made him too optimistic. This man in front of her had learned some life lessons that had solidified into character but not bitterness.

The aroma of coffee hit Sephie's nostrils. She glanced down at the man's hand and saw a mug.

"Got more of that?" she asked.

He offered it to her. "I'm afraid it's black."

Taking the warm mug into her hand, she inhaled its rich aroma. "This is truck-driver coffee, right? One sip and you're electrified for the rest of the morning."

He chuckled. "Pretty much. Can I get you some cream?"

She shook her head and took a small sip of the hot brew. It was indeed strong. "Almost chewable," she remarked.

This time his laugh was heartier.

Feeling the sprinkle of water, they both stepped away from the tent to watch B.D. and Mandy shake off the night's rain before rolling up the side tarps of the booth.

"Family?" the man asked.

"Mandy's my great-niece. Brother-in-law's granddaughter."

"Have any of your own?"

"Grandchildren?" She shook her head. "My daughter and her husband lived the big city fast life. She always said there'd be time for children later. There never was."

He nodded toward the booth where a young woman was taking tarps off the tables under a canopy. "That's my granddaughter." He paused as Sephie drank his coffee. "Family is good. Even made-family. Mandy and Laura have made-family here."

Sephie looked up at him. "You?"

"All of us here, mostly. We're scattered about, but we come together to share joys and sorrows. Made-family is necessary when people don't understand other genders. Laura's family disowned her. Did you know?"

Sephie was shocked. Laura didn't talk about her family, but the old woman assumed it was because she just didn't have stories to tell. Some people gather them better than others. "No, I didn't know."

"I'm glad she has other family that understands."

Mandy, her chore now done, approached them. "Aunt Sephie, I'm glad you met Floyd."

"We haven't been properly introduced," he said, extending his hand. "Floyd Whiteman."

Sephie moved her coffee to her left hand and shook his, noticing that his grip was mainly her fingers and very gentle. She'd experienced that before with other native people when greeting her. "Sephronia Hill. Sephie." Her face then twisted into a question. "White man?"

"I had a Welsh ancestor. My people couldn't pronounce his name, much less spell it. So, he called himself Whiteman. No imagination."

It was Sephie's turn to laugh, nearly spilling her coffee.

"Floyd is Mandan from out West. Part of the Three-Affiliated Tribes. The Mandan, Arikara, and the Hidatsa."

"Mandan," Sephie repeated.

"There aren't many of us left. What there is has more mixed blood. And in truth I'm Mandan and Hidatsa."

"Well, I've got to check how everybody made it through the rain. See if everyone's dry," Mandy said, and headed to the vendor next to theirs.

Sephie drank some more coffee, then said, "Thank you for your help last night. I've never used sand to protect before."

"Salt, sand, corn pollen," he said. "Anything can be used."

She nodded. "Intention."

"Always."

At that moment Sephie felt compelled to ask, "Do you feel that there's something off in Riverbend lately?"

He nodded. "I come in every so often and every year for Solstice. Something's different." His eyes scanned the encampment and then returned to look at Sephie. He smiled. "Come, you should meet Yolanda. You'll like her. She has a good spirit."

When they approached his booth, on the east side, Sephie noticed displays of sage smudges, thin braids of some sort of long leaves, and clumps of cedar and lavender.

"Hello," the young woman inside the booth said.

"This is Yolanda," Floyd said. "And this is Sephie, Mandy's great-aunt."

Yolanda's smile was as welcoming as the sun had been that morning.

Sephie offered her hand to shake. The old woman once more glanced over their wares. This time she pointed to the braided greenery. "I don't know that one."

Floyd picked it up and smelled it. "It's sweetgrass." He put it under Sephie's nose to sniff. "It burns sweet."

"What's it used for?'

"Purification and before prayers. It brings in positive energies."

"I'll get some."

Floyd offered her the braid. "It's yours. A first gift."

Surprised she searched his face. "First?"

He smiled. "Of course, friends always exchange a lot of gifts over their time together."

Yolanda, offering her a bundle of lavender, said, "And another."

"You hungry?" Floyd asked Sephie.

"I can find my own."

"Nonsense. I'll make you an egg sandwich to temper that strong coffee."

He passed behind her, laying a gentle hand on her shoulder as he moved to enter the booth. He removed the tarp on the south side of the booth to reveal a large, commercial propane grill. Quickly firing it up, he said, "We'll have Indian tacos later."

"We feed the encampment and offer some to the public," Yolanda said as she came out of the booth to take Sephie's arm. "Please come sit."

Obligingly, the old woman entered the booth and sat on a folding chair. As Yolanda passed in front of her, Sephie noticed that the young woman's loose t-shirt, several sizes too big, clung snugly around a bulge in her middle.

With his free hand pointing to the other folding chair as he cracked eggs onto the griddle and stirred, Floyd commanded softly. "Sit. You'll be on your feet more than you want today."

Yolanda laughed. "I'm not an invalid." She eased herself down into the other chair.

"Where's your man?" Sephie asked, then worried that maybe she shouldn't have posed such a question.

"He's flying the friendly skies," she said. "He's a pilot. I used to be a flight attendant. That's how we met. But when this little flier appeared, he grounded me." She glanced up at Floyd.

"Besides, Grandfather needs some looking after."

Sephie chuckled. "Seems he's doing all right all by himself. He even cooks."

Floyd grinned at her and returned to his eggs.

"Have you ever been to Riverbend before?" Yolanda asked.

"Once," Sephie said. "About three years after my husband went to Glory. Heart attack. Mandy flew me out here for her wedding, just a day or so. It was all a blur. Got in late, went to my motel, got up to go to the court house, had dinner with them, went back to my hotel while they went to some lake cabin for their honeymoon, took a shuttle to the airport, and gone. I never really saw the town."

"What do you think now that you've seen it?"

"It's a good place." She paused and then added. "Mostly."

Floyd handed her a paper plate with the fried egg between two pieces of whole wheat bread. He offered one to Yolanda before he pulled out a picnic cooler from under the table. Taking his own plate and a mug of coffee, he sat on the cooler. The mug went on the ground after a long drink from it, and he then attacked his sandwich.

"Mmm," Sephie commented. "How come food always tastes better outdoors?'

"I don't think we were ever supposed to live inside," Floyd said. "Just take shelter when the weather got bad."

"I don't know," Yolanda said. "I like my creature comforts. A bathtub, a washing machine, streaming movies, traveling by jet all over the world."

Floyd chuckled. "Guess your husband would be out of a job, wouldn't he, if we lived like our ancestors?"

"And I'd be on my knees at a river washing your shirts."

He held up both hands in surrender. Turning to Sephie, he asked, "Would you care to walk off this breakfast? We can talk about that matter you mentioned."

Yolanda took Sephie's paper plate, and the old woman got up to follow Floyd out of the booth.

"We'll have to open the circle of protection," Sephie said.

Floyd looked at his watch, "It's not too early for it. The public will be down here soon enough."

When they approached the open space between the vendors' booths that he had sealed with sand the night before, he stooped down and scattered what was left of the wet sand with his hand.

"The rain soaked everything," Sephie commented. "Do you think we'll need to reinforce what we did?"

Rising, he said, "It's doing what it's supposed to do. The sand is wet and may be mixing with the earth. The intention is still there and will continue to protect our backs."

Leading the way, he headed down the greenway to the river. It bore a murky color from run off from the rich black soil, caused by the rain throughout the night. When they got to two huge cottonwoods, Floyd leaned against a tree trunk to watch the water flow north. Sephie joined him but was more angled toward the view upstream.

"I like flowing water," he said.

"It cleanses things," she remarked. "That's why I don't understand what's happening here. Laura says it's because of the flooding in the Spring."

"Floods every year."

"That's what I mean. Why now?" She looked over at him. "You do feel it, don't you? Something off?"

He nodded.

"We've seen cat attacks. Could be a big hawk or owl. But the victims act drugged afterwards."

He frowned at her. "You aren't upset just because of that, are you?"

"A nun was scratched, too. Same thing. I applied my dogwood tincture, and she brightened right up the next day. Or the poison just wore off that quick."

"There's more."

"Something hijacked a revival B.D. sang at this week. I put that down to ego, but there was something dark about it."

"And?"

She sighed, half reluctant to reveal the last thing. "I think I'm being stalked by an energy sucker. I know I'm just a crazy old woman, who—"

Floyd reached over and grabbed her hand, making her stop talking. "You're a sensible woman who's seen a lot in your life."

Fear in her own eyes, she searched Floyd's. "I have a feeling this is just the beginning of troubles. Something else's coming. And I don't know how to battle it."

Floyd pushed back from the tree to gently pull Sephie away from her position and moved them up the hill toward the festival encampment. He stopped and released her hand to point at the circle of vendors. "That is where answers are and help."

Chapter 46

Day 13: The Greenway, Saturday midmorning

As Sephie and Floyd approached the encampment, they heard the angry voice of a woman as she shrieked, "Porta-potties? Porta-potties!"

Floyd placed a hand on Sephie's arm to stop her from entering the circle of vendors. They waited, listening. The disagreeable voice sounded familiar, causing Sephie to search through her memory for who it might be.

"I paid good money, and all you can give me is a space by the porta-potties?" the loud woman continued.

"That's where I could fit you in," Mandy explained. "Everybody will pass your booth, and you've got a prominent space for all to see."

"What about over there where that tent is?" She pointed to Laura and Mandy's dome tent.

"We'll need that to change into ritual clothes later," Laura said.

"Why don't you use the porta-potties? Or use one of these booths. Gods only know why you need two."

"It's a small space," Mandy said, seeming to try to bring the vendor back to the issue. Her voice strained to keep her tone calm. "You'd be abutted next to two other vendors. It would be hard to set up."

"But it can be done?"

"Well," she dragged out the word but eventually said a reluctant, "Yes."

Sephie finally recognized the voice. It was the horse-faced woman who'd demanded a space yesterday. Her anger grew at the woman's bullying of her niece, making her want to get up in that woman's face and give her a good piece of her mind. She involuntarily took two steps forward in the direction of the booth and suddenly felt weak, swaying slightly. Putting a hand over face, she closed her eyes in order to take in a few steadying deep breaths. She felt Floyd's arm come around her and his hand rest on her far shoulder.

"Pardon me," a male voice said as he stepped around the two of them.

Floyd pulled Sephie against his side. It felt odd to feel a warm body next to hers after so long, but somehow it was comforting. She felt her strength returning and squinted her eyes at the man who'd just passed them. The old woman caught her breath as she recognized the actor from the theater.

"What's the trouble?" the man asked quietly at the North Star booth.

"There's a problem with the booth!" the horse-faced woman spat out as if he should have known.

"We paid for booth space," he said. "We should have a space."

"That's not the issue!" The woman exploded. "It's where!"

"Let's work something out peaceably," the man said.

"We'll take the space beside yours," the woman said. "Clear that tent out. We need to be ready by noon when the rite starts."

Offering a loud sigh, Mandy relented. "Bring your stuff down. We should have the tent taken down by the time you get back."

At that, the couple huffed past Floyd and Sephie to trudge up the hill to start bringing down their canopy and wares.

Sephie inhaled deeply to further steady herself as Floyd moved ever so slightly to look at her face. "You okay?"

She nodded.

"That's your energy sucker, right?"

Again, she nodded, then asked, "Why weren't you affected?"

"I sensed him and shielded. But he wasn't interested in me."

"I'm shielded, too," she said.

"I noticed. But your shields leak."

"He's targeting me, isn't he? But why?"

Floyd offered her a serious expression. "I think it's your sparkling personality."

The old woman backhanded his chest, but couldn't stop a small smile from escaping to match the one now across Floyd's face.

When they got to the North Star booths, Mandy and B.D. were breaking down the tent. Laura was fuming in the first screen tent. "I've never contemplated homicide before, but that woman has pushed me over the edge."

Calmly, Floyd asked, "Who is she? I don't remember seeing her last year."

"That's Missy Malone."

"Missy?" Floyd chuckled. "I suppose she had college friends named Muffy and Bunny."

Laura eyed him and reluctantly smiled, losing some of her steam. "She moved here a year ago and opened a used furniture store on the north side of town. Someone told me she set up a part of that to sell hexes and cures."

"Hexes!" Floyd said, folding his arms across his chest.

"She thinks she's a voodoo queen," Sephie explained.

Floyd just raised an eyebrow.

"She helped somebody get her husband an early release from jail," Laura continued, "so people think she's the real deal. And she does house clearings. But from what I heard she risks a lot by taking the negative energy into her body and carries it around for days before releasing it."

Having stuffed tent stakes into a bag, Mandy walked over to add, "And she bosses everyone around."

"Who's the man with her?" Floyd asked.

"That's her husband," Mandy said, "Rodolfo Perez."

She moved to help B.D. with the tent.

Laura added, "I once asked Patricia, the Mexican *curandera,* who comes into the shop, about the both of them. She crossed herself and just gave me a stream of Spanish, finally, just saying, '*Mal espiritu.*'"

"Bad spirit," Floyd said before walking over to where the tent was being rolled up. He studied the side of the screen tent next to the empty space. "Keep your tarp flap down on this side." Stepping in to the far side, he carefully untied the gray flap and began to unroll it. Mandy quickly jumped to help, keeping any leftover moisture from dropping down onto the tent B.D. was now tying up. Both Floyd and Mandy tied off the bottoms securely to the canopy poles.

"You have the rest of last night's smudge?" he asked.

Mandy went to their first booth, where Laura was standing, bent down below the counter, and retrieved the burnt smudge bundle and a lighter. She lit the smudge and proceeded to give the flap a good smoking.

"Mirrors," Sephie said to Laura, thinking of repelling protection. "Do you think it would be too obvious to tie little mirrors on that side? Or anything shiny?"

"I don't care if it's obvious. We should smudge and put a circle of protection over us," Laura said.

Sephie stepped to Mandy who had finished smudging the flap. "Do both canopies," she said. When she got back to the first booth, Laura was threading plastic, silver-colored sun Yule ornaments onto string.

"Do you have eight more?" Sephie asked, picking up two that had already been threaded. "Ten would be best."

Laura nodded. "I think so."

B.D. brought the tent and sleeping bags into the first booth. "Is this a good place for this lot?'

"It'll have to do," Laura answered.

Sephie handed two silver suns to B.D. "Tie these to the top corners of that far screen canopy,"

When Laura finished looping string through more suns, Sephie took them two at a time to B.D. to hang from the tent poles. Finally, each of the poles bore a dangling sun. The final two were each tied to a cross piece over the door openings.

When they were done, they all stepped back to look at their work. The suns twisted in the breeze, casting sparkles of light. "Protections that honor the blessed sun," Laura said.

Challenging their cheerful mood, Missy and Rodolfo crossed in front of them, arms full of gear, bickering back and forth. Floyd pulled Sephie away, avoiding Rodolfo's attention so that she didn't feel an energy drain.

"I think I'll go have a word with our vendor neighbor," Laura said and headed toward the booth next to the empty space that was now being piled with gear.

Turning to Sephie, Floyd asked, "I assume you have good prep chef skills."

"You mean can I handle a knife?"

"I've got lots of vegetables that need chopping."

Sephie harrumphed but followed the old man to his booth.

Floyd brought out onions, peppers, tomatoes, and a head of lettuce from a box underneath a long table at the back. These he put between two wooden cutting boards. On top of the boards were two chef's knives.

Sephie picked one knife up and ran her thumb across the edge. Razor sharp. "You don't mess around, do you?"

"Accidents happen with dull knives," he said. He then pointed to a nearby basin filled with water. There was a bottle of dish soap and a towel.

Sephie washed her hands and picked up the towel. Floyd washed his. While she was drying, she glanced back at the activity near Mandy and Laura's booths. "Do you think they'll be all right there?"

"They have good energy," Floyd said, taking the towel from her. "It has charged their goods and that will help keep them protected." He folded the towel and placed it back beside the basin. "It's you who needs protection."

She grunted. She didn't need a man anymore. She wasn't helpless. She had darn well taken care of herself for a long time. Her anger rising, she challenged, "And you think you're the man to pro—"

"I swear I'm gonna wear a rut in the grass going back and forth to the porta—" Yolanda said, entering the booth, stopping abruptly to stare from her grandfather to Sephie, sensing the obvious tension between them.

Sephie huffed toward the cutting board and began peeling an onion. Once she started slicing it, she felt Floyd pass behind her.

"Take care with that knife," he said. "I don't fancy singing soprano."

She sliced a few more slices and then started to laugh. Floyd did, too, then tossed a tomato into the air, caught it, and started cutting it into small dice.

Chapter 47

Day 13: The Greenway, Saturday noon

"Sun Come! Sun Come!" The chant rang out among the vendors and the public alike who had gathered for the Summer Solstice celebration. The directions and the spirits of the land had been honored and the circle had been drawn. Coming from between Floyd's booth and one of his neighbors in the East was a lone man bearing a long pole with a shining sun atop. As he processed clockwise around the gathered group, the chant continued, now punctuated with a drum beat after each phrase. When he had returned to the East, members parted to allow him to enter the circle and place the pole onto a rack on the ground designed to receive it.

The drummers then started a new rhythm and a lone singer began "We Are One with the Infinite Sun." It was sung slowly at first as everyone gathered picked up the melody and sang the chorus, which was in another language, and then the drummers went wild, breaking into danceable rhythms. A pennywhistle carried the melody with the singers over the drummers and those who now added rattles and bells. People began to step into the circle space and dance.

As the energy grew, Laura called out a blessing over the singing, causing them to stop. She asked for good harvests to come, help in times of troubles, and peace among them. Then she bent down to touch both hands to the ground. Everyone did the same, even the drummers.

The man with the pennywhistle began a tune. Beside him, another man added a mandolin, and another added a guitar. The drummers found the beat and joined in. The guitar player began a song about the turn of the wheel. His voice had the same quality as Ian Anderson's of Jethro Tull with a similar British accent. His companions added harmonies on the chorus. As the song continued, everyone joined in.

Next, two teenage boys, dressed in green clothes and wearing leafy crowns, each with a polished staff in his hands, entered the circle. One had a crown of oak leaves and the other a crown made of holly. They circled each other in challenge and began a mock fight with the staves. Ultimately, the oak king fell to the ground, yielding to the holly king. There was a great cry of exultation from the crowd.

Mandy stepped forward. "The Oak King is dead. Hail the Holly King and his reign."

The crowd responded. "Hail the Holly King!"

"We're grateful to see the faces of old friends once again at this solstice gathering. May your time here be filled with joy and profit."

"Huzzah!" the crowd shouted.

"Blessings to you all. We hope to see you again as the wheel turns."

Farewells were made to the spirits of the directions and the circle was opened.

Floyd called out before everyone went back to their booths. "We have Indian tacos at my booth, and my friends over there," he pointed to a booth on the west side of the circle of vendors, "have fresh-squeezed lemonade and lots of cold drinks on this hot day."

As Sephie followed Floyd back to his booth, she asked, "That sun song. What language was that in the chorus, do you know?"

"Lakota," he said.

"How do you feel about the appropriation of native songs like that?"

While he was washing his hands, he said, "We have appropriated since the beginning of time. With contact, one group always influences another, often changing bits here and there." He picked up the towel, and Sephie washed again. "You're from the South," he said.

"Tennessee," she admitted.

"The English ballads that came with settlers into Appalachia were added to and changed. Do you think the English still object to that?"

"No," she said, taking the towel from him. "But they weren't spiritual songs. They were mostly murder ballads and tales of lost love."

"True," he said, "but what about the old hymns? 'Amazing Grace' came from England, 'How Great Thou Art' is from Sweden. 'A Mighty Fortress Is Our God' is from Germany, and 'What a Friend We Have in Jesus' is from Ireland. Nobody squawks about Americans using them."

"But they're all Christian."

He smiled and started frying up onions, green peppers, and hamburger meat. He gestured with a metal spatula toward the open space they had just left. "And what makes that any different from what the Lakota or my people do? It's all honoring nature and the seasons."

As Sephie pulled open the plastic bags of fry bread Floyd had stacked beside the grill, she asked, "How'd you know the history of all those hymns?"

"He's the choir director back home," Yolanda said, handing Sephie a stack of paper plates.

"So, you're not traditional?" Sephie asked.

"I am," he said. "I appropriated what I felt was right."

"So, both. Like B.D."

"How so?"

"Catholic and his bayou orishas."

Floyd twisted to seek out the tall young man at the North Star booths. "That explains his energy. It's earthy, too." He looked down at Sephie. "And you have more than your family's church beliefs, I think."

She nodded, putting a piece of frybread onto a paper plate. "One line of my people comes from Devon County, England, where they practiced the Old Religion. What Mandy and Laura practice is similar, but not the same."

"And you practice something similar but not the same."

She handed him the plate. "Does it show?"

He grinned. "It makes you our people."

Sephie nodded her head in the direction of the North Star booths. "And what about those people next to Mandy and Laura? Right appropriation?"

Floyd paused as he put meat and vegetables onto the fry bread and gave Sephie a look like a patient teacher. "We don't know their circumstances. All we do know is their energy is clouded."

Feeling properly chastised, Sephie let out a soft "meow" to describe her behavior and said, "Sorry."

He chuckled. "We're both learning our way to be with each other," he said. "You're an independent woman with strong opinions and values."

"And you're a protective and wise old fart," she said.

They both laughed as Yolanda took the filled tacos, added tomatoes and lettuce, and handed them to a waiting customer.

Chapter 48

Day 13: The Greenway, Saturday close to sundown

Sephie watched a young man pull the pole with the Sun fixed atop from its holder in the center of the encampment. Another youth with a *djembe* strapped around his waist beat a haunting rhythm as he followed behind. The sun bearer paced counterclockwise around the encampment, which had been pretty much packed up. Most of the vendors had started packing around 7:00 in the evening, taking their time to make sure their wares would survive the journey back to their homes. There had been a lot of swapping goods back and forth before the plastic storage boxes had been hauled to cars. The canopies and tents had been struck and packed in duffle bags and also carted away. Even the two small campers had been retrieved and parked up on the street. Much to Mandy and Laura's relief, Missy and her husband had left around 6:00 before everyone else had begun to pack anything. All that remained were the two porta-potties.

The vendors all gathered in the center of the encampment, facing the West. Sephie joined Floyd and Yolanda as they stood beside the others, watching the last rays of the sun fall behind the buildings on the street behind the floodwall. There was one last quiet, slow round of "We Are One with the Infinite Sun" without the drummers, as all the vendors put their arms around each other, slowly stepping together to form a small circle. Their faces could barely be seen in the fading light.

Laura was crying. Beside her, Mandy gave her a squeeze and spoke quiet words to her before addressing them all. "Once more we are with family." She smiled, but there was the pang of farewell that passed across her face. "We love you all!" She paused again. "At this turning of the wheel, our little town is facing some strange happenings. Laura and I have visited with you about them, and it seems whatever it is has been confined to Riverbend. We ask that you take extra care as you return to your homes tonight. Smudge and clear your auras. Do whatever you do in your practice to protect yourselves and your loved ones. We also ask that you meditate on what you have sensed here. If you've picked up anything or something occurs to you later, please call us. We value your wisdom. And most of all we value your uniqueness and your love. Hail and farewell! We release the protections on this space back to the spirits of the land, who so kindly allowed us to walk here and celebrate the turning of the wheel. Merry meet and merry part and merry meet again! I love you all!"

The circle of arms tightened slightly in a giant hug. Slowly, all gathered there began to pull away and walk up the rise to the street. Before Sephie could move, Yolanda flung her arms around her. "Please stay in touch."

"Take good care of yourself," Sephie said. "May you have a short and easy labor."

Floyd fished out his keys from his jeans pocket and gave them to his granddaughter. "Go rest your feet. You worked really hard today."

Sephie saw Mandy and Laura waiting and thought it was her cue to leave, but they just waved at her as they joined Yolanda to give her a hand up the hill. "Well, it's been a day, hasn't it?" the old woman said, watching the young people.

"A memorable one," Floyd said, putting his hand at her back and offering just enough pressure to signal her to move forward.

"We still don't know what we're dealing with here. And I think we don't know the whole of it."

"It will reveal itself in its own time."

She chuckled. "Well, patience has never been easy for me. I guess in my old age I'll finally learn that one the hard way."

"You can't rush your life away," he said. "We don't have all that much left to squander."

"If I had the energy of youth," she quipped, "I might burn the time I have left and go out in a blaze. But as it is, everything hurts and what doesn't hurt doesn't work."

Floyd's laugh echoed through the night. He stopped to turn to her to say, "I think a few things might still work." He bent down and kissed her, not a peck, but something soft and lingering. When he raised his head to look at her, the sound of wings accompanied by a trilling caused Floyd to duck, pulling Sephie down with him. Right over them, a small owl flew toward the porta-potties. A shriek indicated that the bird had found a mouse lurking there. Following that was a soft, trilling sound.

As Floyd helped Sephie straighten up, the old woman muttered in awe, "What a soothing sound! Almost a purr."

Floyd turned her back toward the floodwall where there was an opening to the street. "A screech owl," he said.

"But it didn't screech."

"Been misnamed. The barn owl screeches. The screech owl trills." He paused, his face grim. "Still, it can't be good. It's a death omen."

When they got up to the street, Floyd walked them past his truck, where Yolanda was talking on her cellphone. He steered Sephie around the vehicle, across the street, and up to the door of the North Star, where lights from the shop illuminated the roses out front. Opening the door, they walked inside to see Mandy and Laura moving some boxes to more convenient places in order to reshelve merchandise tomorrow.

"B.D. go to bed?" Sephie asked.

"Yep," Mandy grunted. "And so should we. I bet you're dead on your feet."

Sephie winced. After seeing the owl, a portent of death, the tired phrase hit too close.

Floyd reached to shake Mandy's hand and then gave Laura a hug. He turned to Sephie, "Got a piece of paper?'

She looked around in confusion. From behind the counter, Laura found a pad of paper and a pen and handed them to Floyd.

As he wrote, he said, "Let me know when more is revealed about what you've been dealing with." He eyed Sephie significantly. "Especially about that recent matter." Then he ripped off the page and handed it to her. "I expect frequent reports."

She glanced at the page. It had several phone numbers and an address. When he handed her the pad and pen, she dutifully wrote down her cellphone number and then her land line and address in Dark Hollow. She smiled, thinking about getting Christmas cards from him as she tore off the sheet and handed it to him.

"Be safe going home," she said. "Keep me posted about Yolanda's baby."

Floyd gave her a big hug and quickly headed out the door.

Laura followed to lock it behind him, and then turned with a grin on her face.

Sephie looked at Mandy who was also grinning.

"What?" the old woman asked.

Mandy put her arm around her aunt, turned her toward the back, and said, "Let me walk you to your door."

Chapter 49

Day 14: North Star, Sunday midmorning

"Hello!" Sephie called out as she passed through the back room of the shop with a mug of coffee and her cell phone.

"Out here," Laura said.

Sephie found her behind the counter sipping tea and shuffling through a stack of DVDs. Mandy was sitting on a folding chair, going through another stack. None of their merchandise had yet been removed from the storage totes and put away.

As the old woman was settling down into her rocker, Laura looked up, grinned, and teased, "Expecting a call?"

Sephie frowned at the cell phone in her hand and then put it on a nearby shelf that held figurines of women. "I need to call Agnesia. I haven't heard a peep from her all this week. I doubt she's resigned herself to my being away from her for so long. It's too early yet, though. She'll be in church for a couple more hours and then off to somebody's house for Sunday dinner. That church does look after her."

"Then why bring it along now?" Laura asked with such innocence Sephie knew she was ribbing her.

"I don't expect to move this body out of this rocker for a good long time today. I'm weary to the bone. I don't know how you kids do it."

"Oh, this is easy," Mandy said, rising to cross the room to retrieve a small footstool next to one of the plastic storage boxes on the floor. "We used to drive to Wisconsin for a huge festival. It was a weeklong event with people coming from all over the country. That was when we had a big truck with a camper topper. We could pack that sucker full."

"It was glorious," Laura said. "All the people and the different spiritual paths. All the music and rituals." She shook her head. "I miss it, but it was so exhausting."

Mandy put the footstool down in front of her aunt and motioned for the old woman to put her feet up on it.

"Where'd that come from?" Sephie asked.

"You remember that guy with the pennywhistle and his mates, the druids. They're woodworkers from Canada. They came to celebrate with us, but they didn't want to vend yet. They left us a few items to sell on consignment. They'll ship more or bring a shipment down themselves."

"Are footstools all they make?"

"Oh, no. We bartered for that. The guitarist used it to prop a foot when he sat to play his classical guitar. They make the most amazing carved staves and wands." Mandy went to a corner in the front of the room and brought out a sample of each.

Sephie turned the staff in her hand, marveling at the carved image of the Green Man at the top and a trail of oak leaves spiraling down the length of it. The wand she examined next was delicate and covered with symbols. "Are these runes?" she asked.

"No, it's ogham, medieval Irish," Mandy said. "They invoke blessings of peace and prosperity. I thought we'd hang it on the wall behind the counter."

As Mandy placed the carved pieces behind the counter, Sephie picked up her mug again to gesture at the DVDs. "Are those barter treasures, too?" she asked.

"A couple of our friends, who came down from a small town near the Canadian border, used to rent videos from their store until quite recently," Laura explained.

"Recently?" Sephie exclaimed. "I thought people didn't do that anymore."

"They did, because the town is so small they couldn't even get one of those red rental boxes there. It was too much to service it. So, they just added a section in their little grocery store. There's decent internet there now, and dish satellite companies serving the community. So, our friends brought down a bunch to sell or barter."

"Anything interesting?"

Laura blushed. "Well, there's some pretty explicit lesbian movies." She pointed to Mandy. "She's sorting through those." Holding up one from her own pile, she added, "I've got some really unusual pagan-themed films here. They're probably awful, but you never know."

"Anything else?"

"Some really bad sci-fi B movies from the 50s and 60s," Mandy added.

"Giant ants and other irradiated animals?" Sephie offered. "Films about the world ending in 1990? And contacts with peaceful aliens that think Earth is too hostile?"

Mandy laughed. "Pretty much."

"Good stuff," Sephie said. "You planning on a movie night?"

"We should do that tonight," Laura said. "There's a big TV in your little house, Aunt Sephie. We can bring the DVD player over and make popcorn."

Mandy looked at Sephie. "I bet you've never turned that TV on."

"Too busy, child. Just too busy."

The opening lyrics of the Grateful Dead's *Ripple* from Sephie's phone interrupted them. She noticed Mandy and Laura exchanging looks before she picked up her phone off the shelf. She frowned at the unknown number but answered.

"Morning, Sephie," the male voice said.

Recognizing it, she replied, "I take it you're still this side of the dirt."

Floyd laughed. "And so are you."

"I suppose you're halfway home by now."

"Actually, we're still in town. Wes, Yolanda's husband, called last night. He has a layover here for a couple of days. So, we're in a motel." He paused.

Sephie sensed there was more. "How's Yolanda?"

"I'm a little concerned. In your womanly knowledge, do you know what to do about swollen ankles and feet?"

Now on alert, Sephie straightened in her rocker, moving her feet to the floor. "Have her put her feet up and rest on her side on the bed if she can. Don't let that man of hers take her dancing or shopping. Dinner out might be all right. Get her some green tea or even black tea. It can be iced tea. And cranberry juice. Though she's retaining water, she has to keep hydrated to make sure everything works so she can get rid of the excess water." She paused.

"Noted. I'll get that."

"Let me think on this a bit more. She might need to get Wes to massage her legs and feet. I need to check whether I brought oils with me. I have tinctures and salves. I'll see what Laura has."

Out of the corner of her eye, Sephie saw Laura rush to a storage container and start to rummage through it. Mandy joined the effort, looking through another box.

"Floyd, she needs to get her blood pressure checked."

Laura popped up. "There's a machine at the pharmacy at the grocery store."

"Laura says there's a blood pressure machine at the grocery store." Not waiting for him to reply, she held out the phone. "Directions."

Mandy intercepted it and told Floyd where the store was. She handed the phone back to her aunt.

"It may be nothing," Sephie said. "But then it might not. She seemed fine yesterday, but that muggy heat after the rain is hard on a pregnant woman. If her blood pressure is really, really high, get her to the ER. If it's only elevated a bit, you may be okay just to wait and watch and then have her OB check her out when she gets home in a couple of days, or have someone here look at her."

"Thanks," he said, worry still evident in his voice.

"You need to be her calm rock, Floyd."

"Well, I am a protective and wise old fart," he said, repeating her words.

Sephie laughed.

"But I think you're the wise one," he admitted.

"I'm the cranky one. Call me after you take Yolanda to the store."

"I will." He paused. "I'm glad you're here."

"Skedaddle."

Laura pulled out several small vials from the box she had been rummaging in. "I've got a bunch of essential oils here. Not sure it's what you want."

Sephie replaced her phone on the shelf and hoisted herself up out of the rocker. Everything was stiff and achy after yesterday's activity. She waddled over to the counter where Laura was lining up the bottles. "Do you have any carrier oil? Anything. Something neutral? Not vegetable or olive oil, though that will do in a pinch for immediate use."

"I think we might have some almond oil in your kitchen. We had a speaker who liked cooking with exotic oils."

Mandy headed out of the room.

"Just make sure it's not rancid," Sephie cautioned before studying the labels on the bottles. "These are equally exotic. Don't you have any chamomile or lavender essential oil? Is there such a thing?"

Laura thought for a moment. "You know, we have some lavender bundles that Floyd gave us." She then went searching through another box. Finally, she pulled out not only a lavender bundle but one paired with a sweetgrass braid, tied up with a thin, yellow ribbon. "What's this?" she asked.

When Laura turned to her, Sephie smiled. Taking the bouquet from Laura, the old woman noticed that a dried, pink prairie rose had been added. She sniffed the flower, enjoying the last bit of scent it had. Then she scowled at Laura, waiting for more teasing.

Putting up both her hands in defense, Laura said, "I'm not saying a word." She pulled out the lavender and sage bundles and placed them on the counter. "Except to say he's a good man."

"How long have you known him?" Sephie asked, moving to put her little bouquet next to her phone and then picking up a lavender bundle from the counter.

"About five years. When we first started the shop, he walked in with sage smudges and asked if we'd be interested in buying any. We jumped at the chance." Then, carefully, she added, "He's been a widower for eight years. He said he'd been lost for a while. I think the smudge making was a way of occupying his time in a constructive way. He drops in from time to time, especially before Yolanda got pregnant and couldn't fly. I think he was lonely." Laura then started restocking the essential oils display with what she had pulled from a storage tote.

Easing herself back into the rocker with the lavender bundle, Sephie commented, "I sense he's had a hard life." She began to strip the flowers off the stems using her thumb and first two fingers, dropping the fragrant bits into the fold she had created to hold the flowers in the bottom of her big t-shirt.

"He did the rodeo circuit as a bull rider. No tame broncs for him. His body has been battered and broken so many times it's held together with a lot of pins. Drink had him for a while and probably women when he was younger. His wife became a rodeo widow, so in some ways he's not really had the stability of a good marriage like you had."

"There's stability," Sephie said, "and then there's ennui or not wanting to change the status quo."

"Ennui!" Laura said.

"What? I read," Sephie said, then admitted. "It was after one of those college boys used the word when he was helping me build my cabin. Said his English professor was full of ennui. I had to make sure it wasn't a swear word I didn't know."

Laura laughed.

"Did Floyd tell you all that about his life?"

"Bits," Laura explained. "It was mainly Yolanda. She'd been raised by her grandmother and saw the fallout every time he went rodeoing."

"Floyd is right. That child has a good spirit."

"When Floyd got too old to bull ride, he took a job as a rodeo clown and then later as a stable hand. When his wife got sick, Yolanda was a grown woman and wanted to travel the world."

"I don't blame her."

"Floyd stayed home and somehow made peace with his wife and the life he'd lived. He started singing in the choir and eventually became the choir director. Still, he felt lost. I think the wildcrafting he does in the backcountry out West has given him some kind of peace. It certainly has fed the wanderlust he still has."

Sephie picked up her mug of cold coffee and drank. "All our lives are complex, whether we want to acknowledge that or not. Even lives of ennui."

"I found some avocado oil," Mandy said rushing into the shop. "It hasn't been opened."

A loud pounding at the front door rattled the bell at the top. Everyone looked up to see a frantic young woman waving at them. Then she resumed pounding.

Mandy put the bottle of oil on the counter and went to unlock and open the door.

"Do you have a phone? I need to call 911."

Mandy opened the door wider, and the woman ran in to the counter. Laura handed her the business phone, and the woman dialed.

"Hello, you need to get someone down to the river. My husband's been pulled overboard." She paused. "My name? Oh, for God's sake! What are you waiting for? He needs help now!" Another pause and then she looked around. "Where are we? The address?"

Mandy told her and the woman repeated it. "It happened on the river right opposite here." Another pause. "Of course, he can swim! He wouldn't be out there otherwise. Yes, he has a life vest on! Just get somebody here quick!" She slammed the phone down before offering more.

"Do you need to sit down?" Mandy asked.

She shook her head. "I just need to catch my breath. I need to get back down there."

"I'll go with you," Mandy said. "But tell us what happened first so we can tell the rescue squad when they get here."

"My husband was fishing in his boat while I was on the bank with our picnic."

"A big boat?"

"No, a little thing with a motor. He'd anchored and cast out a few times. And then these pale-looking arms reached out of the water in the front and pulled him into the river. He struggled a bit and started to swim back to the boat and down he went again. Oh, my God! I've got to get back to him." The woman ran through the shop and out the door.

Mandy patted her back pocket to make sure her cell phone was there and followed, just as sirens could be heard in the distance. Before anyone could say, "Be careful!" she was gone.

Chapter 50

Day 14: North Star, Sunday noon

"They found him," Mandy said as she came through the front door of the shop.

"Where?" Laura asked, turning from the candle display she was filling from a box of stock in the back room. There hadn't been many candles left from the festival.

"About a mile or so downstream," Mandy said, heading toward the back room and the toilet. "He was on the bank."

"Dead?"

"No," she paused to look back into the shop. "He was alive and raving about white creatures in the water."

She turned and nearly bumped into B.D. as he strutted in from the back door, dressed in a charcoal gray sport coat, black trousers, a pale blue shirt with a blue striped tie, and highly polished black shoes.

"Nice threads."

B.D. grinned and went on into the shop.

Making her stop at the facilities short, Mandy quickly returned to watch B.D. as he still strutted around, modeling his new look.

"You had all that in that teeny bag of yours?" Sephie asked from her rocker.

"Mama didn't raise no Bayou Billy," he said.

"Why didn't you wear that to mass last week?"

"Mother Evangeline said it was casual because it was in a nursing home. So, where do you want to go for lunch?"

"You buying?" Sephie asked.

Reaching into an inner pocket of his jacket, he said, "As a matter of fact, I am." He pulled out a fat envelope. "They took up a special collection for me. Man, that church is big!"

"What'd you sing?" Laura wanted to know.

"We did a big medley of spirituals. It sounded great with that big choir in the background. Powerful. But you know, these northern singers sure are good, but they don't have any power. When there was a solo part in the arrangement, it took two or three of them to get the volume of one back home."

"Spirituals," Laura repeated. "And you'll do 'Free at Last' and 'Ole Man River' later. Do you think you're being typecast?"

He shrugged. "Probably. I hope that wears off."

"It reminds me of when I was in college here," Laura said. "During PowWow week, the entire faculty would wear all the turquoise or native jewelry they owned."

"Huh," B.D. said. "They thought that was respectful?"

"They thought it honored their native colleagues," she said. "What really honored them was providing a space for the workshops and talks about native issues that went alongside the gathering of the tribes for dancing."

B.D. looked around the shop that had been put to rights in the morning. "Looks like y'all got everything back where it belongs. I'm sorry I couldn't help with that."

"It was mainly Laura and me," Sephie said. "We had some excitement, and it was a way to deal with it."

"Excitement?" B.D. said, taking a seat on an empty stool.

"Some woman called the rescue squad from here because she thought her husband was drowning. Mandy followed her back to the river while we waited for the fire department and the police," Laura said.

"Strangest thing," Mandy admitted as she sat back down in the folding chair. "The woman said somebody pulled her husband out of a small boat with an outboard into the river."

"Somebody? In the river?" B.D. asked.

"Yep. Said he had pale arms."

"Did you see anything?"

"When I got down there, there was only the boat anchored in the water. No man. No life jacket."

"Was the guy fishing?"

"Yeah, trying for one of those big channel cats in the river. They can get as big as calves here."

"Did the rescue squad find anything?"

"Not at first. They thought they'd have to send down divers or maybe drag the river to find the body. There's a lot of debris in the river from hundreds of years of flooding. But they found him on the bank about a mile away. The EMT told the man's wife that it was odd since there was nothing for the man to grab hold of to hoist him out of the river."

B.D. mused. "Ole mentioned something about beings attacking fishing boats. The Finn Folk or Finnmen, he called them. It was usually about competition for fish. But one guy fishing for one big fish shouldn't have made one of those creatures attack. IF that's indeed what it was."

Laura mused, "We have a big catfishing tournament in August every year. The river is full of boats, teams of fishermen trying to get the biggest one. If the Finnmen were worried about competition, they'd have attacked them years ago. But nothing ever happened."

"Once in a while," Mandy countered, "there is that one guy who gets drunk and falls overboard and drowns. The undertow in places is pretty bad."

"Maybe there was just too much activity on the river then," B.D. suggested.

"Strange that all these incidents are happening now," Sephie said. "It's got to be more than just the usual river flooding."

"And all these incidents or creatures are coming from the folklore of a lot of different people," B.D. stated.

Sephie's ringtone interrupted their ponderings. She didn't even bother to check who it was, but did look at the clock on the wall behind the counter to see the time.

While the old woman talked, B.D. announced, "I'll run next door and change out of these good clothes. Think of a place to eat while I'm gone."

Mandy walked over to Laura and said conspiratorially, "If Bill finds out we're eating someplace else, he'll kill us."

"There's really no other good place," Laura said. "All those places out by the mall are national chains, and I really can't face a McAnything or an-open-a-box-and-heat-it meal from some sit-down restaurant out there."

"Then the Watering Hole it is."

Sephie rose wearily from her rocker waving her phone at Mandy. "Can you put caller ID on my phone?"

Taking it, Mandy asked, "For the last number?"

"No, the one before. Floyd's number. That last one was from Agnesia's pastor. She passed out at church, but she refused to be taken to the hospital. Some church ladies will stay with her overnight and take her to see her doctor tomorrow. He said she's in her right mind but isn't complaining about me like she usually does. I guess he and I both know that's not a good sign."

"Will you need to go home?" Laura asked.

Sephie shook her head. "It doesn't sound serious . . . yet," she said. "We'll see what the doctor says tomorrow. She's got a lot of people there helping her and doesn't need me to raise her blood pressure any more."

Mandy handed the phone back.

"Floyd never called back," Sephie said as she looked at the clock again. Finding his name in recent calls, she was about to press it when the bell over the door rang again. The door opened and Floyd entered, his face lined with worry.

Sephie met him. "How's Yolanda?"

"We took her to a walk-in clinic because her blood

pressure was so high. They did a urine test and think it might be preeclampsia. They didn't do much — gave her a diuretic and told her the same things you told me she should do. The doctors want to wait and watch what happens. I don't want to take her home while Wes is here since they see each other so little lately, but her own doctor knows her."

"What if Wes went back with you?"

"Then we'd have to get him back here in the wee hours on Tuesday for his flight."

Laura interrupted, coming to stand next to him, "Floyd, she's better off here practically next door to a big hospital with Wes. You told me your place on the rez is far out in the country on dirt roads, hours away from a city hospital."

Mandy offered the practical. "Wes' airline is picking up the tab for his layover, right?"

Floyd nodded once.

"When Wes leaves, both of you come over here. We can make room in the little house next door, can't we, Aunt Sephie?"

"Sure, we can," the old woman said. "There's a pullout sofa, and Mandy has cots."

Relief flooded Floyd's face, then it scrunched up and he had to turn away.

"So, where're we going to eat?" B.D. called, bounding into the shop.

Chapter 51

Day 14: The little house, Sunday early evening

"Mandy and Laura need a pickin' porch," Floyd remarked, stepping out into the cooling air in front of the little house next to the shop.

"A screened porch," Sephie said, wondering when the new crop of mosquitoes would emerge after the recent rain. Mandy had told her that the city would send out trucks to spray after it rained and it had dried off a bit.

Loud laughter came from inside through the open windows. Mandy had convinced B.D. to order pizzas while they came over to the little house to watch old sci-fi movies. He'd been able to watch one before going to mass, and the women had put on a film noir mystery while he was gone. When he had returned, the sci-fi marathon resumed.

As for the older folks, Sephie had made good headway with the new shawl she was crocheting. Floyd had fallen asleep on the couch and then left to check on Yolanda. He'd returned a while ago but seemed restless.

"Do you play?" Sephie asked, returning to the reference about the picking porch.

"A little. Guitar," he said.

"You should've brought it with you."

"Naw," he said, stepping down to the little fence in front of the house to rest a forearm on the corner piece. He hunched over to lean there. "It's quiet out here."

"Not much traffic on a Sunday night."

"The town should put benches down along the river so people could watch the water."

"I'm not so sure I'd want to be down there tonight. They almost lost a man there today." Floyd turned his body to stare at her, causing her to give more explanation. "A fisherman. His wife told the first responders that something with bare white arms pulled him off his boat."

Floyd frowned. "That's the owl omen."

"Maybe, but he didn't die," Sephie muttered.

"Owl spirit doesn't always mean imminent death. Just that death's around. It sounds like the man could've died."

Thinking about her sister and the seriousness of Yolanda's condition and even about her age and Floyd's, Sephie shook her head and admitted, "Too much has happened today. My sister collapsed in church this morning. The pastor called and told me. She's got plenty of church ladies to help. But she's old. Who knows what's wrong?"

"You going home?"

She shook her head. "You never know about my sister. She's claimed to have all sorts of ailments all her life and gotten people to cater to her. Even me. This could be the big one, though. But there's nothing I can do there that the church ladies can't. I'm needed here. I have to see this through."

"It's hard, when you're pulled in too many directions." He paused. "Sure you won't have regrets you didn't go home?"

"Floyd, my sister is hard to love, but I do love her. Sometimes you have to make decisions that don't just suck you back into old patterns. Of course, the whole church'll think I'm heartless. But it's not my church."

He let a small laugh escape. It had been a rough day for everyone.

Straightening, he pointed toward the river. "When I was a boy, I heard tall tales about the Riverbend Frog even way back home. A good tale always gets spread around a bit."

"A frog?"

"Yep. A giant frog was supposed to live south of town.

That was way before it was all developed down there. It was a bend in the river where people used to fish from the bank. It sure did make boys curious though."

"Could also be just a good excuse to cover sneaking out to go fishing. Parents could get distracted by the tale and not the offense."

He chuckled. "Probably." There was a buzz in his pocket. Fishing out his cellphone, "Sorry," he said and answered it, listening intently. "What do you think?" he asked the caller. "You don't have to do that. I'll be with her and there are friends—" He listened again. "I understand. Let's take her in again in the morning and see what they say." He sighed and then said, quietly and evenly, "Wes, you got this. We both got this." There was a long pause. "Do you want me to bring you some dinner? Are you sure? Okay. Keep me posted. And call your mother."

He clicked the call off and threw his hands up slightly. "I feel so helpless."

Sephie moved closer to him and put her hand on his back, rubbing it gently. "She needs to know you're there. Wes is her husband, but you are her rock, remember?"

"I look at her and don't know how to help. This is women's business."

"Well, men — a man — helped get her where she is. So, it's men's business, too."

He bowed his head. "But you don't understand. I was gone so much of her life."

"I know," she said. "Laura told me."

"And here I am . . . here, not with her. And Wes will need to leave to go back to work."

"Your instincts are right. You're giving them space. It can get claustrophobic with three people in a small motel room. Why don't we walk down to the Watering Hole and see what you can take back to Wes and Yolanda."

Floyd pulled her against his chest for a long minute and then released her. “I want to take you to dinner sometime,” he said.

“But not tonight,” she said. “I’m full of pizza. Just let me tell the younguns where we’ll be.”

Chapter 52

Day 15: Prairie Hospital, Monday early afternoon

Seeing Yolanda's bright eyes and welcoming smile caused Sephie to let out a sigh of relief. She hadn't realized she had been holding her breath until that moment. Feeling Floyd's hand on her left elbow tighten slightly, the old woman realized that he saw more than she did, or else he was revisiting old ghosts. Moving away from him, she offered Yolanda the small bouquet of prairie roses she had cut and put into a thick jar that had once held artichokes.

"They smell wonderful!" Though Yolanda looked well, her face was flushed and Sephie detected a flash of worry behind her eyes.

"I thought they'd brighten your room since you have to rest, I hear."

"I could rest better at home," she complained, but reached out to cover the hand of the young man beside her bed, who had risen at Sephie and Floyd's entrance.

Wes was a slender man of medium height, his blond hair in a military cut. Though he was dressed in a t-shirt and jeans, there was evidence of discipline and training.

The old woman extended her hand to him. "I'm Sephie, and you must be Wes." She found his handshake very firm, another proof that he was not native. "Air Force?" she asked.

He smiled. "Why, yes. I got my training there. How'd you know?"

"You still carry the discipline," she said, then took the flowers from Yolanda and put them on the night stand beside her bed. Turning to the girl, she asked, "How long are they keeping you here?"

"Too long," she said.

"Ma'am?" Wes drew her attention away from his wife. "Can I get you some coffee or a soft drink?"

Sephie started to protest, but there was something in his tone that stopped her.

"There's a machine in the waiting room," he said. "But you'll have to show me what you want."

The old woman graciously agreed, recognizing his silent message that wasn't about whether she wanted Coke or Dr. Pepper. She followed him out of the room to the waiting area.

"Ma'am, I don't mean to take you away like this, but you're not native and I need someone else to talk to."

"Did you call your mother like Floyd asked?"

"Yes, but, ma'am, she just doesn't understand. She never did." They entered the empty waiting room. "But I think you do. You wouldn't be with Floyd if you didn't. He's very traditional."

She laughed. "I'm not *with* Floyd," she said. "I only just met him."

Wes stopped and turned to her. "But, but—"

"Out with it. You're starting to sound like a motor boat."

"It's just that he lights up when he talks about you."

"And why would he be talking about me? He should be focusing on your wife."

The young man collapsed into a chair, causing Sephie to sit down next to him and put her hand on his arm.

"What do the doctors say?" she asked.

"They've confirmed preeclampsia. It's not serious yet, but it can get that way, life-threatening for her and the baby. We didn't have a clue. It came on so sudden. They said she'll need bed rest until the baby is born or they deliver by C-section early. She's thirty-two weeks, just barely eight months. The baby's too small yet."

"She doesn't show very much," Sephie remarked. "Probably a small baby girl."

"A girl?"

"From the way she carries it." She squeezed his arm. "It will be all right. If they release her, we'll all take care of her here in Riverbend, close to the hospital and to the airport. My niece and her wife and my young friend B.D. are making a place for her and Floyd with us at the guest house next door to their shop. I'm not sure how the beds will all be arranged, but she'll be really comfortable, and she'll have company. Someone will be with her every minute."

"Why're they doing all that for us? Why are you?"

"We're all family, Wes. Your mother may not understand your marriage, and my sister and the rest of my family may not understand the love between my niece and her wife, but we're all here as made-family."

The strains of "Ripple" emerged from Sephie's purse that she had slung over her shoulder. "Sorry," she said, fishing out the phone. Frowning at her home number, she answered.

"Sephie, it's Pastor Woods."

"What's the news?"

"The doctors ran all sorts of tests. They think she had a mild stroke, what they call a TIA."

"Any damage?"

"Not this time, but they said that when there's one, there might be more. They also saw some serious damage to her heart that wasn't found before. She's been neglecting herself."

"So, what do they recommend?"

"They're sending her home. The ladies from the church have organized food and shifts for someone to be with her round the clock for the next few days. Agnesia is much loved by the church, and we'll take good care of her until you come home. Do you know when that will be?"

Sephie rubbed her weary eyes and took a deep breath.

"I don't know when that will be. I'm helping with a medical emergency here."

"Your niece?"

"No, but, Pastor, you know that when we're called to service, we must obey that call."

"Amen, sister. You go do God's work, and we'll take good care of Agnesia. We'll let you know of any changes."

When Sephie had pocketed the phone, Wes blurted out, "It sounds like you have worries of your own, ma'am. You needn't—"

Turning on him, she began, "Now, don't you start telling me what I need to do or not do. I'm here. And I'm here for however long it takes. Even if I have to endure these damn North Dakota winters."

She stood and walked over to the bank of three vending machines. One was for snacks, one for coffee, and one for soft drinks and water. She looked over the selections of soft drinks and started to reach into her handbag.

"No, you don't," Wes said, dropping coins into the slot. "What do you want?"

She pointed to a Dr. Pepper, and he punched in the code. Sephie retrieved it when it dropped. "We can't go back empty-handed."

As they walked back to Yolanda's room, Sephie felt more settled in her mind than she had been in the past few days. Her explanation to Pastor Woods defined her reason for being there, whether she found the elusive Dakota Dracula or not. Though she knew she'd feel the pull back to Dark Hollow in a couple of months when she should be wildcrafting, she had enough materials with her to start working on more salves and tinctures and maybe more oils. She felt the pull of the need to help here far stronger than the one in Dark Hollow.

When they got back to the room, Sephie put her soda can down on the nightstand and fished a bottle out of her purse. She handed it to Wes. "I'm putting you to work, young man. That's lavender oil. I want you to massage her feet and legs up to her knees. Just use a little at a time." She turned to Yolanda. "It's made from your lavender, my dear. It smells wonderful. And you'll feel so pampered. Now, I need to get back to the shop. I'll visit again."

Out in the hallway, Sephie elbowed Floyd's ribs gently. "Stop talking about me," she said, grinning all the way down the hall.

Chapter 53

Day 15: North Star, Monday late afternoon

"I didn't expect to see y'all here lounging," Sephie said as she entered the shop and found Mandy and Laura sitting, leafing through catalogs, and B.D. grinning at something on an iPad. "I thought you'd all have the little house all torn up and still be rearranging things."

"Easy fix," Mandy said. "Linens are on the pullout couch, and we put the cot in B.D.'s room and moved some pillows around."

"And put out fresh towels," Laura added.

"So, no heavy lifting for you?" she said pointedly at B.D. as she took possession of her rocker.

"How's Yolanda?" Laura asked. "Any better?"

"She looks remarkably well, but they want her to rest. They might do a C-section. That baby's not big enough to meet the world yet."

"Any word on Aunt Agnesia?" Mandy asked.

"TIA and some heart issues," she reported and then got up to go into the back room. She looked around and came back into the shop. "Can I have that tablet and a pen?"

B.D. raised his head and Laura looked over at him in question. Mandy, understanding, reached behind the counter and brought out a pad of paper and a pen. She wiggled the pad. "This is a tablet in Sephie's generation." Handing it to her, she asked, "Going to make a Honey-do list for each of us?"

"That's next," she said. "Right now, I need to inventory what I brought with me. After making Yolanda's oil, I thought

I might make some more with different herbs. And then see if I can rearrange the back room in order to put up more tinctures and salves. You'll still have room for your seminars whenever you have them," she said, moving into the back room.

"You know," Laura said, following her, "I've wanted to do a line of shop-made products other than the mint tea and rose hips that we offer. Something other than what other vendors produce."

"Like what?" Sephie said as she wrote down the number of dogwood branches.

"I'd like to do blessed protection oils and blessed love oils."

"Didn't I see the infamous Missy offering love oils and soaps at the festival? I just got a glimpse before the noon celebration."

"I'm glad you stayed away. We didn't feel anything except just hate. Their booth didn't get much business, though. And all of her wares were commercial stuff bought off the internet. You never know where that comes from."

Sephie glanced at Laura, "But you buy commercial products." She bent down to count jars of Lije's shine.

"Candles and jewelry. Altarware and books. Commercial teas. Drums and rattles. But nothing *special*. We trust your tinctures and salves. We know they're made with good intentions and cleanly. I'd like to make blessed healing soaps. Yolanda's are good but are used for general bathing."

Moving to another box, Sephie started pulling out remaining salves. All the tinctures were out on display. "If you plan on making soap, you'll need to get a range in here or a bigger hotplate and put a door to the shop to shut out the smell. Or make them outside like they did in olden days. It's not always pleasant."

Finally, Sephie turned out the contents of two more large boxes filled with dried herb and flower bundles. "You've got enough roses out there to make your love oils and soaps."

She separated all the bundles into piles on the floor: nearly dried chestnut leaves, chamomile flowers, burdock roots, ginseng roots, poke berries, anise hyssop, sheep's sorrel, savory, dandelion leaves, witch hazel branches, St. John's Wort flowers, last year's stoneroot, goldenseal, rue, and Sweet Joe-Pye Weed. She also took out a pint jar of Sweet Gum sap. All of these she noted on the pad. Tucked in the corner was a paper grocery bag of black walnuts still in their green hulls, another of hickory nuts, and another full of nettle.

Bending down over the herbs spread out on the floor, Laura said in awe, "You've got a pharmacy here." She stared up at her wife's great-aunt. "I know their value and some of their names, but I don't know how to use them or even handle them."

Pointing to the bag of nettles, Sephie cautioned. "You leave that bag alone unless you're wearing gloves. Nettle leaves a terrible rash but makes a soothing tea. I'm extra sensitive to it so I don't even drink the tea."

Rising to approach Sephie, Laura said softly, almost in a whisper, "Can I be your apprentice? Will you teach me?"

Sephie was moved by her earnestness and a sense of destiny. She smiled, actually relieved she would be passing on some of her knowledge since her daughter, being a modern woman, had never wanted to learn about anything from the backwoods. When Sephie was gone, it would all be lost except for the snippets she'd taught B.D.

"You'll share that status with B.D., though he's more interested in finding out if there are chants I use in the making of the medicines. There probably were once but they got lost to time."

"Could we make new ones?"

Sephie patted Laura's forearm. "Of course, we can. It's all intention anyway." She smiled. "And I want to learn from you, your ways. They fit closer to the ways my old granny taught me, but she never sang or used the poetry you do."

"In my path," Laura said, "we use what fits, with respect, of course, because not many of us had a granny to teach us, so we read and share and learn bits from here and there."

"I'm seeing that. I was surprised that Floyd and Yolanda weren't up in arms about the native song."

Laura pushed her brows together as if to try to understand better.

"'We Are One with the Infinite Sun,'" Sephie prodded. "The chorus is Lakota."

Laura's eyes widened. "I never knew. It's widely used by pagans everywhere." Then she seemed to think harder. "Oh, geez. That appropriation."

"But it is an example of your community's use of bits they find here and there. Floyd said basically that it was used in the same way that native people viewed the world. So, he was fine with it. Secretly, I think he liked the idea of his beliefs having a place in the ceremony. Being included is important, if it's done respectfully." She pursed her lips. "He educated me."

"Well, we did have those druids from Canada, and Patricia brought her copal incense and did cleansings from Mexico. Oh, shoot, I should have introduced you! She's the *curandera* I told you about."

"We'll meet when the time is right."

"I'm glad Floyd kept you safe at the encampment. Rodolfo is the energy vampire! That is still so hard to believe. But tied to Missy, it's no wonder."

"She's got big energy that explodes everywhere. Maybe she's kept him fed for all this time."

"But why's he targeting you? Now?"

"Don't know."

Laura let a small smile escape before she said, "Stay around Floyd. His energy mixes well with yours."

Sephie harrumphed, then turned to weigh the options for the space in the back room. "If you have a smaller table, you could put the microwave, coffeemaker, and little hotplate on that closer to the sink over here by the stairs and the bathroom. Is there an outlet over there? Then that big table and maybe another could be put along this far wall to use for doing the wildcrafting work. We could run a line above it to hang all the herbs and maybe some shelving underneath for jars and supplies and the moonshine."

Laura went over to look near the sink. "No outlet here. There never were very many in these old houses." She walked over to the short wall facing the foot of the stairs. "See, this is odd. There's one here and the one on that long wall." She looked over at the little microwave. "We could get a microwave cart with a shelf on top over here and put the coffeemaker there. The hot plate, though?" She shook her head.

"You only use it for tea water, don't you?"

"Yeah."

"Then use the coffeemaker to heat your tea water."

Laura opened her mouth and then smiled. "I never thought of that."

"My daughter has one. She just lifts and closes the lid without the k-cup. She brews the strongest coffee they make. I think Floyd would love her for that. But I always brew a full cup then pour half into another and run the cycle again, filling both cups. It's about drinkable then. But don't tell Floyd. He'll think I'm a wimp."

Chapter 54

Day 16: North Star, Tuesday early afternoon

Securing a line made of twine for her aunt's dried herbs, Mandy swayed slightly on the top step of the adder in the back room as B.D. bumped it rushing in through the back door. She slammed both hands against the two adjoining walls in the corner to steady herself. "Rein in your horses, B.D.!"

"Oh!" he said, turning to brace a hand on the young woman's butt to keep her from falling.

Eying his hand suspiciously, she said, "I think I got this."

Jerking his hand back as if he'd put it into a fire, he muttered, "Sorry."

Finally securing the line, Mandy stepped down the ladder, using the wall for support. When she was on the floor, she said, "What's gotten you into a steam?"

"I'm just excited. I just got back from interviewing Ole." He held up a mini voice recorder. "I got some good stuff. A couple of songs. He did something called *yoiking*. It reminded me of the doodling mountain people did around Dark Holler, where you used the voice to fill in the music when there wasn't any."

"Well, that'd be something to hear," Sephie said, coming in from the shop with a bag of clothespins. "Let's use these on each bundle instead of tying them to the twine. It will allow us to add more as they're used." Jerking her thumb at Mandy toward the shop, she added, "It's getting busy out there. Go help Laura. I can put B.D.'s height to use."

As Sephie tied extra twine around one bundle, she left a long tail. Handing it and a clothespin to B.D. she instructed,

"Just clip it over there," and nodded to the line closest to the back door.

"This'll work out great for you. Just like at your cabin."

"I think it will," she said. They proceeded to hang the bundles of herbs and had covered about half of the line when Sephie asked, "You learn anything else from Ole?"

"You mean about our little problem here? Not really. But it's good research. Oh, and he told me there's this singer coming in from Minneapolis to do a show on Saturday. It's sponsored by the Sons of Norway, so she should be pretty authentic."

"Isn't that the day of your showcase at the university?"

"No, that's Friday night, the last day of the workshops on musicals. They're bringing in kids from the high school, too. But this Norwegian singer sometimes does something really unusual called staving. It's singing accompanied by beating a rhythm with a staff on a board on the ground."

"A song to accompany some work, I suppose," Sephie said.

"I think it's like the butter-churning songs I collected in the mountains."

"I remember my grandmother 'singing the butter' as she called it. What was it? 'Come, butter, come.'" She sang off a line. "It was a slow steady beat. The song kept her going because it took a long time for the butter to form."

"Like the corn grinding songs of my people," a voice said behind Sephie as she handed yet another bundle to B.D.

The old woman looked behind her and offered a small smile to Floyd. "Did Wes get off okay?"

"Early, but yeah. I cleaned out the motel room and went back to the hospital. Somehow, that girl managed to get them to release her."

"Probably got her blood pressure to come down."

"I can't understand how. She was pretty upset after Wes left, even though she put on a really brave front when he was there."

"Did the doctors give you any instructions?"

"They gave her a blood pressure monitor. A small thing she wears on her wrist. This one takes readings by the hour automatically. It wouldn't surprise me that somehow it sends the hospital a report."

"Well, that'll help. Is she all settled in next door?"

There was a long silence. It was long enough that Sephie turned to find out what had stopped his tongue.

"I think we have some rebellion on our hands."

"Oh?"

"She won't stay next door. She doesn't want to be away from the action, I guess."

Sephie considered that and then said. "Might be the best for her. Keep her mind off Wes and what's happening. We'll just need to find a way to keep her feet up. Maybe we can get Laura and Mandy to close a little early or just man the store with one person." Sephie turned pointedly to B.D.

"Me? What do I know about your stuff or theirs?"

"You'll learn. After all, you've got a college education." She turned to the last bundle of herbs. "I'm not going to let my herb lore die with me." When she had tied twine on it, she handed it to B.D.

"I'll do it tonight," he said. "I don't have rehearsal. But tomorrow night I'm practicing with that musician Bill got to accompany me. We're supposed to pull a set together for Thursday night. And I have showcase rehearsal Friday afternoon and then the show. And. . . ."

Sephie turned to Floyd. "I think I've created a monster."

Chapter 55

Day 16: North Star, Tuesday early evening

Standing in the doorway to the back room, Sephie surveyed the afternoon's work. She had everything where she wanted it. Mandy had found an old night stand up in their little apartment to put the microwave and coffeemaker on so Sephie had the entire other half of the room for her workshop. The old woman had commandeered the hot plate in case she needed to boil something instead of steeping it in Lije's remedy. Nodding her head, she was well satisfied and ready to begin tomorrow or the next day. Now, she was weary and hungry.

Behind her, she felt strong hands massage her shoulders. Normally, she would have jumped when someone disturbed her thoughts, but the presence behind her was solid and tall and becoming familiar. She smelled a gamey trace of horses and leather mixed with aftershave or cologne, making her lean back against the man's chest, closing her eyes. "If you keep that up, I'll fall asleep on my feet."

"You need to eat," Floyd said.

She reluctantly turned around. "What did the kids order?" She wasn't sure what she had an appetite for.

"They got pizza delivered next door. They're watching movies."

"Another old sci-fi movie marathon, I guess. B.D. out front?"

"Actually, no. Mandy and Laura closed the shop a little early."

She started to move into the shop but the lights had been

turned off. Through the front window, she saw that it was getting dark outside. "What time is it, anyway?"

"About eight-thirty."

"How'd I miss their closing up?"

"Singular purpose," he teased, and then sobered as he studied her face. "You *are* worried about not being able to share what you know, aren't you?"

She rubbed her upper arms as if she were cold. "That owl and my sister and then Yolanda got me thinking."

He turned her toward the back door. "We feel our mortality more at this age."

They stepped outside to find the yard lights had been turned on. Floyd fished a key out of his pocket and held it up. "Mandy got extra keys made." He locked the door and then wrapped her arm around his. "Got the strength to walk down to the Watering Hole?"

"Sure. Anything Bill has to offer is better than pizza again. I think I have it maybe once a year back home when my daughter visits."

Floyd directed her toward the little gate that opened to the alley. When they got close to it, Sephie balked. "Not that way."

Not waiting for an explanation, he steered her toward the narrow side yard between the two buildings toward the front and onto the sidewalk. As they passed his truck parked on the street, Floyd stated, "I'll move my truck behind the house tomorrow. I think there's room for it. I found there's a side of the fencing that can swing out to accommodate a vehicle."

Though his commercial grill and goods were heavily tarped and tied down on his truck, moving them out of easy access was better than leaving them on the street. "It'll be safer back there," she said.

"For everyone."

She frowned. "Meaning?"

"Seeing a truck in the back might be a deterrent in the night."

"You can move that stuff into the little house, you know."

"I will. But I'm not talking about my things."

As they neared the street to cross to the Watering Hole, Sephie realized just what he was saying. "You felt it, too. Was it Rodolfo lurking there again?"

He stopped before they crossed the street. "He's been in the alley?"

"Well, yeah. I thought I told you."

"I thought you meant in the shop."

Hustling her across the street, Floyd rushed them into the restaurant, through the foliage jungle of the foyer, and to a booth in the back where it was quieter. The bar area was filling up and getting rowdy. Floyd gave Sephie a little shove onto the bench and used his hip to move her further in so he could sit. He craned his head out like an ogling turkey to survey the people in the bar. Stretching in front of Sephie to pick up the salt cellar on the table, Floyd unscrewed the lid and took her right hand, turning it upright. He poured about a tablespoon of salt into her palm. From his shirt pocket, the old man pulled out a small pouch and poured a tiny bit of the powder into the palm of his left hand. Then he moved his upturned palm against hers, saying small blessing in a language Sephie didn't recognize. Realizing that this must be a protection, Sephie whispered, "Cleanse and purify and keep us safe."

Floyd twisted her wrist so that the salt fell into his palm. He said something else and then, unobtrusively, he began to spread a line of the mixture across the floor in front of their booth. "May we be seen only by our server," he said. The bit that was left in his palm, he dusted over both of them.

"If he can't see you, he can't harm you," he said softly to Sephie. "You're already too tired to be drained further."

"The theater group should still be rehearsing," she said.

"Maybe he slipped out early. We both sensed something out there."

"It could be something else. Everything is too weird. I've never run into anything like what's happening here."

He put his arm around her, but didn't say anything for a while. "You've been trying to deal with this all on your own. The whole family, all of us from the Solstice event, is on alert. We'll find answers."

She sighed. "Sometimes I think maybe there's nothing really odd about any of this. Maybe we're just wanting to make it that way because we're looking for something, and B.D. and I aren't used to this land."

"I saw what happened on Saturday when you were around Rodolfo. That's real. The owl was real. And the strange incident in the river with the fisherman. The cat attacks are real. We don't know what the whole is or the reason for any of it."

"It's coming from all sorts of practical and mythical areas," she said.

A young woman appeared by their booth. She grinned while she placed their menus in front of them.

Floyd unwound his arm from Sephie and opened the large menu. "What kind of soup do you have?"

"French onion soup and tomato basil," the server said. "Tonight's special is a petite sirloin with either a baked potato or sweet potato fries. It comes with a small house salad." Using her pen, she pointed to a paper addition to the printed menu.

"That sounds great." He turned to Sephie, who was squinting over the offerings.

"You know, French onion soup sounds wonderful," the old woman said, not really wanting much. Sometimes when she got too hungry, thinking of a lot of food just made her ill.

"Bring two specials with two French onion soups. Make mine medium rare."

"And yours, ma'am?" the server said.

"I can't eat all that," she protested.

"That's what boxes are for," he said.

She sighed. "Then medium, please."

"And the dressing for your salads?"

"Italian," Sephie said.

"The same." Floyd answered, collecting the menus and handing them to the server.

"And to drink?"

"Colas," Floyd said, raising an eyebrow at Sephie for confirmation. She nodded.

When the server left, Sephie said, "It would be so nice not to have a worry just once."

"That'll never happen. It's all part of life. You just have to grab the bits that are good and hang on."

"Like a bull rider?" Sephie asked, trying to suppress a smile but failing. "What was that like?"

"Eight of the longest and shortest seconds of your life, not knowing the exact moment you'd be thrown or whether you'd get caught in a stirrup and pulled under those angry hooves. Just living in that moment." He looked embarrassed. "Best high around."

"I guess that would make you seek that wherever you could find it."

"Yeah. Booze. Women. Even mucking out rodeo stables just to be near the thrill, watching others do what you once did and trying to live it with them." Floyd ran a finger along the irregularities of the wood of the table in front of him. "I think it was fear, though." He paused and then admitted, "I was running from stability, from something solid."

Sephie took a deep breath. "Sometimes, seeking stability can be another way to deal with fear. Every woman of our generation sought it, especially when they'd been raised dirt poor. I feared adventure. My mother had a choice between stability — a preacher — and adventure — a coal miner. She chose adventure and regretted it, because she married a philanderer. When hearts get wrapped up in security, there can only be hurt." She sighed. "But adventure." She let the word hang in the air as the fleeting regret it was.

Floyd put his hand over hers. "I'm not afraid of your solid."

She turned her head to look at his life-worn but comfortable face. She could get used to looking at that across the kitchen table every morning. There was something untamable still there, but there was also peace. "It's your nature to roam," she said.

"Maybe," he said. "But I don't see a bridle in your hands."

Sephie realized no woman could ever own this man. It was clear to her that he had been roped and bridled before, but the bit cut deep.

"I'd always come home to your solid," he said.

"Ahem." The server politely avoided looking at them, concentrating on the placement of the cups of soup she had brought.

Sephie removed her hand from Floyd's and leaned over her soup. The fragrant aroma made her stomach growl.

"I forgot to ask," the server said, "if you wanted baked potato or sweet potato fries? We also have something new — what the owner calls tater tot fries. They're made inhouse."

"Sounds different. I'll take those," Floyd said.

"Sweet potato fries," Sephie said, plunging her spoon into the cheese-covered bread. Once she had swallowed a mouthful, she realized that she was so hungry she probably could eat everything on the menu. She applied her efforts to the soup and then to the rest of the meal when it came, which was mostly spent in idle comments about the food.

When Floyd paid the check, he asked the server, "Mind if we leave through the back?"

She looked surprised but didn't question the request. She only said, "Sure. I'll show you out."

Unnoticed, they slipped past the kitchen and the offices

and out the door to the alley behind. Floyd handed the young woman an extra ten as she closed the door.

"Muggy," Floyd said.

"Feels like back home," the old woman answered.

"No breeze," he commented. "There's always a wind."

"Nature's pause."

"Maybe."

As Floyd put his arm around her, Sephie sensed an unease. She glanced up at his face, only to find his jaw clenched as they passed a decorative street lamp from the pocket park next to the restaurant. He also quickened his pace slightly, urging her back to the little house and safety.

Chapter 56

Day 17: The little house, Wednesday morning

The rich aromas of coffee and bacon drew Sephie into the kitchen. At the stove, Floyd cracked eggs into a pan sizzling with pats of melting butter. B.D. was laying the table for six, having squeezed in two folding chairs for the extra places. Laughter, spilling in from the living room, added a new music to the little house.

"Well, now. That's a sight for these old eyes to see. Menfolk in the kitchen and not breaking anything."

"Don't be such a sexist, Miz Sephie," B.D. said. "Y'all know we're both expert cooks."

"That you are." She looked over what was on the stove. "If you've woke me up, I'd have made a batch of biscuits."

"You needed your rest," Floyd said. "Toast'll do. Oops. Better check on it." He opened the oven door, then got a potholder and pulled out a baking sheet of toasted bread smothered in butter. "Grab me a plate, will you? This is hot."

Sephie picked up one from the table and put it on the counter where Floyd slid the buttery goodness onto it. The old woman put the plate back on the table while he put the hot pan in the sink. She went to a cabinet and retrieved another plate.

"Better call the girls," the old man said, dishing up bacon and then eggs onto two other plates he'd pulled from the same cabinet.

"I'll do it," B.D. said, and vanished into the living room.

Sephie found places for the food and then got herself a cup of coffee. She sipped it, expecting it to be Floyd's chewable version. To her delight, it wasn't.

"I made a pot for myself earlier," he said. "I figured everybody else didn't need to be so wired."

"Much appreciated," she said, taking another sip before settling herself into a chair.

When Yolanda entered the room with Mandy and Laura, she looked like the radiant young woman Sephie had first met on Saturday. She looked rested and happy. As they all settled down, the old woman gazed around the table. She wanted to hold that peaceful moment in her mind, to keep it alive to warm the coming days. Laura and Yolanda were giggling like old school friends. Mandy watched, enjoying the banter between them. B.D. gave them a smile before reaching to fill his plate. And Floyd, beside her, observed Yolanda like a protective wolf, vigilant but allowing a smile to escape. He reached for Sephie's hand. The movement drew Mandy's attention. She took Laura's hand and she in turn took Yolanda's. Mandy and Floyd each offered their hands to B.D., and Sephie reached for Yolanda's.

"Could you offer a blessing?" Mandy asked her great-aunt.

Sephie thought a moment, knowing her words wouldn't hold a candle to Agnesia's grace. She took a deep breath and reached into her heart. "We ask a blessing on this food and the hands that made it. We ask that it nourish our bodies and our spirits. May it knit our hearts closer as family. Amen."

Yolanda and Floyd echoed the Amen while Laura and Mandy added "So mote it be."

Food was passed, plate by plate, with only a run to the fridge for apricot jam to break the rhythm. B.D. was teased for taking so much bacon, and Yolanda was warned about the salt. Compliments on the food were passed along with the salt and pepper, and plans were made for the day. The only real schedule was B.D.'s rehearsal at the university in the afternoon and then the one with the guitarist at night. And, of course, Sephie had herbs to make into medicines.

Near the end of the meal, Yolanda's blood pressure monitor buzzed. Sephie caught a glance at the numbers before the young woman looked at it. The numbers were high but not alarming, no more than the old woman's had been before her doctor had changed her medication. Yolanda merely glanced and ignored the reading.

"Let's clear up all this," Mandy said and started carrying plates to the sink, where she rinsed them.

Laura followed with more and put the rinsed plates into the dishwasher. B.D. brought the rest and the silverware. Sephie took the empty serving plates and piled a few cups on them.

Floyd stood and asked Yolanda, "Are you staying here for a while or going over to the shop?"

"To the shop," she said. "There's people to see and things to do."

He smiled and caught Sephie's eye. "Care to take a morning walk along the greenway?"

It sounded pleasant, so the old woman nodded even though an old practical voice told her not to expect such mornings like this to be repeated. They walked in silence out the door and, across the street. Carefully, they made their way down to the cottonwoods. Light glinted off the quietly flowing water, making Sephie realize that these moments with Floyd were like islands of calm in churning seas. She was going to take his advice and grab them while she could. Bird song added a soundtrack to the scene, reminding her of her cabin beside the creek when she watched the swallowtails. The same serenity filled her, and without the spiked lemonade she always drank. She'd not be able to make it up and down that mountain for much longer. Her aging bones and muscles would soon stop her. But here in the flatland, though it was still a labor to walk back up to the road, it was easier. She looked at Floyd who, to her surprise, was studying her.

He slipped his arm around her and then very purposely kissed her, folding her completely against his chest, wrapping his other arm around her snugly.

They lingered a long time as Sephie realized that perhaps he was right after all, and that not all of her parts didn't work. Reluctantly, she moved away to look at his dark eyes.

Floyd straightened a bit, releasing her but not letting her go entirely, resting his hands on her shoulders. "We're going to be living on top of each other for a while."

She waited, not knowing where he was heading.

"It won't be the normal progression of things."

Again, she waited, becoming more confused. Suddenly she needed clarification. "Normal?"

"Dinners, dances, going to church, meeting the families."

She chuckled. "You mean courting? I think we've done most of those things." Then she asked, fully realizing what he was saying, "Are we courting?"

"I just don't want things to get uncomfortable. I don't want you thinking there'll be wanderings in the middle of the night."

Her laugh this time was hearty. "What makes you think I'd let you?" Then she added impishly. "I do have a lock on my door."

Floyd laughed, relaxing. "I didn't want— I thought— some women expect— or would think—"

"Lordy, Floyd. We're not teenagers. Besides we've got work to do."

He pulled her into a hug and kissed the top of her head. Releasing her, he said, "Let's go find out what else weird has happened in this town."

"Hush your mouth!"

Chapter 57

Day 18: North Star, Thursday midafternoon

"I've been tired all the time," Sephie, pausing in the doorway separating the shop and the back room, heard a young woman say to her friend as they looked over the display of tinctures. Behind them, toward the front of the store, an elderly woman ran her fingers over the names of incense.

"It's because you're not sleeping," the young woman's friend said.

"I get to sleep well enough. I'm just so restless and drained. And the dreams."

That statement drew the older woman's attention, causing her to step closer but not interfere.

Bringing in a half dozen little plastic bags with handwritten labels, Sephie said, "You might try some of this chamomile tea. Mix it with some mint."

Laura had already pulled a little bag of mint tea and offered it to the woman as Sephie handed her a bag of her own. Laura then took the rest of the bags to the little table of herbal teas.

The sleep-deprived woman held the bag up to scrutinize the contents. "It's just little dried flowers."

"That's what chamomile is. A lovely little wildflower with medicinal properties. Put about a tablespoon in a tea diffuser — half mint and half chamomile. Put it into a cup and pour hot water over it. Let it steep a couple of minutes."

"It's delicious," Yolanda said, coming in from having gone to the bathroom to take command of Sephie's rocker and put her feet up again. From beside the rocker, she picked up a partially filled paper bowl and a bundle of herbs she was stripping leaves from. She resumed her actions. "I have a cup every night before bed."

"Safe enough for a pregnant woman," Laura said.

"Try it," the woman's friend said, causing the sleep-deprived one to shrug and head to the counter to pay for her purchase.

When they had left the shop, the older customer stepped closer to the counter. "It's a *nattmara* or maybe a *deattan*," she said to Laura. "But these young people don't want to hear about the old ways."

Sephie joined them at the counter, but moved slightly to make sure that Yolanda could see everyone clearly. "Tell me about the *nattmara* and the other creature," she prompted. "They cause nightmares?"

"Yes. They visited me once or twice when I was a girl. My old nana told me about them. They ride you. They sit on your chest and suck your good dreams out. The *deattan* is a witch that can shapeshift into an animal but mostly a big black bird. Some people wake up with claw marks on their chests from them perching there all night."

"How do you get rid of them?"

The customer thought a moment as if sifting through as many years of lore and living as Sephie herself had. "There was an old charm. It had something to do with making them swim through the whole world — some impossible task — before they could come into the house."

Sephie nodded. "If you remember the whole charm, will you come in again and tell us, so we can help other people?"

"Ya. I will."

"Now, what can I help you find?" Laura said.

"Oh, I just came in to get some sweet-smelling incense for my bathroom. I don't know what my husband's been eating but — uff da! — you can't go in there after."

Laura laughed and guided the woman back to the incense display.

Sephie turned to Yolanda. "I can see why you didn't want to stay cooped up next door." She moved toward the back room. "I think I need a sit down. But before I do, you want some of that hibiscus tea Laura got? It has such a pretty color."

"Yes, please. It's quicker if you just heat the water in the microwave with the tea bag. You can do more than more cup. Have one yourself."

"Honey, my blood pressure is low enough. I have to be careful with that. But it sure is tasty."

"There's rosehips or green tea."

"I forgot about green tea. It might help my achy body."

She patted Yolanda on the shoulder as she headed into the back room. Within a few minutes, she was back in the shop with tea. She passed a cup to Yolanda and took a seat in a folding chair. The wave of customers had subsided for a moment and they were alone.

"So, now we add *nattmara* and the other creature to our list of odd occurrences," Sephie said.

"It could just be that people come tell us odd happenings because we're a metaphysical store and they feel we might believe anything," Laura said.

"They're coming for help, though. It isn't just to share gossip," Sephie reminded.

"The way the woman pronounced *nattmara,* it sounds Scandinavian. Could you look that up on your phone or i-whatever and find out?"

"Good idea!" Laura reached for the shelf behind her and picked up her tablet. After a couple of minutes, she said, "*Nattmara* is Norwegian, but there are all sorts of forms of it throughout Scandinavia. What was the other one?"

"Maybe there's a reference in what you found about the *nattmara,*" Yolanda offered.

"There is! It's *deattan*. It's Sami. Who are the Sami?"

Laura wondered. She clicked some more on the tablet. "Oh, here it is. They're indigenous people from the northernmost parts of Scandinavia and a bit of Russia. They're the Lapps. The reindeer people." She scrolled down some more and frowned. "They've been victimized by almost every government where they've lived, like native people in this country." She searched some more. "Oh, these are the people who *yoik*. Wasn't that what B.D. called that singing he heard Ole do?"

"Sure was," Sephie said, then shook her head. "So, that's what passes for a set of Britannica for you kids now? Instant knowledge."

"Well, you still have to look at where you get your information and double check it. This source looks legit. It's from a university."

"You suppose the tablet can tell us how to get rid of a *nattmara* or a *deattan*?"

She shook her head. "I looked."

Sephie stretched out her legs as she leaned back in her chair. "What would make all of these things appear at the same time? From several different cultures?"

"They only seem to be Scandinavian," Yolanda remarked.

Laura put down the tablet and started counting on her fingers. "There are the Finnmen from Finland. The *draugr* from Norway that B.D. told us about. Now the *nattmara,* also from Norway."

"That newspaper article said something about big black birds hunkered down in one of the trees. Was that a *draugr* or a *deattan* from the Sami?"

"And then there was the owl," Yolanda said.

"What owl?" Laura asked at the same time Sephie also asked, "Who told you about the owl?"

"Grandfather," Yolanda answered. "While I was in the hospital. He was so worried I'd die or the baby. . . ."

"Shhhh. Take that thought out of the law," Laura said.

Sephie cast her an odd look.

“It works just like ‘Hush your mouth,’ or ‘Bite your tongue.’” Laura replied.

Nodding, Sephie said, “Just so.” And then continued, “Owls as omens appear in many different cultures. So, we aren’t restricted to Scandinavia.”

“And then there’s the energy vampire,” Laura added, “which could be from any tradition, except Scandinavia. There are no vampires there. But we know who that is, and he’s Cuban.” Once more she searched her tablet. “There are real vampire bats in Cuba. Maybe he was bitten.”

Sephie laughed. “Energy vampires aren’t made. They just are. Just like emotional vampires.”

“Yeah like those needy friends who just suck you dry,” Yolanda said.

Sephie was silent, pondering all of the incidents they’d just recounted. Then she remembered one more. “And there was something else.” She waited, reluctant to introduce it into the mix.

“What was it?” Laura finally asked.

“Something.” The old woman shook her head. “I don’t know what it was.”

“Where? When?” Laura prodded.

“In the alley. When Yolanda came home.”

“When you and Grandpa went on your first date?” Yolanda asked.

Sephie gave her a cautioning look. “It was dinner. But, yes, that night. We both felt something out there.”

“And it wasn’t Rodolfo?”

She shook her head. “I didn’t feel a drain.” Then she added. “But it wasn’t good. Whatever it was.”

“So, an unknown from an unknown source,” Laura said. “And why would Rodolfo target you anyway and not anyone else?”

The old woman shrugged. “Maybe it’s like a wolf picking off the stragglers, the very young, the weak, the old.”

Yolanda stopped stripping the herbs she was working on. "You said something before. What would draw all of these creatures here? Now? Do you think someone is deliberately conjuring these beings?"

"Well, they're not demons. Maybe critters we don't want to be around, but not necessarily evil or life threatening."

"Except for the Finnmen," Laura interjected.

"True," Sephie said, "but they act to protect their fishing rights and they saved the fisherman. If someone called them, then they were only doing what was in their nature. The person who conjured them would be the evil person."

"Who'd have the power to do that?" Yolanda asked. "And why would they do it?"

"Do what?" Mandy asked, startling all three women. She had come in from the back room, followed by B.D. and Floyd.

Sephie twisted her head up to look at her great-niece. "Did you get everything rearranged?"

B.D.'s energy was popping, making him pace around the shop. "Bill had us moving tables and one of the heavy booths so Cal, the guitarist, and I had a place to perform tonight. That booth took the four of us. Cal brought his practice amp, which should be just loud enough to play over talking, and a couple of good mics. Are you coming tonight?"

Floyd had come to stand beside Sephie, placing a hand on her shoulder. She glanced up at him before replying. "I know it'll be great, but I'm going to stay in with Yolanda. You'll be playing there a lot. We'll all come see you tomorrow night at the university. Yolanda's blood pressure is coming down, so I think we can all have a night out."

"We're coming tonight," Mandy said. "We wouldn't miss it for the world!"

"I know you," Laura teased. "You're just hoping you can make that act a trio sometime."

“We talked about that,” B.D. said. “Mandy and I just need to work up a set, just the two of us.”

As they continued to discuss B.D.’s first gig at The Watering Hole, Sephie reached to touch Floyd’s hand. She hoped Yolanda would indeed be able to go out on Friday. Her numbers were still high but had begun to drop a few points every day since she’d been with them all, doing useful things and making attempts at being normal. The gig at Bill’s restaurant would be fun, but B.D. had been really nervous about performing a number from a musical at the university. He’d never commented much about the rehearsals, tipping off Sephie that they had been a lot more stressful than singing with Cal or even Mandy would be. Tonight, B.D. would make his debut with rowdy friends, and she and Floyd would make Yolanda feel as though she wasn’t missing out. It was also the night Wes had more time to talk, and he’d be calling later.

Chapter 58

Day 18: The little house, Thursday evening

The kitchen was quiet, illuminated only by the light in the fume hood over the stove. Sephie and Floyd sat at the table, watching the night shadows creep over the alley through the screen door. They'd fled into the kitchen when Wes had called, to give Yolanda some privacy. Floyd had taken her hand, without a word, as they sat in the silence, content, facing the door.

Sephie found his touches foreign but tender. It wasn't something she'd experienced in her long marriage. Her husband was not a demonstrative man; her family claimed it was his cold German ancestry. But over the years, she had met a few rowdy Germans, so it may have just been his family that was so restrained. Still, Floyd's casual touches that seemed like touchstones for luck or as a means of reassuring him she was there or that he was there for her — she couldn't figure out which — were welcome though unfamiliar.

A dull mechanical hum in the distance broke the silence as *Ripple* came on the coattails of that notification. Picking up her phone from the table, Sephie answered.

"Aunt Sephie," Mandy said loudly over the restaurant commotion in the background. "Close the windows. They're spraying. Bill is hopping mad because the city didn't warn him in time. He's rushing people off the patio. It's bedlam here. Shut the windows, if you don't want to get gassed." Without waiting for her aunt to reply, she ended the call.

"Mandy says close the windows," the old woman said. "Something about spraying."

Floyd rose, replying, "Mosquitoes. I'll take the living room and here."

"I'll do the rest," she said, rushing into the bathroom to crank the window closed over the tub. Then she closed the single window in each of the bedrooms. Coming back into the kitchen, she saw Floyd shut the wooden back door. He pressed closer to the window panes in that door and waved Sephie over. As the noise of the truck sprayer got louder, she crowded in next to him to see a figure in a long dark coat and hat at the back door of the shop. It paused, hearing the truck approach, and fled down the couple of steps to cross to the gate. It opened it as the truck passed, managing to turn its head as it got the full brunt of the insect spray. A fit of coughing followed with some gagging and upchucking in the dirt alley as the figure headed toward the Watering Hole.

"Think that's Rodolfo?" Sephie asked.

"Don't know, but he was up to no good next door."

"We should go take a look." Sephie reached for the door handle.

Floyd put his hand firmly on the door frame, blocking her attempt to go out. "It can wait. You don't want to be going out there in that. Nobody in their right mind is going to be out there after the sprayer for a long time. We'll call Mandy and tell her to check out the back when they come home. And then we can smudge tomorrow morning."

Resigned to not being able to do anything, Sephie went back to her chair by the table. "Well, maybe we should just stop racking our brains about all these strange creatures and incidents and let Karma deal with it. That sure happened tonight."

Floyd thought about that. "And it might just kick things up a bit. People don't always understand that Karma is because of what they've done. Some seem to still want to blame someone else."

She nodded and then remembered the conversation earlier in the shop. "Could someone be consciously calling up all these beings to plague the town?"

He shrugged. "It's possible. But why? And why only the Scandinavian spirits? And the energy vampire is an odd addition."

"Good question."

Chapter 59

Day 19: Erickson Concert Hall, Friday evening

Sephie picked up the program that she had opened and draped over the velvet seat when she had accompanied Yolanda to the ladies' room before intermission. These last weeks of her pregnancy had the young woman hopping up and down to the bathroom. Sephie had left with the young woman, grabbing her arm as if she were assisting the old woman but in truth, just helping her save face because of the commotion it caused for her to get up while the show was still going on. B.D. had gotten them seats all together in a row, but when they sat down Sephie had been placed on the end next to Floyd because the girls all wanted to sit together and quietly comment on the show.

As Sephie now reclaimed her seat, she realized they should have put Yolanda on the end. After all, her own old bladder didn't have the demands a young woman's had, with a baby that was using it as a trampoline. Once more, Sephie paged through the acts of the showcase. It consisted of what they called cuttings from four different musicals. The first one had songs from *H.M.S. Pinafore* that the high school summer theater group had been working on. The second one had songs from *The Music Man* that the program said were performed by college freshmen in the theater and music departments. The second half would have songs from *Working* and *Big River,* that were done by older students, faculty, and community people like B.D.

Behind her, Sephie heard someone say that it was the first time the university had included high school students and the community before. The first part of the program was good, surprising her a bit with the vocal talent of these young people. There had also been bits of dialogue to set up some of the songs and some set pieces. The program notes about the next musical said that it had been based on a book written by Studs Turkel, a Chicago radio personality, who was known for his interviews of ordinary people. *Big River* was a rendering of Huckleberry Finn by country singer Roger Miller.

The lights came down, and Sephie settled in. As the music and lives of the characters of *Working* unfolded, the old woman understood why they had added faculty and community voices. Only people with maturity could make "The Mason," "Cleanin' Women," and "Mill Worker" real. These older voices, some from people in their 50s and 60s, brought a depth of life and feeling that no twenty-something could.

Sephie found herself wiping away tears as these songs were presented. Floyd noticed and passed her his folded white handkerchief. She accepted it without comment, dabbing the corners of her eyes, glad she didn't wear much makeup anymore.

Big River's songs began with the funny songs, "Do Ya Wanna Go to Heaven" and "Guv'ment." B.D. made his debut as the slave character, Jim, barefoot, dressed in overalls and a white shirt, along with the Huck Finn character with the song, *Muddy Water*, an upbeat tune.

Sephie whispered to Floyd, "He didn't tell us he was doing more than one song."

Huck Finn sang "Waitin' for the Light to Shine" with a gospel choral background. The director had slipped in B.D. to help with that one, too.

But it was the final song, "Free at Last," when B.D. stepped out from behind flimsy set-constructed bars and was joined by the entire cast as backup gospel singers that brought open tears to not only Sephie but everyone in the audience. B.D. worked the song, building it like a country preacher to a powerfully felt conclusion, giving every bit of his soul. It would have had people in the New Life Church of John the Baptist shouting, speaking in tongues, and dancing in the aisles. But these North Dakota Scandinavian immigrants were a reserved people. They may have been smiling or surreptitiously wiping away tears, but they wouldn't let their neighbors see. Sephie wasn't so restrained. She was bawling like a baby and feeling good about having those emotions. Floyd put his arm around the old woman, causing her to glance up at him in the dim light. She noticed a tear leave the corner of his eye.

The lights went down and the applause was deafening. Despite that Scandianvian reserve, the entire audience was on its feet clapping. Sephie herself struggled to her feet to add her own accolades. She was sure now that the university had its claws well hooked into B.D., and it would be hard having to drag him back home to Tennessee or even Louisiana. She felt better about his using his musical skills here than with the theater group. If Rodolfo wasn't involved, that would have been another good outlet for him, though she didn't know if he could act or just how many musicals they did each year. As she thought about that young man being close to the energy vampire, she felt dread deep in the pit of her stomach. She sat down as the director of the theater department stepped on stage to address the audience. Sephie was glad for the distraction from her thoughts.

"Good evening. As some of you may know, I'm John Benson, the dean of the theater department here at the university. This summer we're working on musicals with the music department and have been privileged to work with some of the best young talent in the Northern Plains. When I was a young high school drama teacher here in Riverbend, I accompanied a group of students to an international choir contest in Toronto. Some of my drama students were also choir members, and I wanted to support them as a chaperon. When we got to the hotel, the kids mingled with other students from all over the

United States and Canada. I overheard one student in his huddle of choir members from his school ask where our students were from. When they told the group Riverbend, North Dakota, the young man looked crestfallen and said to his bandmates, 'We might as well go home. North Dakota is the Choral Capital of America.'"

He went on to talk about the students and the program and even thanked B.D. personally. When he invited everyone back for the full productions later in the year, everyone applauded and started to leave. It took a little while for Sephie and the others to make it out of the auditorium and into the hall. They waited while Yolanda went to the bathroom yet another time. By the time she had rejoined them, B.D. was there, dressed in jeans and a t-shirt.

Sephie looked down and saw his shod feet. "I see you found your shoes," she teased.

He laughed. Then asked, like a little kid, "What'd you think?"

Sephie pursed her lips together. "Passable," she said, making B.D.'s jaw drop in shock.

"Don't you believe that," Floyd said. "I caught her crying."

"Bawling like a baby," Sephie admitted and hugged the young man tightly. "It was wonderful. This is what you should be doing." She pulled away. "You moved people. Even this reserved lot."

As she released him, an older couple came up and shook B.D.'s hand. "Wonderful performance, young man," the man said. His wife just beamed at him as if she were greeting Neil Diamond or Tom Jones. She grabbed his hand, too, and shook it repeatedly.

The couple was pushed aside by a young blonde woman in a very short dress, who touched B.D.'s arm with both of her hands, covering it with small strokes. "You were great," she said. "I wish I could sing. You're amazing."

A brunette joined the blonde. “Good show,” she said, and dragged the blonde away, who was now giggling. A movement underneath the short skirt caught Sephie’s eye. The slight glimpse of a tail much like that of a cow twitched out and then back under cover.

Sephie’s eyes widened. “Did you see that?” she asked quietly.

B.D. swallowed hard. “What was that?”

“I think she was a *huldre*,” Laura said in some awe but not fear.

B.D. snapped his head around to look back into the crowd. “Isn’t a *huldre* some kind of seductress?”

Laura, tittering a little, took his arm and looked at Mandy, who took his other. “We’ll protect you,” Laura assured him. “My grandmother said they’re harmless. They’re just looking for an eligible bachelor.” She grinned. “Besides, she really needs to work on her seduction technique. Very junior high.”

Chapter 60

Day 20: Sons of Norway, Saturday evening

The petite blonde woman walked across the stage carrying her guitar. She wore a black heavily-embroidered skirt, a white blouse, and a red embroidered vest, with black shoes adorned with buckles. Around her waist was a silver belt from which hung a black bag, also embroidered, with a silver clasp. She took a seat on a folding chair between two others before a microphone stand with a vocal mic and one for her guitar. Two other microphone stands stood in front of the other chairs.

Sephie, Floyd, and B.D. had found seats in the back. Since Bella Anderson's show at the Sons of Norway hall had been mostly sold out, they were lucky to get tickets. Sephie figured Ole had somehow smoothed the way for that purchase.

As Bella adjusted the strap on her guitar and then the mic, she spoke to the audience. "It's nice to be back at the Sons of Norway again. It's been a while. I think it was two years ago."

She fished out a guitar pick from the embroidered bag around her waist and ran it over the strings. "Thank you so much for inviting me back to farm country." She offered an impish grin. "Did you hear about the Norwegian farmer who loved his wife so much. . . ." She paused and the audience finished for her.

Sephie couldn't make it out and asked Floyd, who was chuckling. "What was that?"

"'He almost told her.'"

She pulled her brows together in confusion and then

thought about last night's reserved audience. Her delayed laugh rang out after the audience had quieted.

"Oh, we have a foreigner in our midst," Bella said. "Welcome. Try not to enjoy yourself too much."

The audience offered muffled titters at her remark.

"I usually do an educational program when I perform at Sons of Norway. Sometimes I'm asked to do Bronze Age songs or older ones. Yes, there are even Iron Age songs passed down. I get a lot of calls to do Viking programs because television has made them so popular, though thoroughly wrong and very romanticized. But tonight, I'll bring you a mix of some of the Viking songs and women's songs and then just a couple of instrumental dance numbers. I brought some friends along with me."

At that, an older man with a fiddle and a young man with a round frame drum joined her.

"To start, this is a fun one about *nisse*, helper elves."

She broke into a sprightly tune sung in Norwegian. Sephie didn't understand a word, but many in the audience, mostly people her own age, obviously did. For Sephie, the tune was enough to get her toe tapping, and Bella's voice was a delight to listen to.

The singer did a few more tunes and then paused to talk with the audience again. "I mentioned Vikings before. Their textiles are interesting and not just for the intricate embroidery like on the *bunad* I'm wearing." She gestured at her costume. "These were made of flax because it can be worked into finer woven cloth. Recently, researchers discovered that sometimes flax and hemp were woven together for wall hangings. And hemp could be woven coarser into sailcloth. However, early Viking sails were made of wool. How many sheep do you think it would take to make all the sails for a small Viking boat? Call out your guesses."

"Fifty," someone said.

Another said, "A hundred."

After a few more guesses, Bella laughed. "You're way off. It took 700 sheep to make the sails for a small ship. For those big ships that went up the Danube or for Leif Erickson's ship that left Iceland for the New World, it took over 2000 sheep. That's a lot of spinning that the women did. Now, here's a spinning song."

The evening progressed with other songs that Sephie and her group couldn't understand, though they all enjoyed. Bella even did a song about a *huldre* that B.D. was desperate to get a translation of since his weird encounter the night before.

When the program was over, B.D. went in search of Bella Anderson, leaving Floyd and Sephie as they lingered at the refreshment tables in the back. Older women in *bunads* served everyone from trays of wafer-like cookies in various shapes. Under Floyd's guidance, Sephie took two rolled items and a flat sweet on a paper plate. One, shaped into a cone, was a crisp cookie with a delicate design pressed into it, similar to the one on the flatter cookie. The other rolled thing looked like a flour tortilla.

Moving away from the refreshments, Sephie asked, "So, what's on my plate?"

He pointed to the tortilla-like thing. "That's *lefse*. It's a thin potato pancake with sugar on it."

Sephie took a bite. She wasn't impressed. "Not much to it, huh?"

He chuckled. "I guess it's better than *lutefisk*."

"I like your fry bread better."

He pointed to the other two sweets. "The cone is *rumkake* and the other is a *rosette*."

"The *rumkake* should be filled with something, shouldn't it?"

Floyd shook his head. "It's just a different cookie. Those are rolled out with a decorated rolling pin, cut, and baked. The *rosettes* are made by dipping a decorated iron in batter and deep frying it. Taste them. They're not bad."

Sephie obliged. "I still think the *rumkake* would benefit from a vanilla or lemon filling."

"That's your English background talking," he said.

"What's this *lutefisk*? Is it awful?"

"Oh, it can be," he said. "Funny thing about tradition. It's fish, usually cod, that has been preserved with lye. It was how early immigrants put food by for the winter. People got used to eating it even when it went off flavor."

"Oh, lordy, no!"

He nodded. "Now that people don't need to preserve fish that way, people still eat it when it's rank because that's tradition. My people had the sense not to keep eating bad dried buffalo."

Sephie burst out laughing, causing heads to turn. Then she leaned closer to Floyd and whispered, "I wonder if we'll be asked to leave."

Taking her empty paper plate and her hand, Floyd found a waste container, dumped the plate there, and led Sephie out of the hall into the night.

Outside the Sons of Norway hall, located in the northern section of Riverbend on a less densely populated street, Floyd turned her toward a plaque on the front of the long modern building. The hall wasn't old or even made of brick, but looked like any bigger ranch style home in any suburb. The plaque, protected behind glass, had hand-painted, stylized flowers around the inscription done in careful calligraphy. It told how the hall, at a location closer to downtown, had been destroyed by the flood. With the help of members, the historical papers and art had been moved to safety and had found a new location at the generosity of a member, who had donated his home to the Sons of Norway. He had unfortunately died after the flood but had made provisions in his will.

"Well, that was a generous thing to do," Sephie said. Automatically, her hand reached to touch the glass of the decorations around the plaque. "That's so pretty."

"It's called *rosemaling*," Floyd said.

Sephie smiled up at him. "You know a lot about these people. I expected Laura to fill me in on more since she was born here."

Outside the hall near the plaque, the members had constructed a wooden bench. Floyd guided her to it so they could sit while waiting for B.D. Putting his arm around the back of the bench to rest his hand on her shoulder, he said, "I think Laura struggles with her heritage and her family's rejection. She hasn't grown into the fact that you can own one and not the other."

Stretching their legs out before them, they sat in silence for a bit, enjoying the night breeze and looking out at the few shops and homes illuminated by the flood lights around the hall and the street lamps farther down the road. A movement down the street caught Sephie's eye. A dark figure in a long coat and a hat strode across the road right under the street lamp. The old woman elbowed Floyd gently. "Look," she said.

The figure continued toward them on the other side of the street, but he didn't seem to notice them. He was looking at something in his hand. Reaching a shop door, he paused, retrieved a key from his pocket, applied it to the door, and entered.

"Think that's Missy and Rodolfo's store?"

"Probably."

"What'd he have in his hand?"

"Couldn't tell."

"Was it a phone? But it didn't light up like mine does."

"No, it was bigger from what I could see and odd shaped." Floyd lifted his hand and leaned back behind Sephie to look at his watch. "It's nine-thirty. I wonder where he's been wandering."

Removing his arm from the bench, Floyd fished his own phone from his shirt pocket. After a few maneuvers, he had Yolanda on the line. "How are you feeling?" He paused, returning his arm around Sephie. "We're having a great time. Sephie got a full introduction into Norwegian life. But some of it will need translating." Another pause. "Is Mandy around?" A longer pause, and he gave Sephie a little squeeze as if she knew what he was up to on the phone. "Mandy, have you seen anyone wandering around the back of the shop tonight?" He attempted to say something more, but evidently Mandy was going on about something. "I'm sure the smudging we did yesterday morning is working. And we never found anything out of the ordinary back there anyway." He waited politely again. "We'll be home soon, if we can drag B.D. away from such a good song source. I think he's worried about that *huldre* we saw last night. Yes, good night."

"Mandy giving you hell?" Sephie asked.

"She's being protective," Floyd said, pocketing the phone. "I think she tries too much sometimes. She forgets that even men can't be perfect, and that being her unique gender puts her in a different realm."

"Taking on the man's role and the woman's?" Sephie asked.

"It's more than that, and she hasn't come to that realization yet. Native people understand there are more than two genders, and they aren't always how even the gay community defines them. It's something else. Unfortunately, a lot of that was lost as we became Christianized and acculturated. There are no elders left who remember those ways to teach the young."

"Mandy once told me years ago when she first came out," Sephie said, "that she wished she had a butch mentor to help her navigate her identity. She said that it had happened years before she was born in the 40s and 50s. After the 60s and the press for women's rights, even what she called butch-femme relationships like hers with Laura were pushed underground because it reminded those feminists so much of patriarchy." The old woman sighed. "We are all victims of the eras we're born in."

"So much knowledge gets lost," Floyd said and then added. "I wish I could help her."

Sephie, moved by his honesty, reached her hand to touch the side of his worn face, pulled him closer to her, and kissed him soundly. When he raised his head, he smiled and leaned closer.

Sephie put her hand on his chest to stop him as she heard B.D.'s voice.

"Hey, quit making out for everyone in God's country to see."

Floyd looked over his shoulder behind him. "Respect your elders, son."

Sephie pushed herself off the bench. "Did you get the information you wanted?"

"Sure did. She gave me a translation of one of her songs and pointed me toward a recording that I bought so I can learn the melody. And I got all the dope on *huldre* and sort of how to avoid them. Did you know they lose those tails if they marry in the church? And can really be good wives. Kinda like the stories of mermaids. But they'll hound you to death if you spurn them. Worse than a rejected rock star groupie."

"Let's go find my truck," Floyd said, heading up the street, taking Sephie's arm. "B.D., take her arm. She needs some steadying."

Sephie started to protest, her independence being questioned. But the seriousness of Floyd's face stopped her tongue. She accepted B.D.'s arm, too, and they walked three abreast up the street. As they walked, Floyd quietly sang something in his own language. It was hypnotic, causing B.D. to pick up the melody and hum along. They soon passed Missy and Rodolfo's used furniture shop.

Sephie, protected on both sides, gawked as much as she could at the darkened store front across the street. It looked junked up like some thrift stores did, with little to see through the ample windows, just angles of furniture pieces barely illuminated by a single light in the back. That wouldn't be enough to discourage burglaries, but there might be other wards on the property. Sephie couldn't pick up much except general darkness, not anything inviting for a store wanting customers. Perhaps it was the mix of the latent energies in all of the furniture they'd acquired.

As she continued to survey the property, she felt as if she were being sucked into the dark there. The pull became so strong she collided against Floyd, who was on the outside of the sidewalk, and her vision began to dim.

Chapter 61

Day 20: The little house, Saturday late evening

Sephie stirred in the front seat of Floyd's truck as B.D. moved away from her to open the door.

"What was that all about?" she heard B.D. ask.

"Inside," Floyd said, moving also. "Are you back with us?"

"What?" Sephie blinked, looking around. "We're home already?" She laughed. "You get ideas after that kiss? What did you do? Pick me up off that bench and carry me to the truck?"

He frowned. "I'm a gentleman, remember." Gently guiding her over the driver's side, he said, "Watch your feet." Once she was on the ground, he said, "Stand on one foot."

"What?" she muttered.

"Humor me. Stand on one foot."

She did, but wobbled so much Floyd grabbed her arm to steady her. "Put your foot down," he instructed, then shut the door and locked his truck. Putting his arm around her, he guided her quickly inside, avoiding the kitchen, and into the living room where he eased her into the big overstuffed chair facing the couch. Squatting down next to her, he said quietly, "Look at me."

She complied, becoming more alert. "Have I got something on my face?" she asked.

"Can you stick out your tongue?"

She laughed. "Whatever for?"

"Just do it." He paused and then added, "Please."

She did so like a naughty school girl.

"Now smile."

She gave him a silly grin, moving her face closer to his.

"Raise both your arms."

"What has gotten into you?" she remarked but complied.

"What did we do with B.D. tonight?"

"We saw that Norwegian singer, Bella Anderson, at the Sons of Norway. Now will you tell me why you put me through this circus?"

He lowered his head as he still squatted beside her. Finally, taking a deep breath, he rose to his feet. "Just checking."

"For what?"

"Stroke," B.D. said, watching from a chair beside the foldout couch where Yolanda, Laura, and Mandy had piled in like a teenage slumber party. "We did that all the time with one of my aunties." He turned to Floyd. "Why'd you think she had one?"

"Missing time," he said. "Or I thought. And then her sister."

Mandy added, "Sure. Aunt Agnesia had a TIA."

"It can run in families," Floyd said.

"Agnesia is probably milking that for all it's worth, having all those church ladies running around doing her bidding," Sephie spat out.

"Do you remember anything after I caught you and Floyd making out on the bench?" B.D. blurted out, bringing them back to the matter at hand.

It caused Sephie to turn bright red and sink back into the chair cushions.

Floyd threw B.D. a warning glance, but it didn't stop the young man.

"Well, you were," he said, sticking to his ground.

Sephie caught the exchanged looks between the young women on the couch. She would have come out with all her verbal guns blazing at B.D.'s words, but she just didn't have the fight left in her. The little bitter comment about Agnesia had taken any steam she had out of her engine.

Floyd squatted again. "Do you remember going past the used furniture store?"

Sephie rubbed her forehead as if the action would massage the memories back into her brain. "Sort of. I was giving the whole place a good once over," she said. "Then I kinda got pulled into some sort of blackness." She then added a critique. "I don't know how they attract customers. That place has no appeal."

"Well, it drew *you* in," B.D. said. "Almost like a magnet. We both had ahold of you, but you slid into Floyd like you were being pulled across the street and he was blocking the way."

"Maybe you were," Laura said.

"There was something else," Sephie began, trying to bring the thought forward. "Something before, when we — that Floyd and I saw before."

"Rodolfo at the door of the store," the old man prompted.

"Yes. He had something in his hand."

"What was it?" Laura asked, leaning forward.

Floyd turned his face to her. "We couldn't make it out. It was odd-shaped but small enough to grasp by one hand."

"Was it a tool?" Laura asked. "Something magical?"

"Are you saying we're dealing with a cursed object like in some movie?" Sephie scoffed.

"I've been thinking about all these weird occurrences all happening now," Laura said. "Maybe they found something hidden in some piece of furniture."

"You know, Bella Anderson told me tonight that the old people think that the *huldre* came to America by steamer trunk."

"You mean they hid in them?" Mandy asked.

"Not in the trunks. On them. They magically hid in the rosemaling."

"That pretty decorative work?" Sephie asked.

"Yes. Somehow, they were able to step out of the paint and come alive again."

"But the paintings are of flowers and leaves."

"Magic often works in strange ways," he said.

Sephie mused. "Can't say that I've encountered anything like that. I work with herbs, and it's more art and science than magic. But contrary magic, not ordinary magic, operates here and from cultures I don't know."

"Obviously, something was done to you tonight," Laura said. "And Rodolfo is targeting your energy." She looked at Floyd and B.D. "But I don't see how he could've gotten through the protections you both put over her. You did protect her, didn't you?"

Mandy searched their faces. "She's an old woman! She's vulnerable!"

Yolanda grabbed Mandy and Laura's forearms as if to hold them back.

Floyd stiffened his back, slowly rising to his full height as he tightened his jaw and worked to keep the outrage from showing on his face.

Had Sephie the energy, she would have ripped into all of them for challenging an elder, who knew more than they did. She took a breath anyway, determined to lay into them, but Floyd put a hand on the old woman's shoulder, calming her even as he battled to keep his own anger contained.

"Of course, we did!" B.D. said, on his feet and ready to get into the fray like some school yard kid who wanted to get in his own licks. "Floyd was chanting and I helped."

In a soft voice, Yolanda asked, "Why're they targeting Sephie? Why not Mandy and Laura? They live here. The rest of us don't."

B.D. added, "You can't tell me that the rest of us can't detect magic when it's used. We all have abilities."

All faces turned to Sephie. "Why her?" Yolanda repeated.

Wondering the same thing, she met their gazes but had no answers.

Quietly, Floyd said, “She’s the matriarch.” His manner had relaxed, and he gave Sephie’s shoulder a squeeze. “Her energy, whether she does it consciously or not, covers all of you. Like a hen spreading her wings to cover all of her chicks. And she pulls me under those wings, too. I do the same. But for some reason, I’m not a threat to them, though I feel their energy against my shields.”

“It’s because they don’t understand your energy,” Yolanda said, causing all of them to stare at her. “And you’re male.” She looked at B.D. “They’re staying away from you,” she said, “because you’re the real deal.” Her attention moved to Floyd. “Same with Grandfather.”

“And we’re not?” Mandy bristled, turning to challenge Yolanda.

“Yes, you and Laura are.”

“But you don’t have the experience,” Floyd stated.

“I’m the only one here without a magical bone in my body,” Yolanda said. “I wasn’t trained. Grandmother taught me women’s ways but not the paths that Grandfather knows.”

“Yolanda,” Floyd said humbly, “I turned my back on all that — or thought I had.”

“You came back to it and found yourself again. I see that old knowledge in you, coming out more since we’ve been here this time. It’s foreign to me. I really never had an interest. I’m a modern woman, Grandfather, married to a White guy. I’m not a threat to them.”

“Thank God for that,” Sephie said.

“But you,” Yolanda focused on the old woman. “You have knowledge that goes back generations, back to the beginning of your line. Like Grandfather.” She looked at B.D. “And you have access to knowledge just as old. You just haven’t opened yourself to it all yet.” She looked back at Floyd and Sephie. “You can teach Mandy and Laura.”

“That makes so much sense,” Laura said. “But then there’s the same old question. Why?”

Silence filled the room. Then Sephie said simply, "I'm not the threat."

Chapter 62

Day 20: The little house, Saturday near midnight

Pajamas on, Sephie settled herself into her bed in the little house. The day had been too long and her weariness coupled with the pain of her arthritis was almost more than she could bear. She had downed four ibuprofens before she'd crawled under the top sheet, hoping that the pain reliever would kick in soon.

The discussion in the living room had gone on for a bit. Her pronouncement about not being a threat, though she may be a target, had produced more speculation and more questions. She had come all this way to help, not become the problem. With no answers forthcoming, they had all left it until tomorrow when hopefully they could thrash out something more concrete. Mandy was going to do more internet searches and Laura was going to call members of their community to enlist their help. B.D. was planning to call a family member to track down Papa Mamoud and get him on the phone. Yolanda was settled in for a good night's sleep and Floyd — he was somewhere.

She reached over to the little beside table to turn off the light when she heard a soft knock at her door. *What now?* she wondered. "What is it?"

The door opened, and Floyd stuck his head in.

"You doing a midnight ramble?" Sephie said. "If you are, I'm dead to the world."

He chuckled and entered the room, closing the door behind him. Pulling a wooden chair to the side of her bed, he said, "I wanted to check on you." He sat down. "Sounds like you're back to normal."

"You need to be looking after Yolanda, not me," Sephie chided, wanting to divert attention away from everyone's worry over her.

"I checked her blood pressure," he said. "It's holding steady. Still a little high but not enough to rush her to the ER again. She's got a few weeks yet before that baby is big enough to greet the world."

She reached a hand out to him and he took it into both of his. "I don't want that baby born into this chaos. She needs serenity."

"She'll have that back home later. The land will nurture her. It would've been good for Yolanda and for her young one, but I think my granddaughter has become too much of a city girl."

"Wes may take her to a big city."

He frowned. "That would be hard. To bring up a child without family around."

"Maybe they'll find a place near his family."

Floyd nodded. "I don't know much about them. I think they live in Wisconsin."

Sephie yawned. The ibuprofen was slowly kicking in, beginning to take the edge off her pain. For some reason, it always made her sleepy. She squeezed Floyd's hand. "You planning on camping out in that chair all night?"

He smiled. "Thinking about it."

Pulling her hand from his, she raised the sheet with her other hand, an evident invitation. "Take your boots off and turn off the light." She scooted across the bed as he did as he was told. When he lay next to her, she put her head on his shoulder and rested a hand on his chest. Though Sephie felt protected and warm against his body, she set her boundaries. "Sleep is all I can do, old man. I doubt if I'll ever remember how to do anything else."

He automatically enfolded her in his arms and kissed the top of her head. "Go to sleep, old woman. Stop your fretting."

Chapter 63

Day 21: The little house, Sunday morning

The tantalizing smell of coffee roused Sephie, but it was the thud of the mug hitting the night table that opened her eyes. Floyd stood beside her bed. She smiled and pushed herself upright, bracing her back against the headboard with her pillow. She reached for the mug, but Floyd was quicker and put it into her hand.

"You're going to make me unfit for solo company. You know that, don't you?" she said as Floyd sat down on the bed next to her.

He smelled of soap and cologne and that trace of leather that seemed to seep from him as if totally ingrained into his skin from his rodeo days.

"Think that's a bad thing?"

She and Floyd were living in a vacuum, brought together by circumstances. She wasn't a young woman out on an adventure and meeting her future love on a flight to Paris like Yolanda must have. This could only be temporary.

She shrugged. "This isn't—", she began before sipping her hot coffee, not willing to talk further about distance and eventual separation.

"It is what it is," Floyd said, glancing away briefly. "The bathroom's free. B.D. left already for the early mass. He said he wasn't singing today but wanted to spend some time in the chapel before the residents came in."

She nodded. "Any word from next door?"

"Laura called and said that some people from the

community were coming this afternoon. I think she's setting up a big meeting of the spiritual minds."

"We could use some fresh ideas."

"We need to know more about what we're dealing with. We think we may know the source, but we don't know what they're doing or even why."

Sephie frowned. "Mandy and Laura are in danger. Not me."

"I think so, too." He tightened his jaw as if to keep other words from escaping.

Sephie didn't miss that action. "What?" She pressed further. "What do you know?"

"Those young women need to know how to shield better."

"They did all right warding this house."

He nodded. "We're safe, but we're the only ones going in and out of here. There should be something a lot stronger on the shop, especially since Laura and Mandy live there. And that yard. Rodolfo shouldn't even have been able to penetrate the gate."

Sephie frowned. That was certainly true.

"Laura and Mandy are using their energy to protect you, and you and I and B.D. are protecting them. We all can't keep casting our shields over everybody," Floyd added. "Even the best B.D. and I did couldn't keep Missy and Rodolfo from getting to you."

The old woman tilted her head slightly as she raised an eyebrow. "But if you hadn't. . . ." She shook her head, leaving the rest unsaid.

Floyd frowned. "Exactly." Touching her hand, he added, "I feel their power against me, too, Sephie. Yolanda's right. We carry the old knowledge." He glanced down at their hands. "For far too long, I left what I was taught, chasing that rodeo high. I've asked for forgiveness and tried to make amends, to be of service. But my knowledge is incomplete. I don't know what you know."

Sensing more than sharing spiritual understandings in what he was saying, Sephie brought their discussion back to how to help her great-niece and her partner. "The whole community has different kinds of knowledge. Some of it is probably as old as what bits we know. Shoot, B.D.'s traditional roots are just as old and as foreign as what you know is to me. But somehow it resonates and in an odd way is the same."

Giving her hand a squeeze, he nodded. "Laura may be wiser than we're giving her credit for. Sharing knowledge may be the only way to combat this."

Drinking down the last bit of her coffee, she handed the mug back to Floyd. "Guess I better get stirring," she said, signaling for him to stand, which he did. She whipped off the covers and stood herself. "You making breakfast?"

He smiled. "Of course. Pancakes, okay?"

She patted his arm as she passed him to go to the closet. "Perfect."

Chapter 64

Day 21: North Star, Sunday early afternoon

"I didn't expect you to get here so quickly," Mandy said, opening the door of the unlit shop to three young men, the McCarthy brothers from Canada.

"We left right after Laura called," Bruce, the one carrying a guitar case, said as he walked inside. "The border crossing was quick."

"Laura sounded pretty frantic," said Bryan, the one bringing in a small case that looked like it might hold a mandolin.

The last, Alistair, with a pennywhistle stuck in his shirt pocket, grinned. "We're still not sure what you need from us."

Closing the door, Mandy said, "We'll tell you. Go on through to the back. Everyone else is here." She followed them and retook her seat beside Laura. The chairs had been arranged in a tight circle in the back room. Sephie's rearrangements had narrowed the free space a bit, but Mandy had managed to place thirteen chairs together, having participants sit almost knee to knee.

Yolanda had been restricted to the little house so that she wouldn't be affected by the energies generated in the shop. Laura had asked the *curandera,* Patricia, to bring her youngest daughter with her second baby, now six months old, to visit with Yolanda and talk about new mother joys and little inconveniences.

Mandy now looked over the community. Laura was on her right with Sephie beside her. Floyd was next to her great-aunt, with Patricia, who wore a white cotton dress with bright embroidery on the hem and a necklace of crystals, to his right. The next two seats were occupied by Bryan Pederson, affectionately called Dr. B., and his partner Daryll, who were high magicians of the Golden Dawn; both were dressed in jeans and cotton shirts. The Canadian druids filled the next three seats. On Mandy's left sat B.D. Next to him was Chris Olsen and his wife Freya, who both practiced Asatru, or Norse heathenry. Chris was a distinctive mountain of a man, tall and massively built, with long muddy-blond hair that boasted two thin, tight braids on each side of his face that were held in place by a bead with a rune carved into it. His wife, a woman with strong angular features, wore her long brunette hair in more elaborate braids; two very long but tightly plaited thin ones on each side of her face with the top part in a thick loose braid that fell from her forehead down her back. Her hair was kept in place by thin bands. The only ornamentation she had around her face was a pair of silver earrings with more runes on them.

"Thank you for coming," Mandy said.

"I apologize for the short notice," Laura added, then spewed out a rush of words. "We probably should have had a meeting at Solstice, but we really didn't know what was going on — not that we really know now — nor how bad it was going to get. And it may get worse, but we need each and every one of you and your gifts. We can't—"

Not looking at her wife, Mandy clasped Laura's wrist and the stream of words stopped. Laura took a shuddery breath, causing Sephie to put her hand on the young woman's other wrist. While maintaining a neutral expression, Mandy herself took a deep breath, smiled, and began again. "We talked to some of you at Solstice, but we didn't go into detail. If you've been reading the weekly paper or even talked to people down here, you've heard about strange sightings along the river. People seeing big bird figures, *draugrs*, *hiisi*, and *huldre*. There have been reported cat attacks where the cats seemed drugged. There was even one attack on a nun. Someone complained of a *nattmara* coming into her room while she was sleeping. And there has been one near-drowning that sounded much like the Finnmen, pulling a fisherman into the river. This may all be wild imaginings of people who think they saw something and were trying to give it a name. We know there's an energy vampire here, who has targeted my great-aunt and has attacked her on more than one occasion."

Frowns lined the faces of everyone in the circle, even the high magicians who both sat with their legs outstretched into the empty space of the circle and with their arms across their chests, absorbing and pondering. The Norse heathens sat erect with their hands on the knees of their wide-open legs as if ready to rise and do battle if called upon. Patricia had made the sign of the cross at least twice during Mandy's introduction; once at the mention of the nun and the other about Sephie. The McCarthy brothers were the only ones who took the news differently. They each sat with one leg bent with an ankle resting across a knee, while their fingers seemed to run patterns across that bent leg. Having lived these experiences, B.D. and Floyd just frowned.

During this pause, B.D. added details. "From talking with people who hold the folklore knowledge who helped identify some of these creatures," he said, "nearly all of the sightings have involved Scandinavian beings. Mostly from Norway, the Sami in their northern locations, and the Orkneys, which are in the North Sea off the coast of Scotland but share some of the same folk stories. The physical attacks (the cats and the nun) are different but could be attributed to one of those beings or a raptor or even bats. But that doesn't explain the poison in the wounds. The energy vampire, though, is an outlier and doesn't fit into this mix. This has never happened here before, I'm told. So, why now and why all of them?"

Mandy picked up the telling. "What we need today from

all of you is your help finding out exactly what this is. We can do a meditation and/or a scrying in our various ways. Then we need help protecting this shop, where Laura and I live, and the entire property outside. The energy vampire has come into the back yard."

"What about next door?" Patricia asked.

"It seems safe enough now," Mandy said, realizing that the woman was worried about her daughter and granddaughter. "But we need to put wards on the land around it."

Dr. B shifted in his seat, bringing his legs perpendicular to his chair. He leaned forward, bracing himself with his elbows on his knees. "That's a lot to do in one afternoon. Just the search for what this is could take a while, and it could get fairly exhausting. For Daryll and me to even think about doing a protection rite will take a few days for us to research and write it and then gather the proper tools." He looked over at the Norse heathens and then at Patricia. "I'm sure it will take you time to gather what you need." He smiled at the McCarthys. "The rest of us aren't like you boys, who seem to always be ready with the right music." He looked over at Floyd and everyone else on that side of the circle. "I'm sure you've exhausted all that you know, or we wouldn't be here."

"There are a few more things we can do," Floyd commented, "but we can't until we know what we're dealing with."

"Then is it possible to do this on two different days and not all at once?" Dr. B. suggested.

Mandy considered that and then nodded. "That's why we need all of your input." She finally released Laura's wrist, giving her hand a little pat. "We've been trying to shoulder all this alone. And it's been upsetting. We're trying to protect those we love."

Dr. B. offered a reassuring smile. "That's why we're here. We're here to protect those we love, too."

Alistair McCarthy interjected, "We don't want to leave

without doing some kind of protection. We probably wouldn't be able to get back down here until later in the week. But we'll at least set bardic wards on the property today after we scry. B.D., I've heard your bonny voice. Will you help us?"

Giving them a smile, he said, "Teach me. I'll sing."

"The rest of us live in town or nearby," Dr. B. said. "We can come back."

For the first time, Chris Olsen spoke, "In a way, that might be better, because we'll be adding layers and layers onto the protections. But before we leave today, we'll lay runes on the back gate and fence and on the back doors. You'll then have Druid and Asatru protections." He looked over at Floyd. "Sir, will you smudge?"

Floyd nodded. "Sage and cedar. Inside and out."

"I brought some *palo santo* to burn," Patricia said.

"I have a bit of dried rue," Sephie said.

Dr. B. clapped his hands together. "So be it. We'll have smudging, runes, and bardic protections today. Daryll and I will come back on Wednesday night and do a full rite. Mandy, Laura, we'll need your feminine energies to balance our male ones. Will you assist?"

For the first time, Laura smiled and nodded.

"Gladly," Mandy said. "We'll close the shop early and announce the change to our customers." Leaning back into her chair, Mandy said, "So, do we begin with a meditation? I have candles and mirrors and bowls for water. Whatever you prefer to scry with, if you need a tool."

There was a brief scramble for tools while the McCarthy brothers opened up their instrument cases and set a meditative tone for the scrying.

"Before we begin, and with your permission," Mandy said, "Laura and I will cast the circle and create sacred space. We have to protect ourselves as we do this work."

The directions were honored, the circle inscribed with

salt, and the protections of divinity were invoked. As Mandy and Laura took their seats again, Chris stood and in a loud and booming voice said, "Hail, Odin, god of Wisdom, grant us a bit of your knowledge for the need in this community. Open us."

Without prompting, everyone settled into the seats, closed their eyes, and took several deep breaths. And then the scrying began.

Chapter 65

Day 21: North Star, Sunday later in the afternoon

"So, what did you pick up?" Mandy asked those in the circle.

"You already know who the energy vampire is," Patricia stated.

"Yes, you know," Freya echoed.

There were nods all around the circle.

"And I think we do, too," Bruce said, seeking his brothers' agreement, and they each gave a nod.

"We'll leave that for now," Mandy said. "Anything else?"

"This has been conjured," Daryll said.

Mandy cast a glance at Sephie and Floyd. "That's what you both have been thinking?"

Before they could reply, Dr. B. said. "It's been done by an amateur. Someone who doesn't know what he or she is doing."

"I agree. But there's a female signature all over it," Chris added.

"It's not a young teenager," Daryll added. "There's reasoning behind it. A goal."

"Jealousy," Patricia offered.

"Aye, jealousy," Freya agreed.

"But the woman—" Chris shook his head. "There's a muddled read about her." He shot a look at Mandy. "But not like you," he said. "You read both energies equally. You own it, as my Freya owns her strength," he slapped a heavy hand on his partner's knee without producing a wince. "But she embraces her womanhood. This one. . . ." Again, he shook his head.

"There's no music in her," Bryan McCarthy said. He scanned the faces of all those present. "We're fully initiated Druids. We own that we are Bards, and that's where our gifts lie. We'll never be Ovates, healers, or leaders like master Druids." He smiled. "You all sing with such wondrous music. All of nature sings. But this one. . . ." He shrugged and shook his head and idly fingered his mandolin.

"We're dealing with a wounded soul," Dr. B. said. "The jealousy is deeply rooted in trauma. Mostly in her childhood. Abandonment. Rejection. She pieces things together to fit. That's why the conjuring."

"No," B.D. said. "She didn't set out to call all these beings. She found them embedded."

Freya leaned forward in her chair, twisting to face B.D. "Embedded, meaning like in runes."

B.D. snapped his own head toward Sephie and Floyd. "Rosemaling," he said. "It's in the rosemaling. Just like how the *hulde* got here in the first place."

"Wait," Sephie said. "It doesn't explain the valerian in the claw attacks on the cats."

B.D. leaned back in his chair, his idea deflated.

Suddenly, Bryan's diddling fingers flew over his mandolin into a recognizable tune. His brothers, staring at him, now recognized the tune and both said in unison, "Of course!"

Alistair turned toward the group as Bryan slowly stopped playing. "She has a bird!"

Bruce added. "She lets it out at night to feed."

"How'd you make that leap?" Laura asked.

"The tune, 'Blackbird.' It just came to me," Bryan said.

"So, she dips the bird's talons in valerian," Sephie commented.

Mandy started to chuckle, and that turned into a full belly laugh. "We've been such idiots!"

Dr. B. leaned back in his seat. "Just uninformed."

"You kept looking at each individual incident and event," Daryll added.

"Look, it took thirteen people to find the truth," Chris said.

"Now that we know, what are we going to do about it?" Patricia asked.

"Just as Dr. B. suggested. First, we'll smudge and bless," Mandy said. Looking at the McCarthy's, she added, "And you'll sing and protect." Then at the Olsen's, "And you'll put runic wards on the property."

"We can say a blessing and consult with you today," Dr. B. stated. "But we'll be back on Wednesday to do a full rite."

"So mote it be," Mandy said. "Now, let's release this circle."

Chapter 66

Day 21: The little house and the North Star, Sunday later in the afternoon

Though Mandy and Laura thought the little house didn't need anything done inside, Sephie, Floyd, and Patricia started there.

"There are innocents here," Sephie said, and she began the first pass with rue.

Both the front door and the back door had been opened to let the smoke and any negativity out. It was extremely necessary with the rue, which was very pungent. Floyd followed with a sage and cedar bundle that was highly fragrant but didn't reek as much as the rue. And Patricia followed with the sweet smelling *paolo santo*. During each pass, Patricia's daughter covered her baby's head with a thin blanket so it wouldn't breathe so much in.

While Sephie smudged, Patricia followed her, placing a line of salt over the doorstep and each window sill, adding to what was already there. As Floyd smudged, she placed tiny shards of black obsidian by each window and over each door that led outside.

After Patricia smudged, she raided the kitchen for a bowl and some spices from a drawer. Sephie asked her what she was doing as she poured a lime-scented alcohol from an elaborately-labeled bottle into the bowl. "This is Florida water. I'm sure B.D. knows it and has used it before. It acts as a medium to disperse herbs and spices because it evaporates as you sprinkle." Then she proceeded to add whole cloves and whole allspice. Taking a stick of cinnamon, she put it on the counter and hit it with a meat mallet she found on a hanger with other kitchen utensils. She scraped the crushed bits into the bowl with her hand. She held the bowl up for Sephie to see. Smiling, she said, "Now we bring the sweet blessings of hearth and home."

Patricia went into the living room and proceeded to bless it and each room. Afterwards, she poured the contents into the sink, letting the strainer hold the spices until they could be disposed of later.

"Now to the shop," she said.

Next door, they proceeded to do the same thing, working around Mandy and Laura as they talked with Dr. B. and Daryll. The hardest part for Sephie was going up the steep, narrow stairs to her niece's living quarters. It was a small attic that been refurbished into one large room with a full bathroom. Sephie remembered Mandy telling her that the little building had once been the post office, but the town had outgrown it as it began to expand. Originally, the attic was used for storage and had had a small cot up there for when the postmaster couldn't make it home during a blizzard. Laura's touches had made the space charming and as inviting as the little house.

They opened a window up there, despite keeping the air conditioner running, but made sure the unit got extra smudging and wards. Patricia put a big piece of obsidian on top of the air conditioner to collect any nasty bits that came in from the outside through the air intakes.

After closing the window, they came downstairs to do the back room and then the shop. As before, they opened the back door and the front door. The high magicians had left, and Mandy and Laura headed outside to assist Chris and Freya with their work on the back fence. It was trickier putting protections on a shop where people came and went, but Sephie, Floyd, and Patricia decided to clean the whole space to the bones, spiritually, and then put in porous wards on the front door only. Salt went down on the doorway but with it was added cornmeal and the caveat that only those who were seeking help from the negativity around them could pass. It wouldn't let someone with black intentions enter.

As the three elders gathered more smudges, Sephie said, "The only problem with wards and protections for a shop like this is that there are people who are spirit-blind and can't sense the warnings."

"Ah, but they'll itch," Patricia said. "They'll be uncomfortable and won't stay long. We do that with our little taco business. We don't want trouble, so we ward the seating area. We've seen people come in and sit down and then get up and get their order to go instead." She chuckled. "It's like we put itching powder on the seats."

After Patricia had blessed the shop with spice-infused Florida water, Sephie asked, "So, we do the outside now?"

"How you holding up?" Floyd asked.

She challenged him. "You getting tired, old man?"

"I'm just as tired as you are. Let's get this done."

Outside, the McCarthy brothers and B.D. were finishing the protections on the shop and were going to move to the little house. They had been singing a chant, without their instruments, with each one of the men singing from a different corner. When the chant was done, they'd rotate one corner, until all four had been done. It was a haunting chant that sent Sephie's spine tingling because the power they were raising was so strong.

She stopped Alistair as he passed her. "What is that chant? I've never heard the like before. It sounds really ancient."

"It's not," he said. "It's simply called 'The Banishing Song' and was written about twenty years ago by a man named Bradley Murphey of the Dunn County Clerics. I heard it on a recording, and then I was at a big pagan event in Wisconsin where the Clerics performed. They opened the event with that chant. With all of the energies of three hundred people, you could feel the wards forming." He smiled a little embarrassed. "We try to do our best with it."

Sephie patted his arm. "I feel it. Your work almost makes ours unnecessary."

"Smudge anyway," he said. "Chase out the bad and we'll contain the good."

A flock of crows circled overhead. As the young men began the eerie chant again, the birds descended onto the eaves of the shop and the little house. High above both buildings, a larger black bird flew past and then returned to sit on the chimney of the shop and then move to the chimney of the little house.

Sephie nodded, sensing another protection uncalled directly by B.D, but maybe because of him and his enchanted voice.

Three passes were made around the shop: one of rue, one of sage/cedar, and one of *paolo santo*. They moved completely around the shop, and then Sephie and Floyd stepped into the backyard of the little house and chased the negativity out the back gate as the singers finished their chants. Patricia followed and then told Sephie and Floyd to cut some roses and sprinkle their petals around both yards.

"You never leave a space empty," Patricia said. "Voids will always be filled. If you don't put good things back in, bad things with use the space."

After all of the protections were done outside, everyone gathered into the back room of the shop. "Thank you all so much," Mandy said. "I know we're all exhausted, but Laura and I want to feed you for all that you've done. I know you've used a lot of energy today."

Freya protested. "No need. We have to get back to the young ones. We promised them pizza tonight and a movie." She leaned toward Laura, "It's the least we can do for their having to put up with my mother. She can be such a Valkyrie sometimes." She hugged Laura and then Mandy. Chris did the same.

"Call us when you have more news," he said, and they left by the front door.

"Then it's all of you," Mandy said. "We'll all go down to the Watering Hole."

"I need to get my daughter and my grandbaby back home," Patricia said. "Go collect Yolanda. I'm sure she'd like to get out."

Alistair commented, "Thanks. We'll stay for a bit, but we'd like to make the crossing and get into the city well before midnight." He looked at his brothers. "We do have day jobs tomorrow."

"That means one of us has to be the designated driver," Bryan said. "We'll draw lots at the restaurant."

Chapter 67

Day 21: The Watering Hole, Sunday early evening

Normally, it would have been hard to find three empty booths in the bar, but it was early on a Sunday evening and dinner patrons were at the tables. The drinking crowd (even on a Sunday there was one, according to Bill), would arrive much later. Bill was happy to see his bar area full of patrons, and he was beaming when Mandy pulled out her credit card and told him all three tables were on her.

The McCarthy brothers and B.D. occupied one booth with Mandy, Laura, and Yolanda in the middle one, and Sephie and Floyd in the other. When Floyd scooched in next to her, she challenged, “Are you deaf in one ear and need me to sit near your good one?”

“The rodeo did a lot of things to me, but it didn’t take my hearing,” he answered, picking up his menu.

Sephie harrumphed as she looked over hers. She figured he wanted to protect that side of her, while the wood and half wall on the other side would do the same. In light of what they had all been experiencing, she wasn’t surprised, but she still wanted to protest her independence. She did admit, “I’m weary to the bone tonight. I’ll eat and fall into my bed.”

“Want some company?” he asked quietly, studying the dinner selections intently.

She backhanded his arm. “Behave yourself, old man.”

“I’m not that old.”

Bill came bustling over. “Miz Sephie, you look dead tired. You want a G and T?”

She shook her head. "If I have something that strong, I'll be face first onto this table before the appetizer is served."

"A glass of wine might be good for you," Floyd commented.

Before Sephie could retort, Bill said, "Good choice. Red or white?"

Glaring at Floyd, she said, "White and nothing super sweet."

"And for you?" Bill asked.

"The same."

When Bill left to take drink orders from the girls, Sephie demanded, "You planning on a frisky night? Well, you'll be doing your frisking alone."

"My body aches just like yours," he said. "It was an exhausting day both physically and spiritually." Changing the subject, he announced. "I think I'm going to get fried chicken. I don't think I could handle anything fancy."

"You know, that sounds good. And with something sweet after."

As he put his menu down, he looked at her and asked, "Was last night so bad?"

She tried not to smile, but it escaped. "No," she admitted.

Bill's loud laugh drew their attention. He was at the boys' table, and he'd discovered the instrument cases propped against the wall on each bench. "Tell you what I'll do. If you boys will play a couple of tunes, I'll comp your meals."

"Mandy's paying," B.D. reminded.

"It'll save her some money then," Bill said.

Bruce said, "We'll consider it."

Alistair said, "If you'll throw in a round, we'll do a half dozen."

"And what would you be wanting?" Bill asked tentatively.

"Guinness, of course."

"Done!" Bill said.

Bryan asked a practical question. "Do you have a house microphone?"

"Cal left his gear here from Thursday," Bill said. "He went to the Cities over the weekend and doesn't have another gig until this Thursday with you, B.D. You do know how to run it, don't you?"

"Sure," B.D. answered. "Cal have a gig in Minneapolis?"

"No, he just went to see this girl he met."

B.D. thought a minute. "There was some girl hanging around Thursday."

"Guess so." Bill headed for the bar.

"You sing here?" Alistair asked B.D.

"Started this past week," he said. "I hope to sing here all summer."

"Then you'll have to sing with us. Do you know. . . ."

The conversation was lost when Laura and Yolanda started laughing about something. Mandy was the object of their humor and started protesting loudly. More laughter followed.

The bartender brought over two glasses of a chilled sparkling wine and set them in front of Floyd and Sephie. Floyd took a sip and raised an eyebrow, then waited for Sephie to taste her drink.

"Is that champagne?" she asked.

Floyd couldn't help grinning. "You think Bill's doing some matchmaking?"

She grunted. "I hope not." She took a bigger drink. The wine was already beginning to kick in. "This is quicker than waiting for ibuprofen to work," she admitted.

"It can numb a body." He took only one more sip and pushed the glass away.

Sephie noticed. "Old memories."

"Some," he admitted. "It doesn't have a hold on me. But, frankly, I ordered a glass so you wouldn't refuse a second one. I think you'll need both." He pushed it toward Sephie, who had nearly finished her first. "But I'd slow down. We need some food."

Bill circled back from stopping at the bar and sending a server to the back offices for the gig equipment and was turning toward the kitchen. Floyd raised a hand to catch his attention, and Bill said, "Ready to order?"

"We'd both like the fried chicken and two salads. Italian dressing. And do you have pie or cake tonight?"

"We have a New York style cheesecake," he said.

"One slice but two forks," Floyd said, "I think after all that food neither of us will be able to eat a full piece."

Sephie downed the last of her champagne glass when Bill left and leaned back in the booth. "I hope what all we did today will help."

"It'll help. That's the level of protection that should've been on the shop from the day they opened."

"We still don't know exactly what Missy is doing. If Missy and not Rodolfo or someone they know is the one doing this. And really why? Jealousy? Dr. B. is a psychologist teaching at the university, Mandy said. Of course, he'd find childhood trauma."

"It's all too common," Floyd admitted. "But you're right. Is it just to get back at Mandy and Laura? Or to build their own business? Or draw customers to them for their spiritual help?"

"And what about the rosemaling? Could B.D. be right about that? Could they have let something loose when they brought in an old piece of furniture? Or did they get ahold of a real cursed object that worked on the rosemaling? How would we ever know?"

"And how do you combat that? You can't do big magic if you have some vague idea somebody is doing something."

Sephie was quiet for a few moments. Then she said, "Somebody needs to go do some reconnaissance."

Floyd turned on Sephie. "Oh no, you don't! We'd have to scrape you off the sidewalk after you walked out of that place.

If you could walk out of it."

"If not me, then somebody else."

"There have to be two people. And not Mandy or Laura."

"Who's left? You and B.D.?"

The old man frowned. "Not me. Though I think my energy confuses them. B.D. probably. But I think he should be paired with female energy. I think maybe someone connected with the Church."

"You can't possibly think a nun would willingly go into the lion's den? We can't ask Mother Evangeline to do that. No matter how fond she is of B.D."

"No, I was thinking about Patricia. She and B.D. practice ancient paths, and I think she goes to mass regularly like B.D."

"Would they know what to look for?"

"I think they'd let Spirit guide them. Once we know for sure if it is Missy, we can undo what she's doing."

Sephie thought about that. "Knowledge is the key." She nodded. "Let's ask him when we get back to the little house."

Floyd pulled out his phone and ran through his contact list. He found a number and placed the call. He connected just as their salads arrived. Bill fled politely. "Patricia, this is Floyd. Have you got a minute?"

Chapter 68

Day 22: The little house, Monday morning

The soft rumble of snoring at the back of Sephie's head roused her. She felt Floyd's warmth behind her and his arm flung across her ample middle. She smiled at that closeness. Her late husband had always been eager enough for his marital duties, but he flailed across the bed in deep sleep, usually leaving her without covers and on the edge of the queen-sized bed, holding on. Even though these ordinary intimacies with Floyd were not sexual, they echoed within her, making her amply aware of something deeper that a marriage could hold that she never had. Sephie had loved her husband, even though he could be as hard to love as her sister at times. This with Floyd was foreign and yet wondrously tender. It had drawn her closer to him than even marital rompings and very quickly. Yet, she reminded herself, they were in a vacuum, in non-ordinary time, working together spiritually in ways that knitted them closer but were only temporary, born of the urgency to protect those they loved.

She fitted her fingers through Floyd's on her belly and brushed her thumb across his hand. The snoring stopped.

"Good morning," he said and kissed the top of her head.

"Morning," she muttered, still trying to make sense of this moment and others like them with him. "Guess I'll go make coffee."

"I'm the only one who makes the coffee in this family."

She turned on her back to stare at him. "Family?"

"Uh-huh."

"This makes us family?"

He frowned and then nodded as if he suddenly understood. "You're old fashioned. You need something legal."

She sat upright in the bed and clutched her head between her hands. "No," she said wearily.

Raising himself on an elbow, he asked, "Then what?"

She sighed heavily. "We live in different worlds, and we'll go back to those one day." She paused. "Soon."

He raised himself to wrap his arms around her. "We've been put into each other's paths for a reason." He held her in silence for a few minutes and then added, "What makes you think I'd let the only woman I'd stay off the rodeo circuit for slip out of my hands?"

"You're too old for the rodeo, old man," she teased, but what she said had some truth in it.

"That I am." He kissed her temple. "But I don't feel the pull around you." A few seconds later he added. "Life around you has its own adventure."

"You mean around Riverbend. I've never experienced a place like this before."

Swinging his bare legs out of bed, Floyd reached for his pants but not his shirt to cover the white, sleeveless undershirt he had on.

Sephie chuckled. "You need to buy some pajamas."

"I'll take Yolanda for an outing to the Mall, and she can help me pick out some," he said, standing and hiking up his jeans before reaching for his boots.

"Don't tire her out," Sephie cautioned. "She's been doing so well."

"I get dibs on the shower," he said, sitting back down to stuff his feet into the well-worn leather of his boots.

"I'll need lots of coffee first," Sephie said. Upon hearing water running, she added, "But I think B.D. beat you to it. He's up awfully early."

"I think he's meeting Patricia later at a Catholic church that does daily masses. They wanted to be as protected as they can be before they do any reconnaissance this afternoon. Patricia said something about doing a *limpia* before and after."

"Isn't that a cleansing of some kind?"

"With an egg. I have a feeling there are eggs under every bed in this house now."

Chapter 69

Day 22: The little house, Monday morning

Coming out of the bathroom with a towel wrapped around his middle, B.D. gave Floyd a grin as the old man closed the door of Sephie's room. The young man eyed the undershirt he had on and not the usual cotton Western shirt he wore.

"Respect your elders," Floyd said, following him into the room they shared.

"I'm not saying a word," B.D. said, pulling out clothing from a drawer in the dresser.

Floyd selected a clean shirt and jeans from those hanging in the closet. "You've got more on your plate today than other people's business," he said.

B.D. looked at his phone to check the time and then started putting on clothes. "I've got to hustle. I have to find Our Lady of the Waters Church."

"It's on Sixth Street, about a block from the New Life Church of John the Baptist."

As he dressed, the young man asked, "How'd you know that?"

"Yolanda likes visiting big churches. Ours back home is about the size of this house."

"Catholic?"

He nodded. "I direct the little choir. The people like to sing, so it's not hard."

"How are they managing without you?" B.D. said, sitting on the bed to put on his shoes.

"They're learning to sing by themselves. I think someone from the choir is stepping up."

"So, if you decided to. . . ."

Floyd shot him a questioning look. "If I decided to what?"

Standing, B.D. said, "Oh, maybe hang around here."

Reaching into the dresser for underwear, Floyd said, "I think that's already a given. Even if someone hasn't realized that yet."

B.D. grinned. Then his phone rang. Picking it up to check the caller ID, he immediately answered. "Did you find Papa Mamoud?" A pause. "I'm so glad to hear your voice, Papa." The conversation soon dipped into a flood of Cajun French.

Floyd left B.D. to his phone call and headed to put his clothes and his shaving kit in the bathroom before making two pots of coffee.

Chapter 70

Day 22: Used Furniture Store, Monday early afternoon

Walking up the street to Missy's used furniture store, B.D. expressed his concerns to Patricia. "I don't know about this. What're we supposed to be looking for, anyway?"

"It will find you, my boy. Just open up your senses," Patricia encouraged.

"Isn't that dangerous?"

She raised a finger to flick the brown mojo bag at his neck. He grabbed her hand before she got any nearer and said, "I wouldn't touch yours."

She nodded. "*Mea culpa*," she said. "I was just going to say you're protected. By the Church and our prayers before we got out of the car and with that," she pointed to the bag around his neck and then to a leather pouch hanging from a beltloop in his jeans. "And . . . I would suspect there's another."

"Yes, but you don't need to know where that is." He had spent most of the morning scrambling through Sephie's herbs and stock in the shop to find the things that Papa Mamoud told him to put into the mojo bags. Then he had "fed" the bags with sprinkles of Lije's moonshine.

B.D. gestured toward the big cross Patricia wore around her neck among the layers of shells and multiple rows of blue beads. "So are you."

Patricia gently stroked the blue beads and shells. "Yemaya is my orisha. She will protect."

B.D. nodded. "Where did you get so many cowrie shells? I could have used a couple for the bags this morning."

"A gift from someone long ago," she said. "It seemed fitting to use their protection today."

When they got to the storefront, they both paused to take a deep breath. B.D. asked, "You remember the cover story? We're here to get something for your grandbaby. I'm just the muscle."

Patricia gave him a nod, and they entered. "Split up," she said, taking the left part of the dimly lit store.

B.D. had sensed no wards on the front door or even on the nearby objects for sale. There was no bell or chime to signal their presence when they entered. As he made his way, looking at furniture and knickknacks on the right-hand side of the store, he surveyed the corners of the big display room, looking for security cameras. He found none. There also was no one in the room but them, yet there was a closed door to a back area. Theft could be easy here, if the object was small enough, or several people came in to make off with a piece of furniture. Perhaps Missy just hexed the thief after the fact, if something was stolen.

Opening himself to the furniture in the store, B.D. ran an idle finger along pieces as he wandered, as if he were looking for something like any customer would. He passed upholstered chairs and camelback sofas, dish cabinets and dining tables, iron bedsteads and desks. There were lots of small tables of various sizes and uses, as well as lamps, china, and lots of old picture frames. He passed a desk and then stopped. There was a tug of energy. Turning around, he saw a wooden box with a rounded lid, much like a little trunk, about the size of a large old-fashioned bread box, that was covered with rosemaling. B.D. stepped closer and put his hand on each side to examine it in greater detail. The pulsing energies within were electrifying. He jerked his hands away just as a deep female voice said, "Are you looking for anything in particular?" Looking up, he saw Missy swaggering toward him from the back.

Glancing toward the left, he spotted Patricia, who had noticed Missy's movement. She rushed over, gushing enthusiasm, something totally out of character for her. "Did you find something? Oh great! There are so many beautiful things here. I don't know what to get her. What is it? What did you find?"

Immediately, she was at B.D.'s side looking at the box near his hands. "Now this is charming!" She rolled back the lid and examined the large space inside. "And so spacious! We can use it to hold special keepsakes for my grandbaby. This is lovely!"

Missy now was beside them. "It's local," she said. "The painting is old."

"How much?" Patricia asked.

"Fifty."

The *curandera* looked over it. "I don't know. Would you take forty for it?"

"You're a haggler," Missy said. "Sorry, but it's fifty. Firm."

Patricia pretended to consider. Turning to B.D., she asked, "What do you think?"

He wasn't sure she should pay that much for the box or even have it in her possession. "Does it feel right to you?" And then added quickly, "For your grandbaby?"

What B.D. saw in her eyes verified his own sense of the energy in the box. "Oh, yes. I know just what to do with it."

He nodded then.

Missy gloated. "Come to the back to the register."

B.D. started to pick up the box, but Patricia did instead, and they followed the woman to a desk along the back wall and near the door he had noticed before. B.D. saw a wooden dining room table with a display of hex oils and red, black, green, and white candles. There were also three different Hand of Glory candles, a number of small dolls made of muslin, and a bag of divination bones. There were oils, soaps, and potions for love, and a cluster of things used to curse your enemies. B.D. tried to keep his face neutral as he passed.

Standing behind the register, Missy said, "Fifty-two fifty." and held out her hand for the money as Patricia pulled her wallet out of her purse and passed a fifty-dollar bill, two ones to her and then dug into the change section for fifty cents.

Missy rang the order up, stuffed the money in the till, slammed the drawer, and ripped off the bit of register tape. "Keep that. You'll need it if you want to return it within thirty days."

Missy's gaze fell on B.D.'s mojo bag. "I never took you for one of Papa Legba's followers. I heard that you sing in churches all the time." Her focus left his mojo bag to examine his body. "I bet you're a Shango devotee."

B.D. bristled at the sexual implications of her remark, since Shango represented male prowess through dance. But that *orisha* also judged morality and had a very powerful, vengeful side.

"Shango cannot be fooled," he said.

She nodded as if she understood, but B.D. could tell it was only a surface knowledge or she wouldn't have made the comments she had. As they stared at each other, something else was being said.

Patricia picked up the box and began to chatter again. "I can't wait to show this to my daughter. She'll just love it. Come on," she urged and turned toward the door.

B.D. pulled away from the spiritual standoff with Missy and followed Patricia out the door.

As they walked quickly to Patricia's car, she said, "This is the source. But she doesn't know it. I think she's doing something else."

"You can bet on that," B.D. said. "She's dangerous because she doesn't know what she's doing. Shango will come with vengeance."

"I saw that look she gave you," Patricia said. "She wants you. We'll do another *limpia* at the store. Now, let's salt this box before we put it in my car."

On the sidewalk by her little compact car, Patricia reached in the trunk and retrieved a round box of salt. She immediately poured most of the contents over the wooden box, turning it to salt the bottom, and then the inside. When she was done, she shook the salt off the box and then proceeded to salt B.D. and then herself. "I think that'll do for now. We'll need Floyd and Sephie to smudge it before I take it home."

"You aren't planning on keeping that thing, are you?" B.D. asked, horrified.

"It's not the object's fault," she said. "It has stories to tell, and who better to tell them to than me, who has been a keeper of generations of stories? I know how to keep them from walking again. Besides, I paid fifty-two fifty for it."

Chapter 71

Day 22: North Star, Monday early evening

The raw egg slid into the clear glass bowl next to the rosemaling-designed box. Its black yolk caused the group gathered around the counter of the North Star to gasp.

B.D. backpedaled quickly away from the omen. "It's a bad egg."

Patricia, hand on her hip, shook her head. "It came from the same carton I got from the store," she said.

"But yours wasn't like that and neither was the one you used before we left."

"This just shows she has her claws in you."

"Like a *huldre*," Laura pronounced.

"No," B.D. protested. "*Huldres* are just unfortunates, but this, this—"

"Is not so innocent," Patricia said.

Mandy pulled a shallow, wooden box from behind the counter and placed it on the glass top. Opening the lid, she said, "I'll do a cutaway to get rid of anything else attached." Then she pulled out a silver ceremonial dagger.

"No, I'll do it," Laura said. "We need strong feminine energy to combat this woman."

"Wouldn't male energy be better?" Floyd said. "She seems to ignore that."

"That's the point," Laura said. "She ignores you. This is the first time she's targeted a man."

"What does she want with B.D. then?" Sephie asked.

"Sexual energy," Patricia said.

All faces turned to B.D. “Don’t look at me like that. I’ve been too busy since I got here. I haven’t even had a date.”

Floyd chuckled. “Maybe you need to go find that *huldre* and settle down.”

“Too young,” he said in a pout.

“I’ll do it.” It was Yolanda’s quiet voice. She had gotten up from the comfort of Sephie’s rocker to look at the egg. When everyone turned at her voice, she chuckled and clarified. “I’ll do the cutaway. There’s no one more feminine here than me.” She ran a hand across her round belly.

Mandy walked around the counter and pulled B.D. into the center of the shop. Laura brought the knife and put it into Yolanda’s hands. “All that you’ll do is slowly run the knife along his aura. Don’t touch him. Front. Back. Over his head and under his feet.”

Laura stood beside Yolanda. “We’ll set the intention and monitor the energy.”

Mandy took a position behind B.D.

Both Laura and Mandy rubbed their hands together before holding them up palm first toward B.D. Laura nodded at Yolanda as she began to run the knife about six inches from B.D.’s head and then slowly down to his toes. She repeated this action many times, as if she were shaving his image, working her way to the back where Mandy stood. When she was done with the back, Mandy said, “Here.” B.D. twisted his head to see Mandy pointing to a spot in the middle of his back, a place where it would have been hard for him to scratch from any direction. Yolanda repeated the virtual scraping.

When she came around to the front again, Laura said to B.D. “Raise your foot.”

B.D. complied with one foot and then the other so that Yolanda could run the blade under him.

“Head again,” Laura said and Yolanda pulled the knife sideways over his head and then front to back.

Mandy and Laura relaxed. Taking the knife from Yolanda, Laura said to B.D., "You're clear." She handed it to Mandy and turned to the pregnant woman, "You okay?"

Yolanda nodded and smiled. "I'm glad I could help."

Taking her by the elbow, Laura guided her back to the rocker. "You should rest now. I'll make you some hibiscus tea with honey."

When Laura had left for the back room, Mandy explained as she sprinkled salt from behind the counter over the knife and put it back in the box. "There was a big attachment in the middle of your back," she told B.D.

The young man touched his mojo bag. "Why didn't Papa Mamoud's protections work?"

"They did," Patricia said, resting her body in a folding chair. "It would have been worse if you hadn't come so well protected."

"Why'd she need sexual energy from me?" B.D. asked. "You'd think Rodolfo would be enough, especially with all the energy he can absorb. Though I can't for the life of me figure out why a man as good looking as he is got himself hooked up with her."

"Mutual need," Sephie said, also finding a chair to sit in. "I think he was attracted to her big energy."

"Then why's he out looking for more?" B.D. asked.

"Could be he's fueling the magic she's doing," Floyd suggested, "and it drains his stores."

"You mean, he's the battery, and she's draining him now?" Mandy asked.

"I think you're right, Floyd," Patricia said. She turned to B.D. "Were her spiritual wares charged?"

He thought a moment. "Come to think of it, they weren't. But they're the standard things you can buy on the internet or in tourist hoodoo shops back home. She probably has a working altar in the back where she makes offerings. But I doubt if she's ever seen, much less participated in, a real ceremony."

"So, she's doing some kind of working that released all those beings hidden in the rosemaling?" Mandy asked. "What about the bird the McCarthy boys sensed?"

"It's there," Patricia said.

"I didn't see a bird," B.D. countered.

"I smelled it at the register."

"I didn't."

"I have an allergy to birds. That was one reason I rushed us out of there. My eyes were beginning to itch."

"Why didn't you tell us?" Mandy demanded. "We have feathers here."

"Not many, and yours have been cleaned. I react to live bird dander. Missy obviously doesn't clean the cage very well, either. And she doesn't keep a parakeet. It's big."

"What does she use the bird for?" Sephie asked.

"Maybe like Papa Mamoud," B.D. offered. "He uses an albino boa constrictor in ceremony to represent the loa *Dambala*, parading that big beauty on his bare shoulders. That snake has power. Probably from being at so many rites over the years."

"Do you use birds?" Laura asked as she returned with tea for Yolanda.

"Only for sacrifice," B.D. explained and then quickly added, "It's not Hollywood. My people sacrifice chickens during the rite, and the women then cook them up for a feast afterwards."

There was a small silence then Mandy asked. "But why is Rodolfo targeting Sephie? I know we talked about this before, but why not suck all of us dry?"

"She's vulnerable and generates power," Floyd said.

"I am not and do not," Sephie protested. *En masse*, all faces turned to her. "All right. I'm old and maybe my shields leak like my bladder."

Smiles and a couple of giggles slipped out.

"And maybe he wanted to cut you off from your aunt's help," Patricia said. "I don't think he or Missy expected there to be so much help around you both."

"Did they come to last year's Solstice celebration?" Sephie asked.

"No," Laura said, climbing up on the stool behind the counter. "They moved in sometime in the Spring. They must have seen flyers about it last year and this year."

Sephie nodded. "So, it was a way to introduce their wares to the community without doing their own marketing."

"A safe way," Mandy said. "I doubt if Riverbend would appreciate knowing there was a voodoo shop in town."

"Hoodoo," B.D. corrected. "That's all spell and hex work I saw. Nothing was charged or blessed."

"That reminds me," Sephie said. "I need to get back to my herb work. We'll need more blessed goods."

B.D. noticed the box on the counter. "Miz Patricia, are you really going to give that box to your daughter?"

"Why not?"

"It's a cursed box, isn't it?"

"No, it's just a box. The beings put into the rosemaling mean no harm, just like the *huldre*. It just is. As long as the box is loved and appreciated, the beings will be happy to share my family's joys."

"What about all the ones that got out?" Mandy asked, frowning.

"I don't know much about Scandinavian lore, but these spirits aren't necessarily bad, I think. Just beings. They will go about their ways."

"Well, the *nattmara* is keeping people awake at night," Laura said.

"And the Finnmen tried to drown a fisherman," Mandy added.

"People have drowned in the river before and—" Patricia said.

"But the Finnmen don't kill people and they didn't this time, remember? They put him on the bank," B.D. interjected. "Maybe it was just to warn him not to take too many fish or someone made them do it."

Eying him, Patricia continued, "And people have insomnia all the time."

Mandy frowned. "So, you are saying this is all coincidence?"

"Not all of it."

"And the cat attacks?" Laura offered.

"That could have been intentional. The scrying said some of this was intentional."

"But why?" Mandy asked. "Does Missy release her bird at night just to terrorize cats?"

"Maybe it was to train the bird," Yolanda said softly.

They all looked at the young woman in the rocking chair.

"To terrorize cats?" Mandy asked. "But why?"

"Maybe cats were just the beginning. They attacked the nun, too. An elderly woman, unguarded, alone outside at night."

It was Laura's turn to ask, "But why?"

"Jealousy," Floyd pronounced.

"Jealousy over what?" B.D. asked. "You said she wanted me, but this was happening before I got here."

"Yes, she wants you," Patricia said but stepped in front of Laura and Mandy. "But it's business jealousy. Your shop has been here a long time. People come to this shop for education and tools. You run a solstice festival and people respect you."

"But jealousy," Mandy said. "That's silly."

"No," Floyd said. "Jealousy prompted the first murder. Cain slew his brother because he was jealous. It's a powerful emotion."

"So, what do we do?" B.D. asked.

"We do nothing about the spirits," Floyd stated. "They're part of the natural world and the history of the people of this place. They'll be dealt with by those who know who and what they are. It's these humans who are at the heart of dangerous matters." Turning to Laura, he asked. "What is Dr. B. planning? The rite. What will its focus be?"

"I'll call him this afternoon with a report. We're trying to work out the details, and he's supposed to give me a list of tools to gather. This is pretty rushed work for high magicians. They operate in power words so everything must be precise. Now that I can tell him the source, he and Daryll will draft the exact rite we need." She looked from face to face. "When we do this Wednesday, we'll close the shop, and no one but us should be here."

"Good," B.D. said. "I need to get back to the university to whip those young singers into shape. And I need to get with Clay to rehearse." He smiled. "I didn't tell you, but the university offered me the part of Jim in the full production, and the music department is talking about seeing if they can work with the history or anthropology department to create a Master's in folklore that includes music. They've been wanting to get Ole in for some workshops, and they think I can persuade him."

Floyd clapped the young man on the back. "It looks as if you've found a place for yourself."

Sephie frowned, but quickly smiled, offering her congratulations.

Chapter 72

Day 22: North Star, Monday evening

Turning back the covers of the bed in her room in the little house, Sephie, in her white cotton pajamas with little pink flowers, looked up to see Floyd enter, barefoot, wearing his own pajamas in robin's egg blue. She raised an eyebrow and tried not to smile. "Yolanda made a good choice. Blue's a good color for you."

"I wanted the red ones, but she talked me out of it," he said drolly.

Sephie let a laugh slip and sat down on the edge of the bed as she watched him hang a clean shirt over the closet door. "Planning on moving in?" she teased.

"Just want to be ready for the day. B.D.'s been smirking way too much at me."

Laughing again, she added, "I think he's realizing that he has a very long life ahead of him."

"Rightly so," Floyd said, waving Sephie into the bed and crawling in. He immediately switched off the lamp.

"It's still only sleeping, old man," she said, putting her head on his shoulder as he curled his arm around her. "Even if you look handsome in blue."

He chuckled. "You'll know when I want to make a move, old woman."

"How's Yolanda? She seemed a bit tired tonight."

"She loved getting out of the house. And I made her rest often, faking my own feebleness."

"Playing the age card," she commented.

"It works sometimes."

His arm gave her body a squeeze. "You were tired at dinner."

"It's no wonder. I spent all day doing everybody's laundry. Mandy and Laura had been letting it pile up because they didn't want to come in here and bother anybody. It's their house. Lordy!"

"Did you get it all done?"

"Yep. Even yours, old man."

"Whoa, you didn't need to do mine! I'm capable of not putting reds in with whites."

"You're quite fastidious with your clothes, for a rodeo cowboy," she commented.

"I do own a suit," he said. "Back home."

"Does it still fit?" she teased implying that it wasn't worn often.

"Sephie, you're a pest!" he complained. "Of course, it fits. I wear it to church every Sunday."

"Sounds like you might need a new one, then." She couldn't resist teasing him. This time she pushed his buttons so that he retaliated by leaning over and silencing her with a long kiss.

"Now, shut up and go to sleep before we expend far more energy than our old bodies can spare right now."

She smiled and nestled against him, closing her eyes, wondering how it would be to spend all of the nights remaining to her next to this man. Her thoughts didn't linger there as she replayed the day's events. She remembered Floyd commenting that B.D. was making a life in Riverbend, far away from Dark Hollow and even his beloved bayou. She was far from her home, too, far from Agnesia and obligations about her property. Summer was swiftly moving and soon there would be roots to dig and season-end herbs and wild fruits to gather. She should check on Agnesia tomorrow. Mentally, she started making a list of things to do for the rest of the week, only drifting off to sleep long after Floyd had begun to snore.

Chapter 73

Day 23: North Star, Tuesday early afternoon

Sephie eased her tired body into a folding chair in the shop. She reached down to the tapestry bag on the floor beside her and pulled out the yellow shawl she had started. Examining her previous work, she wasn't pleased with how little progress had been made, but her time had been occupied elsewhere. She had been bottling oils today from all of the herbs that had been stripped. A few of them had been put into new tinctures, since people had been buying them. It was work she always did on her feet so she could move quickly from step to step. She supposed someone else would have sat through it all, but somehow that just didn't seem right.

Floyd had helped a bit until she told him he was getting in her way. He had fled to the shop and sat reading the weekly rag.

Now, sitting opposite him, she took up the soothing handwork to relax with and only slightly envied Yolanda the use of the little footstool.

"I wish I could do that," Yolanda said from the rocker. "I just don't have the patience." She frowned and rubbed her abdomen.

Sephie noticed from her crocheting, but figured it was another uncomfortable kick. The baby was very active, which was a good sign, but could be so exhausting for the mother carrying her. "I don't think you'll have the free time anymore when your little one is born. I've got the time, and it feels like praying, in a way."

"I found this book left over on a flight once and took it home. It was called *Quilters* and was about pioneer women's lives and how the women were all bound together by the quilting they did."

"There's a play about that," B.D. announced as he bounced in from the back room.

"I thought you were rehearsing those kids all day."

"I am," he said, "but I got a call from Our Lady of the Waters to meet with their choir director during the break. Somebody spotted me with Patricia yesterday, and now they want me to sing. I guess I'm hard to miss. Are there any leftovers from lunch? I'm starving."

Laura and Mandy, who were poring over esoteric books at the counter, said in unison, "All gone," like someone telling a child or a dog that the treats had run out.

"Sephie, you would've loved that play, *Quilters*," B.D. said. "There's this awful scene where one of the women gets news that her husband got killed working on the railroad. She goes into shock, and the women put a needle and thread in her hands and small quilt pieces, and they sit and sing. She copes because she's hanging onto the bits of life she's always known." He pulled out his phone. "I don't have time to go down to The Watering Hole."

Floyd rose and pushed the young man toward the back room. "I'll teach you to fry an egg, son."

B.D. grimaced, "I don't think I can look at another egg. Besides, I can fry it myself."

"A grilled cheese sandwich, then."

Following him out, the old man bent down and kissed Sephie in front of everybody.

The old woman turned bright red but challenged, "What's that for?"

He winked at her. "Just because."

When he left, the girls all said, "Ooh-la-la."

"Hush up," Sephie said, applying herself in earnest to

the stitches. She wasn't exactly sure how Yolanda would feel about her grandfather being interested in someone other than the woman who had raised her. But she needn't have worried.

"I helped Grandfather pick out pajamas yesterday," she said impishly.

"I don't want to go there," Mandy said, throwing her hands into the air.

"We're two old people sleeping. Who's got the energy for anything else?" And then Sephie added, "I got tired of looking at those long, skinny legs of his."

They all started laughing, and Sephie soon joined in.

Chapter 74

Day 24: North Star, Wednesday early evening

Floyd pulled a kitchen chair into the living room in front of Sephie, who had plopped herself down on the chair near the couch. He physically picked up the old woman's feet and put them on the chair. "I noticed your ankles were swelling."

"Floyd, you gotta stop fussing," Sephie protested, as she straightened out her crocheting to examine it.

He eased his own body into the overstuffed chair facing her and commented. "I don't like all my women folk having puffy ankles."

On the pullout couch, Yolanda titled her body to the side to gape at her feet. "Mine look better today," she said.

Over her work, Sephie agreed. "Yes, they do." Satisfied with her previous stitches, she began another row. "What did you pick to watch tonight?"

"I'm tired of silliness," Yolanda said, nodding toward the stack of DVDs Mandy had brought. "I figured out how to add free movie apps to this TV while you all were cooking dinner. I put a bunch on a Watch List." She fingered the remote. "How about a good Western, Grandfather?"

"Sounds great." He crossed the room near Sephie to stretch out next to Yolanda. He was careful to keep his booted feet off the covers.

Sephie looked at the clock on the DVD player Mandy had brought in days ago to use for those movie marathons. It was well past 8:00. "They've been nearly two hours over there," she said, meaning the participants in the ritual next door.

"It takes time to set up and break down," Floyd said. "You know that."

She sighed. "I suppose." She made a few more stitches and then set her work down. "I just want this to be over. It would be nice to not have worries for a while."

Floyd reached for her hand. "It won't be resolved tonight. It takes time to set in motion, and then there'll be pushing against the work and reinforcing."

"Maybe Sephie needs a Navajo blessing," Yolanda said.

Floyd turned to her, "What do you mean?"

"I flew with a Navajo woman who told me a lot of things she wouldn't tell our White co-workers," Yolanda explained. "She said most of the healing that Navajo healers do are blessings that help people be at peace with what they're dealing with. Sometimes that results in a physical or mental healing, but not every time. Always, though, it's a spiritual healing."

Floyd thought about that and nodded. "I think we all need that." He squeezed Sephie's hand and said to her, "We need a walk in the woods."

The old woman smiled as Yolanda punched the remote to start the movie, but they didn't get very far past the opening credits when B.D. came in from the front and Mandy and Laura from the back door.

"Is there food left?" B.D. asked.

"Chili and cornbread and some sliced tomatoes," Floyd said, starting to heave himself off the couch.

"I can get it," he said, moving into the kitchen past the young women. "How did it go?"

"We're exhausted," Laura said. "But it's done."

"I'll nuke you some chili, too, if you're ready to eat," B.D. called.

Mandy said, "I'll help, and give you the gist while Laura tells the story to the rest."

Laura collapsed into the overstuffed chair as Yolanda paused the movie. "Working with Golden Dawn high magicians isn't for the unfit. We've been standing and chanting and moving ritual pieces and chanting and more chanting. There are so many layers that they set up."

"What kind of rite was it?" Floyd asked.

"Basically, it was an unbinding."

"An unbinding?" Sephie asked in shock. "Not a binding?"

"No. As Dr. B. put it, a binding would only infuriate Missy and her helpers."

"Helpers?" Sephie repeated.

"I'll get to that. Bindings have been done since Greek and Roman times. They restrict what a person does. But that can create resistance and fuel anger and revenge, sometimes resulting in the bindings being broken and worse actions released. But an unbinding is an undoing of every magic that has been put in place, making it harmless. What Dr. B. and Daryll created was a way to generate a continual unbinding every time Missy does magic. It will automatically unbind what she's done and nothing will happen. She won't be able to detect that it's something from the outside."

"That can be done?" Sephie asked.

"Dr. B. is good. He locked it into her ego," Mandy said, bringing in a bowl of chili on a dinner plate with tomatoes and cornbread for Laura. The *ding* from the microwave in the kitchen drew Mandy back for her dinner.

"You mentioned helpers," Sephie said, bringing them back to what Laura said earlier. "You mean Rodolfo?"

"They might have gathered followers," Laura said, and then tasted the chili. "Floyd, did you make this? It's great and not too hot." Taking another mouthful, she chewed and then continued. "Dr. B. said it was possible she might have followers, and they should be part of the unbinding. Also, he said she might have tried or still might try to conjure something worse than the creatures her energy released from the box."

"So, what happens now?" Sephie said.

"We live happily ever after," Laura announced. "Let's all go to the Watering Hole tomorrow and watch B.D. perform."

"I second that," Mandy said, perching herself on the arm of Laura's chair.

B.D. came in and found a spot on the floor. "What movie are you watching?"

"*True Grit*," Yolanda announced. "The newer one with Jeff Bridges."

"I remember that one! My uncle took me to see it when I was nine, maybe. He didn't think anyone could ever top John Wayne, but Jeff Bridges won him over."

Yolanda hit the play icon on the TV and then rubbed her abdomen, frowning.

"You okay?" Floyd said.

She smiled, minimizing what she felt. "I think the chili is kicking up more than the little one."

Chapter 75

Day 24: The little house, Wednesday late evening

Sitting on the edge of the bed, Sephie hung her head, feeling defeated. Maybe it was all the anticipation about tonight's rite or just the weary days catching up with her. It just didn't feel over, as if a big boot or two were hanging overhead waiting to come crashing down on them all.

She looked up when Floyd came in with another clean shirt on a hanger and closed the door. "What's got you in a mood, old woman?" he asked, hanging his shirt over the closet door. When he sat down next to her, he put his arm around her and shook her gently. "What's on your mind?"

Searching his face, she could only say, "Laura said we'd live happily ever after. Floyd, it's not over."

"Some of it is." He studied her. "What are you picking up?"

"Just a feeling." She crumpled her face and then took a breath to steady herself. "My mother used to get these feelings, but I never was blessed or cursed with them. I had other gifts." She twisted to put her arms around him and let him enfold her. "I'm afraid, Floyd." The tears came quietly, even though Sephie tried to curb them to keep him from noticing, but the wetness against his cheek betrayed that plan.

He held her in silence for a long time. Finally, Floyd said softly, "We will walk through whatever it is together."

She gasped, pulled him tighter against her, and cried openly, her body heaving against his like a child until she was spent. Through it all, he held her, rocking her slightly, and softly began to sing. It was a sweet little tune; sung in a language she didn't know.

Finally, she pulled away and began to wipe the tears from her cheeks with both her hands. Floyd leaned across her to pull tissues from a box beside the bedside lamp to hand to her.

"What was that you were singing?" she asked.

"It's a lullaby."

"From your people?"

"No," he said as if apologizing. "Those among the Three Affiliated Tribes have a rhythm, but the melodies aren't very pretty. I learned this one from a Pequot native from Connecticut who had joined the rodeo circuit after coming West to ride horses. We'd get drunk, and he'd remember his children back home who had long since grown up and left. He'd sing. I heard it so much I learned it. I had our little choir sing it at a couple of christenings.

Sephie blew her nose. "Trying to put me to sleep?"

He gently stroked her back. "Something like that."

She put the used tissues on the bedside table. "I'll be all right."

He stood and pulled the rest of the covers back so she could stretch out more comfortably. Then he turned out the lamp and crawled in beside her, gathering her gently into his arms.

"I'm glad you're here," she said as he continued to hum the sweet lullaby.

Chapter 76

Day 25: The Watering Hole, Thursday early evening

The day had passed pleasantly enough for Sephie. She had spent it finishing up the herbal oils she had been preparing and set some other herbs steeping in Lije's recipe. There had been no customers rushing in, frantic, needing something to deal with unusual phenomena, and no reports from the spiritual community about sensing any activity. That respite had been much needed. She even had tried to put a call through to Pastor Woods about Agnesia but only got his answering machine; the same with her landline back home. She figured she'd get a call if there was bad news.

Laura had buzzed around the shop, dusting statues and candles, actually humming. Sephie even caught her dancing to music from a CD she had playing. Mandy only watched, never joining her. Sephie guessed her niece was working out chords for the tune in her head. B.D. was in and out per usual, darting between rehearsals and preparing for tonight's gig. And Floyd — Floyd was ever-present, slipping out to the little house to prepare meals. Yolanda was in the rocker with her feet up, trying a couple of simple crochet stitches Sephie had showed her, but she was getting restless. She had smiled wistfully at Laura's dancing, probably wishing she was on a dance floor somewhere with Wes.

The atmosphere that night at the Watering Hole was one of joyous celebration and pretty much confined to the booth the girls were in and around B.D. and Clay's little stage area. Sephie had passed on Floyd's offer of a cocktail with their dinner, opting for a soft drink, as he had. She had shrugged off last night's dark mood, but it had been replaced by an edginess that was born of anticipation of the unknown. It was a remnant of what she had felt the night before. She wondered for the first time how her mother had ever borne the burden of her gift, to know but not to know completely, not to know on whom that big boot above was going to land.

Floyd had never mentioned last night's crying jag or even asked her about her feelings today. He just was near . . . always.

Sephie felt a sudden pang of loss and gasped.

Floyd just put his arm around her. "The camel burger was good," he said neutrally.

She nodded, taking a long drink of her soda. Suddenly, she felt a tiredness come over her. She sighed.

She noticed Floyd look over her and the low wall of the booth. Immediately, he said, "Face me," and looked intently at her.

Sephie complied, pushing her eyebrows together in question.

"I want to you put a special shield on. Think of it as a big opaque cloak with silver sparkles on it."

"Pretty fancy," she muttered.

"Start at your back and pull it over your head and down the rest of your body. Charge it with power to operate but not be noticed. Think of being invisible, but not to those you love."

It was an odd shield, but she worked to create it. As she did so, she felt a bit of Floyd retreat from her, though she still could detect his nearness. She also felt her strength returning.

"Now, hold that."

When Floyd flagged a server who quickly came over, he ordered a cheese and fruit tray. The server said, "Just for you? It's a big platter."

"I'll manage."

The server picked up their plates and then asked, "Did your lady friend leave?"

"No," he smiled. "She just. . . ."

The young man smiled. "Oh, she went to the ladies'," he said, and took the dishes away.

"He didn't see me!" Sephie said in awe, relaxing.

"Don't release it," Floyd warned.

"It takes so much effort," she complained, but quickly reinforced it as she saw Rodolfo swagger through the bar, moving his head from the back of the restaurant to the front as if looking for something or someone. He walked right past them without recognition and stood at the end of the bar, waiting for B.D. and Clay to finish the song they were singing.

"What's your favorite song?" Floyd asked abruptly.

"What?" Sephie turned back to him.

"Favorite song?"

"Uh. 'Stand by Me' or 'Lean on Me.' Same message."

He chuckled. "No 'Dance Monkey' or even 'Sweet Home Alabama'?"

"Never been to Alabama," she said.

"Only you would pick deep meaningful songs."

"I like Ben E. King and Bill Withers. What? You think I live so far back in the hills we only listen to hillbilly music?"

He laughed. "No, it just suits you. Now, why don't you take Yolanda to the ladies' room and there you can relax your shielding for a while. And I'll go make a song request. I don't think B.D. would call himself a professional singer without knowing either of those you like." He rose from the booth and offered her a hand. "Keep your shield up."

She walked with him toward B.D. and Clay but parted at the girls' booth. "Yolanda, care to make a trip to the ladies'? We gotta always go in pairs, you know."

The young woman slid out of the booth that she had been crammed in. Sephie looped her arm around Yolanda's, pulling it close to her body. To others, Yolanda would just look normal. They supported each other up the two steps to the area that led to the restrooms. Inside, Sephie relaxed her shielding and used the facilities. She was at the sink washing her hands when she heard Yolanda grunt. Figuring it was only normal bodily functions, she dried her hands on a paper towel and waited.

Yolanda opened the stall door and went to the sink. When she was drying her own hands, she grimaced and put a hand on her abdomen.

Sephie gently placed her own hand on the young woman's expanded belly. Feeling the contraction, her eyes widened. "How long has this been going on?"

"Here and there for a couple of days now. It's probably just Braxton Hicks contractions. They come well before labor."

"And maybe not. Didn't you just have one when you were in there?"

She laughed. "No, the baby really kicked hard."

Sephie gently ran both hands around Yolanda's abdomen. "The baby's dropped. You're ready any time."

"But it's still early."

"But not too early," Sephie countered. "If those contractions get regular and closer together, we'll need to have a little car ride. Is there a way you can count the minutes?"

"I've got a stop watch app on my phone. Wes put it on his and mine before he left." She smiled. "He wants to be there when it happens."

"I think you need to call him and see if he can take some time off soon." She opened the door of the restroom. "Babies come in their own time, and they wait for no one."

In the hallway, Sephie paused and pulled the invisibility shield over her. Yolanda's questioning look prompted the old woman's response. "Your grandfather taught me a new shield."

"Good thing. I saw Rodolfo come in. You okay?"

"It works, my dear."

When they returned to their seats, B.D. and Clay were taking a break and stood talking with Floyd and Rodolfo. Sephie passed the old man and slid into the booth. He separated himself from the discussion and joined her.

"Rodolfo's trying to get B.D. to come to the theater for rehearsals. B.D. put his foot down. He said he only agreed to do a showcase number this weekend at a park and not the full melodrama. Rodolfo is using every charming tactic he knows to try to persuade him. But look."

They saw B.D. adamantly shake his head and rudely walk away from Rodolfo to join the girls. Rodolfo looked frustrated and angry. He took one other look around, finally dropping his gaze onto Floyd.

"Hold your shields," Floyd said raising his soft drink glass toward his mouth to cover his words. He drank, mildly meeting Rodolfo's glare, causing the young man to rush out of the restaurant.

"Well, now," Sephie said, dropping the invisibility shield. "What do you think he wants from B.D.? Is he procuring for his wife?"

Floyd turned his face to her. "Maybe. But he still wants you. Didn't you see him keep looking around for you? I think he wants to get close to B.D. so he can put a more permanent drain on you." Taking another drink from his glass, he said. "It seems Missy is running out of energy to do her work."

"Don't get smug," Sephie warned.

"I'm not," he protested. "I can't help it if I enjoy evil people squirming."

"She may be more ignorant than evil. More's the pity."

Putting his arm around her, he pulled her close and then swooped in for a kiss.

At that moment, the server brought the cheese and fruit tray. "I see you found your lady." He grinned and left just as B.D. and Clay returned to their microphones.

"This is going out to two very special people in my life who have been there for me and for each other," B.D. said, as he brought out a *cajon*, a box drum, that he sat on. Clay did a short guitar intro and B.D. softly began "Stand by Me," building up his soulful delivery. Its effect caused many of the restaurant patrons to pause their conversations and eating to listen. Sephie grabbed her napkin to cover her mouth, and Floyd pulled her closer.

When the song ended, there was silence for a space and then intense applause. B.D. grinned at Clay and nodded. The guitarist then broke into Stevie Wonder's "Higher Ground," letting B.D. loose on the *cajon*. The entire set was filled with soul, funk, and reggae music, ending with a special song.

"This last song is dedicated to all of those in the diaspora and their descendants like me," B.D. said. "This is in honor of the motherland of all mankind, *Alkebulan*."

They then began a reggae/island-like song called, "Mama Africa." Through it, B.D. encouraged patrons to sing the Mama Africa chorus. He even waved for Laura to come up to dance. Floyd pulled Sephie out of the booth while Mandy helped Yolanda out. They all moved to the beat of the tune. Soon, others joined them, filling the aisles. Bill and Sugar came out of the kitchen, and Bill grabbed his wife into dance position and danced her around the back. The kitchen staff paused and came out to dance as well. Floyd caught Sephie up in his arms and moved her around the floor as Bill and Sugar were doing. For a time in that most unusual restaurant, the joy of carefree, tropical life permeated them, creating memories and lasting smiles.

Chapter 77

Day 26: The little house, Friday midmorning

Yolanda's cry forced Sephie and Floyd from the kitchen where they had been lingering over extra cups of coffee. They had all slept in, even the girls next door. Mandy had called to tell them all not to come in until noon.

Sephie and Floyd found Yolanda standing in the middle of the linoleum over a puddle on the floor, her socks soaked. "What's happening?" Yolanda cried.

The old woman took her by the arm. "Your water broke, child. Let's get you cleaned up." She moved her into the bathroom. "It never happened to me, but it did to many other women I know. It's nothing to worry about. But we'll need to take that ride today."

Handing her a washcloth, Sephie added. "I'll get you some fresh clothes so you'll feel more comfortable." When she returned to the living room to search through Yolanda's suitcase, Floyd was mopping the floor. "Any blood?" He shook his head. "Then it's normal."

He paused, leaning on the mop, fear evident on his face. "It's early," he almost whispered.

"But better than a few days ago."

"She did too much."

She passed Floyd and touched his arm. "Babies come when they're ready. She's been having contractions. Perhaps this is best."

Within a few minutes, they had put Yolanda in the truck and were on their way to the hospital. Yolanda was on the phone, trying to find Wes, and was in tears when she left him the message about the baby coming. Both Floyd and Sephie put a comforting hand on each of her knees.

It didn't take long to admit Yolanda, and Floyd and Sephie were banished to the waiting room. Yolanda was going to be alone, since there was no way Wes could be there in a couple of hours. First babies often took a long time, but there was no guarantee. Floyd tried sitting but paced the floor. "We can't leave her alone," he said, and stepped out to negotiate with the nursing staff. From the loudness his voice had risen to, it was clear to Sephie that he was actually doing more battle than tactful bargaining.

The altercation soon drew the old woman out into the hall to join them. Placing a calming hand on Floyd's back, she interrupted. "Excuse me. Our granddaughter shouldn't be left alone. It isn't the way of our people."

Floyd's head swiveled so fast to look at her that the movement caused her to steady herself by putting her arm fully around his middle. Sephie didn't allow the nurse to reply. "Her husband, her labor coach, is a commercial pilot, and he can't get here in time. I've helped coach a few women in labor before, but I'm not a certified midwife. I know the signs. In fact, I alerted her about her blood pressure and possible preeclampsia a few days ago."

The nurse relaxed. "Well, in that case." And then she admitted, "Your granddaughter is pretty upset right now." She patted Sephie's arm. "I'll see what we can do. I won't be long." The nurse headed to the nursing station to talk with her supervisor.

Immediately, Floyd turned to Sephie, grabbing both of her arms. "Our?"

"Well, how else could I justify getting into her room?" she said, slipping out of his grasp and hiding her smile as she headed back to the waiting room.

Chapter 78

Day 27: The little house, Saturday in the wee hours of the morning

"Did we eat today?" Sephie asked as they dragged their exhausted bodies into the kitchen of the little house.

"I don't remember," Floyd said.

"That's a new one for you. You're always trying to feed all of us." Collapsing into a chair, she added, "Cute little baby, isn't she? All that hair. I'm jealous. My daughter was bald as an eaglet, but she soon made up for it."

"Runs in the family," he said, rummaging through the cabinet. "Will tomato soup do?"

"Sure," Sephie said. "I'll make some grilled cheese." She went to the fridge and got out butter, bread, and cheddar while Floyd put the soup into a pan and added milk.

Soon, they had bowls of hot soup and gooey cheese sandwiches on a plate. As they took their first bites, the sound of "Ripple" filled the room. Sephie frowned at Floyd before looking at the caller ID. When she did, her frowned increased. It was Pastor Woods.

"Sephie, I've got some news."

"Yes?" the old woman prompted.

"Our dear Sister Agnesia has gone to Glory. It happened tonight."

Sephie took a deep breath, letting the news sink in. "When's the funeral?"

"We can't hold it before Monday due to state law. We're planning on Tuesday."

She put a hand to her head and then rested her elbow on the table. "I'll be there. It'll take a few days."

"Do you have any requests?"

"No, I'm sure she discussed her wishes long ago with you."

"That she did. Sister Agnesia was well prepared to meet the Lord."

"Thank you, Pastor," she said and cut the call because she didn't want to discuss the Lord with him more than she had to.

Floyd reached for her hand. "Your sister?" When she nodded, he added, "I'm sorry."

B.D. came in from the front door. "What did Yolanda have?" he asked.

"A little girl. Six pounds, twelve ounces," Floyd said, his concentration on Sephie.

"Nice. I was—" He stopped when he saw Sephie's face. "What happened? Is she all right?"

"She's fine, B.D.," Floyd explained. "It's Sephie's sister."

"Agnesia?"

"The funeral is Tuesday," Sephie said. "I'll start back in the morning."

B.D. came around to squat next to Sephie's seat. "I'm so sorry. I'll make some calls in the morning and let people here know. And then I'll drive you."

"No, B.D. I'll go by myself. You're making a wonderful life here. I've never seen you get so many singing gigs or you be so happy. You can help Mandy and Laura a lot. And then there's that graduate program."

"I can come back."

She shook her head. "I'll be down there for a long time. I have property to tend to. Agnesia isn't there to look after it."

B.D. stood. "Talk some sense into her. She can't make that trip by herself. It took both of us driving a while to get here. And she's mourning."

Floyd nodded and then tilted his head toward the back, a clear signal for B.D. to make himself scarce. When the young man was gone, Floyd took both of the old woman's hands. He leaned closer to her and said, "Sephie, I told you that I would come down into that dark valley and walk it with you. And this is certainly a dark valley."

"I can do this by myself. You have Yolanda and a new grandbaby."

"Mandy and Laura and even B.D. can look after them until Wes gets here. Right now, you can't do this by yourself. No matter how strong and stubborn you think you are."

She looked down at their hands. "Get me down home and then come back to your family."

He leaned back into the hard, wooden chair, frustrated. "You don't get it, Sephie. I'm coming with you. I'll help you clear out your sister's belongings. I'll help with house repairs, anything you need. I'll stay until you decide to come back here."

She thought about her little cabin and the long, hard trek down to it and back up to her modern house and how her body ached every time, even though her spirit was always refreshed by her experiences in Dark Hollow. It was really too much for her. She saw that, here with Mandy and Laura in this flat land devoid of the lush woods, kudzu vines, and chiggers — all those chiggers that still plagued her even in her old age. Maybe it was time to sell. Her daughter would be hopping mad at this change, but she could buy the homestead if she wanted it.

Lifting her head, she teased, "Are you making an honest woman of me?"

He laughed. "There's not a more honest woman than you on earth!" Then, he leaned in close. "Sephie, won't you give us a chance?"

She paused. "We'll see."

"You're infuriating!" he said and kissed her long and hard.

Chapter 79

Day 27: Greenway, Saturday near dawn

The dark figure rose slightly on its gnarled feet, grasping the cottonwood branch, allowing it to shake the cloak free from its shoulders. Its hunger had not been well satisfied these past weeks. The gleanings from the river had been paltry, just enough to keep its essence alive. Something else had invaded its space, chasing all the easy food inside, away from beasts with the right to hunt.

Nasty little creature of the night, attacking but never feasting. Truth, though, it could not eat with that leather thing on its head that let it see but not eat. Unnatural. And that even nastier large creature flailing its arms around the downed food, never allowing a proper beast to finish it off and eat.

The dark figure shook itself again, causing something to happen along its flesh.

Soon, the hunting will be mine again. A proper beast knows how to slink softly, pounce, and. . . . Then feast. A proper beast knows how to rid the hunting place of unwanted strangers.

A third time the creature stretched even taller and shook its body fiercely, its dark skin shimmering, changing, as it jumped down from the branch to land in the long, dew-filled grass on four, black, furry paws. The beast extended its claws on its front paws and then tried those on its hind ones, digging deep into the soft earth. The muscles along its black fur rippled as the creature tested its new form. Letting out a low rumble from its throat and a hiss of satisfaction, the creature stalked off in search of its competition.

Oh, to feast again! Soon.

About the Author

Janie Franz comes from a long line of liars and storytellers with roots deep in east Tennessee and honed by the frigid winters of the Northern Plains and the ever-changing landscape of the high desert and mountains of New Mexico. She is an author, a professional speaker, and reviewer. Previously, she ran her own online music publication (Refrain Magazine) and was an agent/publicist for a groove/funk band, a radio announcer, and a yoga/relaxation instructor. Readers' comments welcome at janie@janiefranzauthor.com

www.ingramcontent.com/pod-product-compliance
Lightning Source LLC
LaVergne TN
LVHW020040110826
845155LV00029B/571
9781942166825